DIVIDED

THE ALLIANCE SERIES: BOOK FOUR

EMMA L. ADAMS

1

ADA

I walked under a starless, pitch-black sky. My entire body ached, and my mouth was dry, my skin already cracked from the blistering heat. It was cooler now night had fallen, after countless hours of walking over dry, dead ground. On either side of me walked a warrior. Not a human. Even if they looked like people, I couldn't think of them like that. Not when they'd captured me.

Not when they'd beaten Kay, brutally. The one hope I had left was that he was still alive despite what they'd done to him, because if I dared consider the alternative, I'd fall down and never get up.

I'm alive, Kay. You'd better be alive too, because I'm going to find you.

I didn't even know which world I was on, but chanting those words in my head kept me from cracking and trying to make a break for it. When I'd shifted out of line, one of my captors had grabbed my arm and hauled me back into place, gripping hard enough to leave a bruise. A reminder that these... creatures weren't human. They called themselves Stoneskins, and with the magicproof adamantine woven into their skin, they formed an unbreakable wall on both sides of me. I couldn't fight them with magic or physical force, and no weapons seemed to work on them. Kay's Alliance dagger had broken the instant it made contact with their skin.

Oh, god, Kay.

We'd been so damn *stupid.* We'd run into the Passages without a plan and walked right into the hands of the enemy. It was hard to believe less than twenty-four hours ago, I'd been at Kay's flat. Now, we were literally worlds apart. Last time I'd seen him, he'd been bleeding on the ground in the jungle of Vey-Xanetha, before the Stoneskins had dragged me through the doorway and cut us off from one another.

I'd given up trying to see what else was ahead. Nothing but the unbroken line of the horizon. Whoever was navigating must know where they were going, though how they did so was anyone's guess. We human prisoners had been shunted into a line, like cattle, caged in by stone-skinned, invincible warriors. They carried no weapons, but then again, they *were* weapons.

When the Stoneskins had dragged me through the open door, I'd known immediately they hadn't brought me into the Passages—the blue-lit metal-walled corridors lined with doors to all the worlds in the Multiverse—but to another world entirely. An empty one. Where *they* came from, I didn't know, because the ones who spoke English refused to tell me. It couldn't be Earth, nor any of the other worlds Earth's languages had spread to, like Valeria. Because those were Alliance members. I'd met people from twenty-odd worlds, and as an Alliance employee, I'd had access to information on all species across the Multiverse. But I'd never seen creatures like these before. Which meant either they weren't from any of the worlds registered in the Multiverse, or they'd been hiding. But how had they known my name? Not just my given name: my real name. They'd called me

Adamantine. They'd said they needed me for something. But what?

Time had shrunk to a bubble, but night had fallen in the past hour. Walking under the burning sun had been nothing short of torture. The back of my neck burned, and my throat was dry even though one of the Stoneskins had been thoughtful enough to hand me a flask of water. They didn't seem to need it themselves.

The one on my left was male, human in shape, dressed in a long, robe-like garment. Not that he needed to protect itself from the sun, because his skin was literally rock, marbled in shades of brown, black, and grey. He paid me no attention. The female Stoneskin on my right kept glancing at me, curiosity in her expression. It made her look almost human, which screwed with my head more than the notion of being kidnapped by these creatures.

The group stopped. The Stoneskins moved deliberately, decisively, though I didn't see who gave the orders. The guards spoke to one another in a language I recognised— Klathican—and I shifted, trying to hear the others. The guard at my side shouted something at the guard opposite, who shouted a reply. As if I didn't stand between them. I knew spoken Klathican, though I was a bit out of practise. The first speaker had said, *Watch the humans.* His companion had replied, *I know.*

Someone had to be leading the group. There must be a chain of command, because from their disgruntled expressions, the two guards weren't best pleased about having to watch over me rather than walking up front. The other humans at the back walked in parallel lines. They didn't need chains when no one had anywhere to run. In the hours we'd walked, no one had even tried to make a break for it across the wilderness.

Prisoner. Slave. The word left a bad taste in my mouth. It

3

wasn't the first time I'd been held captive. The Alliance had arrested me once already, back when I'd been illegally trespassing in the Passages as part of my work helping other people escape the war on my homeworld. But even when shit had repeatedly hit the fan, I never could have imagined there existed a creature capable of enslaving magical forces and even Cethraxian monsters.

The Stoneskins had almost destroyed the Multiverse in their quest for magical sources. They'd played everyone for fools, including the Alliance. When they'd failed to drain all the magic from Vey-Xanetha, and the doorway had closed, they'd been reduced to searching for an alternative... me. And I still didn't know *why.*

One of them pushed me, lightly, but enough for me to stumble forward. "Go to the other humans," he said, in English. The guy's voice even sounded like a rockslide.

I couldn't argue. Not like there was anywhere to run. Just rock and dust and empty sky. There didn't seem to be any kind of animal or plant life either. We might be the only people left in all the world. In this world, at least. No signs of human habitation anywhere, and no landmarks. How did they know where they were going? It wasn't like you could get satellite navigation out here. Even the Alliance's maps didn't cover everywhere, and doorways didn't always match. These guys had somehow created a doorway themselves. With a world-key, maybe, but those were limited to certain higher-up Alliance members. Kay had used one, before—

Don't think about him. Don't. Besides, it probably wasn't as bad as it looked. When the Stoneskins had dragged me through the doorway, I'd seen them knock Kay down. But they'd blocked the way, and I'd only seen from a side angle. Kay had survived more than one attack from an angry god, for crying out loud. He'd survived *third level magic,* which was fatal if it struck you directly. He couldn't—couldn't have—

I pressed the heels of my palms into my eyes. *Calm down, Ada. Calm down.* Panic out here and I might as well be dead already. *Kay would tell you to survive.*

I drew in a deep breath. The Stoneskins were herding the other humans to one area. Rather than taking my place amongst the others, I hung back at the edge of our 'camp', watching them. There were at least fifty Stoneskins, and despite the adamantine in their skin, they moved so much like humans. Except... now I watched closer, some appeared to have webbing between the fingers. Some walked barefoot on clawed feet.

Another possibility sank into my heart. The Stoneskins were from more than one world. They had to be. Their marbled skin and bald heads made it difficult to tell at first, but the physical differences left no doubt. They couldn't have started out that way. Somehow... they'd been changed.

I shut off that train of thought—with difficulty—and tried to see if I could spot their leader. I made out the shape of some kind of cart up ahead, at the head of the group, but it was too dim to see any more. The darkness had crept in, all lights on the barren world extinguished. The Stoneskins themselves became shadows, some remaining on guard while the others set up tents. A couple carried lanterns, but didn't deign to bring any over to the humans.

The prisoners didn't have anything as fancy as tents. Just one blanket each. At least a river ran on the other side of the camp, which I ran to, gasping for a drink after walking all day. I couldn't remember the last time I'd eaten, either. I didn't have a way to keep track of time. I'd never packed for an impromptu kidnapping. Sure, I'd put a bunch of items in the inside pockets of my coat, like my communicator and my house key. My *house key.* I'd never been further from home. Ever.

As for my communicator, the signal was out of range.

After briefly checking for a signal during one of our stops, when I was sure nobody could see me, I'd switched it off to save power, until we reached wherever it was we were going. I had no doubt the Stoneskins would confiscate my communicator if they knew I carried it with me. I should have brought one of the earpieces; they worked on any world. But like an idiot, I'd given it back to Central yesterday, along with my weapons. The one defence I had was magic, and the Stoneskins could absorb it without even trying.

Adamantine. I'd faced antimagic before—I could absorb it, in fact, because antimagic *was* magic in some sense. But the usual rules didn't apply to these... creatures. They must have an insanely high level of adamantine in their skin. Higher than I did, even, though with me, it was in my blood. The Stoneskins were practically *living* antimagic. My bruised arm throbbed where the guard had grabbed me. I was lucky it wasn't broken. Because out here in the middle of nowhere, there was no way to fix it.

All things considered, being the Alliance's prisoner had been more fun. The thought made me want to laugh and cry simultaneously. Back then, I'd had a way to contact my family. They'd think I was dead.

Even the humans made me wary. There were maybe fifty of them, and four hovered in a close-knit group near some rocks. The others stood apart from one another, like they didn't want to get too close. The Stoneskins had set up their tents so they surrounded us on all sides except the one where the river ran alongside camp, too deep to swim across. I wasn't desperate enough to try my luck against the raging current. *That must mean we're near an ocean,* I thought, scanning the dark horizon. There was no point in looking too closely. We'd be gone tomorrow.

I gritted my teeth and walked into camp, where some people had set up a makeshift fire. *Find allies,* whispered a voice in the back of my head. It sounded like Nell—practical, cool in a crisis.

"You're the one they stopped for?" a woman asked as I approached. She wore a tattered suit, torn and mud-stained, but clearly from an Alliance world. Earth? She handed me something I vaguely recognised as the kind of factory-made instant energy bars they made on Valeria.

"Oh, thanks," I said, ripping off the plastic. The unidentifiable gravel-like substance didn't look particularly appetising, but at this point, I didn't care. "Where'd you get this?"

"At the last pit-stop," she said. "Swiped a bunch of them. They let us gather supplies. Kind of nice of them. There's nothing out here in the wilderness."

"This is Valerian," I said, between mouthfuls.

"Yeah, some cross-world traders were shipping them. Pity we couldn't steal any of their tech. Then we might have a chance in the stars of getting out of here."

I looked at her. "You know a way out?"

Someone laughed. "Who is she?" asked a claw-footed man —had to be Avian—who had two claws missing from one foot, giving him a pronounced limp. He spoke English with a halting accent.

"I'm Ada," I said. "I'm from Earth. Where are they taking us?"

A guy leaning on a rock laughed, showing slightly elongated teeth disturbingly similar to my once-friend Delta's. "Where, she says. Haven't a clue, have we?"

"Ignore him," said the woman in the business suit. "I'm Gervene, from Valeria. They caught me in the escape tunnel. Is that where they got you, too?"

Huh? "I don't know about escape tunnels," I said slowly. "I was in the Passages…"

"The escape tunnels are in the Passages," said Gervene. "I assume you were running away, right?"

I shook my head. "No. I was in there investigating something, and the Stoneskins came through a door. It wasn't supposed to be there."

"Wasn't supposed to? Who are you, the doorway police?" The long-toothed man laughed loudly at his own joke, and Gervene smacked him on the arm.

"Quiet," she said. "They'll hear us."

"They were looking for you," said long-toothed man to me. "Heard them talking about a girl."

"But—that's impossible," I said. "They found me by total accident. I wasn't even meant to be there."

"They have their ways," said another man, who was covered in so much dirt and blood I couldn't tell where his hands ended and his sleeves began. Nor if it was his blood, or someone else's.

"Tracking," said Gervene. "They've been combing the Passages for months. Sending their creepy little Cethraxian spies."

"What?" This situation was getting more bizarre by the minute. "You're saying they have Cethraxian spies… looking for me?"

"Considering we've finally started moving again now they've found you? I'd say so." The long-toothed man shuddered theatrically. "I hope it's quick."

"I hope they destroy themselves," said Gervene.

I looked from one face to the other, frowning. The other girl in the group appeared no older than fifteen, terrified, and hadn't spoken a word.

"What am I missing?" I asked. "What's their deal, anyway?"

"No clue," said Gervene. "Whatever they're planning, they need a lot of magical energy. They picked up any magic-wielders they ran into while searching the Passages. They caught me fleeing Valeria through the escape tunnel. You really don't know about it?"

"I'm seriously missing something here," I said. "So you're all magic-wielders?"

Several nods.

"And they need us for their plan… okay. But me? What do they need me for?"

Probably to blow something up, an unwelcome voice whispered in my ear. I might as well be a walking bomb, given how the adamantine in my blood made me able to channel unlimited amounts of magical energy. Here, away from the Alliance, on a high-magic world…

I didn't dare think about what they might want to use me for.

"They said they needed my *help,*" I said. "But seeing as they're deluded psychos, I've no clue what they meant."

The long-toothed man's mouth twisted into an odd smile. "I have a feeling things are going to get interesting around here."

"Where are they going, anyway?" I asked. "Is this their world?"

"No," said Gervene. "At least, I don't think so. It's not their destination, anyway. From what I could pick up, they're searching for a certain place. Whichever world they're going to, they haven't found it yet."

"You're Valerian," I said slowly. "Why were you running away?"

Gervene's expression closed up. "I get to keep some secrets," she said. "I don't believe for a minute you were there by coincidence."

"They were tracking powerful sources," said the avian man. "That's what they said."

Sources. Oh, shit. They must have picked up my trace, like a tracker, when I faced the god. I'd channelled so much magic, it had been like I'd sent a beacon across the Multiverse. Of course someone would have noticed. It wouldn't have surprised me if the signal had gone to all the Alliance's trackers and scrambled them. And the Stoneskins must have caught the signal, opened a door... and waited. Then I'd gone into the Passages less than twenty-four hours after I'd been on Vey-Xanetha, and stepped right in front of the door. I'd practically broadcasted my location without even realising it.

Dammit, Ada. I could practically hear Nell's lecturing voice telling me to consider the consequences of my actions. But really, who could have predicted I'd wind up kidnapped by these thugs? What did it matter, anyway? I needed to get out of here.

"So there's no way back to the Passages from here?"

The long-toothed man laughed.

"Stars, no. Don't you think we'd have run for it by now?" said Gervene.

"All right," I said, crossing my arms defensively. "Just checking. They got through to the Passages in the first place, right?"

"Yeah, they have their ways," said Long-Toothed Guy. "Well, the StoneKing does."

"StoneKing," I said. "Right. That's their leader?"

"Yeah, can't say I want to meet him," said Gervene. "They say he personally executed the last person to try to run."

"Not surprising," muttered the bloodstained man.

"What happened to you?" I asked, unable to restrain my curiosity.

No answer. The guy shifted his feet, eyes fixed on the ground.

"Okay. Just wondered."

"Might as well try to escape while you can," said Long-Toothed Guy. "Before you lose hope like the rest of us."

"So that's it? You're planning to march to your deaths?"

"To wherever they're taking us," said Gervene. "Every other world-stop's a transit point on Cethrax, I know, but we can't run off alone in that place, not right in the middle of wyvern territory. None of the worlds we've been through have been survivable. I don't have anything on me, none of us have any weapons—nothing can hurt those Stoneskins. Just keep quiet and hope they don't kill you first."

"Wow." I shook my head. "Real optimistic, guys. Why Cethrax?" Also, *wyvern territory?* Like things couldn't get worse. *As if, Ada. You've jumped from the frying pan onto the surface of the sun.*

"I heard it from one of them," said Gervene. "Cethrax overlaps with most worlds at some point, through the escape tunnels."

Again with the escape tunnels. "You're not talking about the hidden Passages, are you?" I asked. I didn't actually know how far the only Passage unknown to the Alliance extended, but it did overlap with Cethrax. A lot...

"Guess they're hidden from most people." Gervene shrugged. "They're used for illegal trade amongst the allied worlds, if they're willing to risk the monsters. No Alliance guards."

Holy hell. "That's how the offworld trade gets around Alliance laws," I said, before I could stop myself. "I always wondered..." I cut myself off before I gave the game away. Not three months ago, I'd lived under the Alliance's radar in London, working with a whole network of people to help other offworlders fleeing worlds like mine. Nell had wanted me to have as normal a life as possible so she'd never told me the details of what went on behind the scenes, but I'd figured a lot of it out. There were hundreds of people involved, from the volunteers at the world-transit points who helped teach offworlders how to blend in on the new world they'd be living on, to people like Delta and me, who helped them travel safely through the Passages to their new destination without being caught by the Alliance or eaten by one of Cethrax's monsters. I'd always thought of the hidden Passage as a lucky coincidence.

But it made sense other people used it, too. The illegal offworld technology Jeth experimented with had to come from somewhere. Delta's family had used those tunnels to keep contact with Cethrax, and so had the Conners.

Then it hit me what else she'd said. "Did you say Cethrax overlaps with most worlds?"

Gervene blinked. "New doors open all the time. Usually they're drawn to the Passages, but sometimes they're drawn to other sources."

Sources. Like Vey-Xanetha. Cethrax had a connection with that place, and the Stoneskins had used it. Hard to believe no one had thought to look into it before. But so few people knew about magic sources. So few, an operation like this had slipped through the Passages unseen.

"Damn," I said. "That's how the Stoneskins dominated the vox-kind?"

"Cethrax?" said Gervene. "Of course. The Cethraxians believe the Stoneskins to be the incarnation of the undergods they worship."

I shivered. My last experience with living gods hadn't ended well.

I have to escape. There has to be a way.

I woke to the same, starless black sky.

I hadn't meant to fall asleep, but I'd been walking for hours, and I was numb all over with exhaustion and shock. *Kay,* was the first thought that came to mind. I curled up, biting down on my hand to keep from crying. He'd tell me to stay strong. He'd tell me to fight.

You're all right.

A few tears escaped, but I fiercely brushed them away. I'd make these bastards pay.

Around me were the sleeping forms of the other human prisoners. Some had huddled under the blankets, others had folded them to make the rock-hard ground less uncomfortable to lie on. I glanced over at the Stoneskins' tents and didn't see any movement, but for all I knew, they could disguise themselves as rocks or something. You never knew.

Don't think. I stood up to pace around the camp. The ground was rock, the sky was blank, and we might have been the only people left in the Multiverse.

The thought made me shiver uncontrollably. I couldn't believe I'd let myself get captured again. Nell would give me the lecture of a lifetime if I ever got home. Another sharp pain pierced my heart. My family didn't know where I was. That I was alive. Would the *Alliance* think I was dead? How could anyone follow me if they didn't know which world I was on?

"What are you doing, walking around?" hissed the avian man who lay nearby.

I shrugged.

"Another mad one," said a nearby male. "They always kill those first."

"Nah, she's pretty. They'll want to keep her."

"StoneKing did say he was looking for a queen," snickered the long-toothed guy. I shot him an angry glare.

"Seeing as everyone's awake," I said, quietly, "can anyone tell me why they haven't just opened a doorway to wherever they're going?"

A pause. I suspected their sources—whatever they'd used

to open the door—had burned out, but how much did the others know?

"They ran out," said the avian man. "They tried using some of the prisoners as sacrifices, but it didn't work. They had an… instrument they stole from the Alliance. That didn't work for long. I can't understand their speech."

Klathican. They spoke Classical… but that didn't mean they came from Klathica. It was the most common language in the Multiverse, after all. But who *were* the Stoneskins?

"Right," I said. "They don't seem worried they'll lose us in the wilderness."

"We're expendable," said the man. "Useful, but expendable. They're planning to sacrifice all of us, you know."

"Nah, they're planning on sucking the magic right out of us." The long-toothed man shuddered theatrically.

"That's not possible, idiot," snapped Gervene, with a glance at the terrified-looking teenage girl huddled nearby.

"Are you definitely all magic-wielders?" I asked.

"I reckon so," said the first man who'd spoken. "There was a girl who didn't have magic they caught, they killed her right away."

"Shit," I said, my throat closing up. *They're amassing magic-wielders for something. An army?*

I held back a shudder. I'd escaped a similar fate on my homeworld. For over twenty years on Earth, I'd thought I was safe, secure in the knowledge I wouldn't be used as an assassin, like if I'd remained on my homeworld, Enzar. Enzar's war had consumed whole worlds, and magic-born magebloods fought against the ruling Royals, who'd injected their children—like me—with magic to give them a fighting edge in magical warfare. Safe, with my family. We'd been happy. Not always financially secure, but happy.

Breathe, Ada. Panic threatened to crush me from the inside out. I concentrated on my anger at the Stoneskins instead. I shot a blistering glare at the three stone-skinned warriors stalking the edges of camp. For all their catlike movements, they weren't stealthy at all. They were slow-moving rocks. But they weren't stupid, and they'd see an attack coming a mile off. Could *anyone* fight invincible monsters who were immune to magic as well as all weapons? Even the Alliance?

"This place isn't high-magic," said Gervene. "Quiet as death. I think it's a defunct world."

"I thought so, too," I whispered. "I can't feel anything."

"Oh, gods, you're one of those," said someone else—the bloodstained man from before, and he was lying not far from my feet. I edged away from him, slightly unnerved by the way he just lay there covered in blood, making no attempt to clean it off even with a river ten metres away. Maybe he wanted to scare people into leaving him alone. It seemed to be working.

"One of what?"

"The freaks."

"Ignore him," said Gervene. "He's sore because one of those enhanced magic-wielders kicked the crap out of him the other day."

I walked over to her. She'd sat up, rubbing the back of her neck.

"Is that where the blood came from?" I asked, in a whisper.

She shook her head. "He was like that when we found him on Cethrax. I think something jumped him and the people he was with, and he was the only survivor."

I ran my hands over the goosebumps on my arms. "What did you mean about enhanced magic-wielders? Not the Stoneskins?"

"I thought that's what *you* were," said Gervene. "Magic-wielders who weren't born that way. There are a few … I'm not one of them," she added. "They can feel magic changes in level when we move between worlds. There's not much to feel anyway."

I nodded. I wasn't about to tell her I was no normal magic-wielder, with the adamantine in my blood giving me the ability to absorb any nearby magic, even take a deadly level three hit and walk away with no damage. But it didn't matter when faced with an enemy literally made out of stone. I wasn't unbreakable. I broke as easily as anyone else.

"Yeah," I said. "How many are there?"

"Three. The two Klathicans are a little strange. And that guy over there's not friendly. No one talks to him."

I turned to see where she pointed. A large, blond man sat on the rocks across the camp, wearing… Alliance guard gear.

Aric Conner.

2

KAY

I was dying. And it was the Multiverse's final laugh that I'd be able to feel every second of it. Every stab of dull pain as the wounds from the stone-skinned warriors' attacks shut my body down. Every failing breath, punctured with more agony.

The one consolation I had was that my life didn't flash before my eyes. I couldn't see anything at all. Not even Ada. The faded image of her face was slipping away by the second.

I can't die here.

Whoever said the pain faded before you died was a lying bastard.

"Fuck you, Multiverse," I whispered.

A rational voice in my head told me I shouldn't even be able to speak. I should by rights be dead already. I was pretty sure those Stoneskins had broken every bone in my body. I was no stranger to pain, and this wasn't the first time I'd hung on the edge, wondering when I was finally going to die. But there was no way I could have survived. I knew a thousand ways to break a person, and getting beaten halfway to hell by concrete monsters outclassed all of them. Nobody could lose so much blood and live.

But if I really was dying, I shouldn't be able to think so clearly. The all-encompassing pain had dulled, and was fading by the second. My eyes flickered open and I blinked, my vision clearing to show a web of branches above my head.

What?

No, there were vines, and they were moving. Sensation twitched back into my limbs, and creeping tendrils moved over my skin. I gasped for breath, and almost doubled over from the pain. But something held me pinned down. *Vines* held me pinned down.

The pain was fading. I could breathe. It hurt like a mother-fucker, but I could breathe.

Breathe, Kay. Keep breathing...

The tendrils withdrew, cold against my bare skin. My clothes were soaked with my own blood. But I wasn't dead. I drew in a ragged breath, a sharp voice awakening in the back of my head. *Get up. Get up.*

I sat up, regretting the movement instantly as dizziness washed over my vision. I could move. I wasn't trapped. But how had I not bled to death? Whatever the reason, I was alive.

Which meant Ada was really gone.

The thought hit me with a force a thousand times stronger than a steel fist.

A face came into focus, a few feet away, and I started, my body shifting before I was even aware I'd got to my feet. The room swam again. *Focus. She's just a kid.* A girl, no older than ten. I recognised her—from the Vey-Xanethan forest, after she'd escaped being sacrificed. The summoner of Xanet. She'd healed Ada.

My heart pounded. She'd done the same to me. Why?

Because we'd saved her? I couldn't think clearly. But she'd saved my life, healed me with the power of her god.

"*Vakath*," I whispered. Thank you.

I could say no more. I was alive. As long as I was still breathing, I could find Ada.

And the door. I'd been lying on a bed in a house—on the inside of a tree, judging by the bark-like lines on the walls.

The girl backed away from me, wary now. I must be in the city where the summoners had almost sacrificed those kids, deep inside the Vey-Xanethan jungle.

How did I even get here?

I lurched to my feet, even as pain shot through my entire body. Nobody stopped me leaving. The city appeared to be deserted, but frightened faces peered from the windows. I had to think. I didn't have a world-key, but the doorway must be close by. Another doorway had been opened in the jungle before, so it was logical that the same spot might be used again.

The door closed.

No. I wouldn't accept it until I saw it with my own eyes.

It wasn't hard to pick up the trail of my own blood, spattered over the tangled tree roots which covered the town. The girl had dragged me—no, someone else must have helped. I'd come *that* close to dying. Hell, I *should* be dead. Part of me thought it was a trick, because magic was a force of destruction. Now it had saved my life. I was here, on Vey-Xanetha, and Ada was... gone.

My steps were unsteady, my breaths shallow. *Get it together, Kay.* The city merged with the jungle so successfully I couldn't tell where one ended and the other began. The houses were more like hollowed-out trees, and the branches formed a canopy so thick it was like being closed in a dome. My breath quickened. I needed to get back to Earth, but how was that even possible now?

I hauled myself over thick tree roots, out into the jungle proper. The blood staining the ground became thicker, and if not for the pain of the exertion, I'd have triple-checked I was actually alive. But magic couldn't bring back the dead.

I scanned the undergrowth-choked paths, willing my head to stop spinning. I'd been here before. Not two days before. I could find my way.

There. A clearing. Blood spattered the ground and the nearby trees, and the undergrowth was flattened. But no doorway.

"No way," I muttered. I dropped to a crouch, searching under tree roots—for a clue, anything. It was impossible to open a doorway without a world-key. They needed a source, or a sacrifice. So they'd either killed a summoner or left evidence behind.

My hand closed around a small, ice-cold object. *Got it.* It was a piece of metal, all right, but the colour was dulled, like the power had drained from it. If it had been used to open a doorway...

I didn't know whether I could amplify sources that were already dead, but there was a metric crap-ton of magic here on Vey-Xanetha. No time to debate or question. I'd nearly died once already. I reached for the magic inside the cold piece of metal.

Blackness filled my vision, like all light had been extinguished. Like the opening sequence of a simulation, stuck on pause. I couldn't even see my own outstretched hand. It was like empty space. I tried to move forward, but couldn't. Hell.

I concentrated on the only sensation I could grasp—magic. The maddening buzz of static. Not a physical sense, but like when I amplified a tracker to pick up the trace of a specific magic-wielder. Like when I tuned into the signal to make myself invisible when holding a Chameleon.

This signal seemed to be coming from all around me, not

that it was easy to tell in pitch-darkness. It had to come from the world-key. And all world-keys were tied into the same place.

The Passages. Get to the Passages.

I staggered forward, almost tripping over a tree root. Still in the jungle. But the piece of the Passages remained in my hand.

I didn't have a clue about the specifics of how world-keys worked, but standing here like an idiot didn't have any effect. When I used the key in the Passages, I had to sketch out symbols for a specific world. And it *did* work in reverse, I remembered. The Passages themselves had a symbol for instant access. They were the one point which could be reached from any world.

I reached into my jacket and pulled out my communicator. Or, what was left of it. It was all but in pieces, the case shattered thanks to the Stoneskins. And I'd handed the Chameleon in at Central again, seeing as the battery had drained out of it.

But I had the tracker. My own, actually, since they'd never asked for it back. And I could use it to pick up a magic signal.

Ada's magic signal slammed into me with a shock of pain, right through my bones. Her signal was mixed in with my own, like two radio signals, indistinct. And... that was it. There were faint traces of others, people who'd passed this way to the city, but none were linked to the Stoneskins. They had no traces of magic at all.

With Ada's signal, I could find her. If I opened a door.

I looked up, at the nearest tree. Symbols had been carved into the trunk. A mark like a trident turned on its side, and three smaller symbols intertwined with each of the three points. Those were the symbols the Alliance used to open doorways. I'd used them myself.

Following instinct, I traced the lines of the symbols

carved with the edge of the piece of Passage, keeping the amplifier on, building the charge higher, and above all, concentrating on the trace of Ada's magic. I gripped it like a safety rope. *Take me to her,* I thought fiercely, like it would make a difference. I blinked, and the outline of a Passage door seemed to impress itself over the symbols. I blinked again and it was gone.

I finished tracing the last symbol, a circle with an indentation in the centre. The world-key, whatever it was, fitted exactly. When I let go, the magic faded, and the little colour remaining in the piece of metal faded. I'd amplified the little magic left in it, but the Stoneskins had already burned most of it out.

But it was enough. Power surged around me, and a doorway opened right over the symbols, through the centre of the tree. A familiar corridor.

The lower Passages.

I stepped over the threshold, and the door vanished, a blast of magic carrying me over the edge. I struck the ground hard, rolling over through... mud and water. Cethrax's area.

But Ada wasn't here. Nobody was in the corridor, which, unlike the upper Passages, was stone-walled, poorly maintained. Murky water swirled around me.

Pushing myself to my feet, I became aware in one instant I was covered in blood, alone and weaponless, in the middle of the most dangerous area of the Passages. Not only that, Cethrax was working against the Alliance, with those Stoneskins who'd taken Ada.

A slithering movement sounded nearby, and a shadow detached itself from the wall.

Of all the timing.

I swore. The creature had already seen me, and was taking its time. Piece by piece, the shadows pulled back, revealing a very solid and very ugly opponent. Curved tusks hung from its overlarge mouth, and wild red eyes fixated on me, deep-set in its boulder-like head. This creature had four short arms, and three thick, tree-trunk-like legs. Stooping under the low ceiling, it dared me to challenge it. Just what I needed right now—a chalder vox.

Dealing damage to one of these bastards only made them stronger. I'd faced them countless times before, but never unarmed. The goddamn Stoneskins had shattered my dagger. I had nothing more than a tracker, and that was no use here. I had to do something I'd never done in a fight before—run away.

I ran for the nearest archway, hoping it led to the stairs up to the first level. My feet skidded on the wet floor, and I ducked a swinging fist. It slammed into the wall, knocking pieces of rock over my head. The recovery from near-death had slowed me down, but I pushed my newly-healed body to its limits all the same, running through one chamber after another. The beast was on my heels—literally. Cursing the Multiverse, I put on a last burst of speed and found myself in a smaller chamber. The door was too narrow for the beast to follow me.

I didn't know this part of the Passages, because it was hidden. But there *had* to be a way to the first level. Ada had used these Passages all the time, even with the threat of Cethrax around the corner.

Speaking of which… A sloping corridor was on my right, and I was willing to bet the murky stone walls led right into the heart of Cethrax. No way in hell was I going in there.

A slithering sound told me the chalder vox had figured out how to follow me through the narrow doorway. Just what I needed. An enemy with an iota of intelligence.

I backed away, swearing. Only one way to run, aside from the tunnel into enemy territory. There had to be a way out.

Crash. Stone crumbled under the chalder vox's fist. The

ceiling was too sturdy to cause a cave-in, but the walls trembled. I ducked as a small boulder soared over my head, shattering on the opposite wall. I backed further up, feet skidding in swamp water—and blood. Old blood. Wyvern. I *must* be near an exit.

The chalder vox had sunk into shadow again, and I threw caution out the window and ran full-pelt across the chamber. Yes—a door lay ahead.

Something heavy struck me in the ribs and for about the tenth time that day, the breath was knocked from my lungs. I slammed into the wall, gritting my teeth against the pain. The stone fist withdrew into the shadows. Clever bastard. Few of the vox-kind made use of their semi-corporeal state.

I dropped to the ground to avoid another punch, ignoring the sharp pain. I was pretty sure the bastard had cracked a rib or two. I crawled, pressed flat to the floor.

I need a goddamned weapon!

I dragged myself through the door, and saw the shroud of magic hiding a concealed stair. *There.* I pulled myself to my feet again and sprinted. It hurt like hell, but I ran up the stairs, and fell onto cold metal. The first level. Gasping, I rolled onto my back. The blue light of the Passages swam before my eyes.

Get up, Kay. I staggered upright, sending swamp water flying everywhere. Shadows moved behind me. Damned monster had followed me.

I let magic gather above my hand. "Get out of here."

Quick footsteps. Voices, echoing. A spark bounced off the nearest wall. An Alliance stunner.

A voice spoke. "Kay, what are you doing in here?" Carl, head guard. He must be leading a patrol. Before I could speak, the beast reformed itself from shadow in layers of rock, and Carl swore, shouting out a warning to the other guards. A concrete foot slammed down, and I ducked out the way as a guard fired his stunner, sparks of magic rebounding.

"Don't do that!" Carl shouted. "It'll enrage it."

Too late. The beast roared, and charged. Carl was on the case, moving between the beast and a petrified-looking guy who was clearly a novice-in-training. Carl fired the stunner at the ceiling, forcing the beast to lower its head and giving him the chance to climb the monster's back and stab it behind the neck. Instant kill.

"You lot, clear this up," he ordered the others, climbing back to ground level. The three novices all seemed to have frozen behind him, eyes wide with terror. "You get used to it or you get out. Kay, *what* are you doing in here? Is that *blood?*"

"Cethrax is using the hidden Passage," I said. "That's how the monsters kept getting out. It's probably where the invisible ravegens came from, too. But it's not them." I paused for a painful breath. Like I needed to be incapacitated now. "It's not them. Not Cethrax. I've never seen anything like them before, but they took Ada with them. They nearly killed me. I couldn't save her." I breathed in, fists clenched, trying to hold myself steady while the world tilted under my feet. "I have to go after her. They opened a doorway."

"Kay, slow down," said Carl. "We need to deal with this situation first. Did you say Cethrax's lot took Ada? What are you waiting for?" he yelled at the guards, who jumped to attention so abruptly that two of them nearly slipped on the swamp water-and-blood-soaked Passage floor. "Get down there and check every doorway. Kay, why in the name of all gods didn't you send in a report before running in here? You're saying one of our employees is missing because you decided to take it upon yourself to enter a restricted area alone and unprotected?"

Finally able to get a word in edgeways, I said, "It wasn't Cethrax, and we weren't unprotected. Those creatures are like nothing I've seen before. They're made of—" I glanced at the novices, who were blatantly listening in. The information was probably classified. "I need to talk to you. Alone. This is urgent. The chalder vox can wait. We're talking a legitimate threat to the Alliance here."

"Kay, did you get *stabbed?*"

I'd reached to brush hair from my eyes and probably left a trail of blood. It didn't show on the black uniform, but now Carl's eyes widened. Dammit. The novices gaped at me.

I shook my head. "I'm fine," I said. "Look, I'm telling the truth. I realise I broke the rules, but they have Ada. They might be in any world, doing... anything to her." Every second we wasted in here they might be torturing her. They said they needed her for some reason, but that didn't mean they needed her in one piece.

The walls were tight, confining. I clenched my teeth, willed the ringing in my ears to disappear. *She's not dead. Don't think.*

"Go back to Central," said Carl, his face tight. "You need the infirmary."

"You're shitting me," I said. "You're not going to hear me out?"

"Kay, you're dripping blood everywhere. You'll draw every monster this side of Cethrax. I'll let your boss know you're injured, but there are stories of wyverns down in the—"

"Those Stoneskins were worse."

"Those *what?*"

"Stoneskins." Each time I said the name, the very idea of those creatures sounded more absurd. If anyone had tried to tell me the same story, I'd have disbelieved them. Even the Passages had a limit. "If you see them, don't fight, run. They're—it's like they're made out of rock."

Carl's expression grew even more incredulous. "Made out

of rock. Kay, you just described half the population of Cethrax. I'm not authorising you to go chasing after runaway vox-kind while injured. Guards, what did I tell you about getting downstairs? One of our employees is missing, probably in Cethrax. Get moving!"

"It's not Cethrax—" I swore as Carl sidestepped the chalder vox's body and ran after the novices. "Fine. I'll tell Ms Weston and get a report to the council. And you guys watch your backs in here," I added to the novices, who looked more terrified than ever.

Once in a corridor alone, I paused. This was my last chance to find Ada's signal again. I pulled out the tracker, which wasn't broken—unlike my communicator. Noise drifted down from the corridor on my right, which led to the main Passage.

The last thing I needed was to get arrested. If anyone saw me covered in blood, in a place I wasn't supposed to be, I'd be in even more trouble than I already was. At least I had my Alliance ID as proof I wasn't a random drunk wandering in off the streets, not that it would be any consolation to anyone who saw me like this. But I couldn't worry about that now.

I took the tracker instead, and tapped into the amplifier. *Ada. I need to find Ada.* I'd been vaguely aware of her trace as I'd been in the lower Passage… but it had disappeared.

No way. I'd kept the amplifier on. I *should* be able to sense her, even if she was on a different universe. Perhaps I'd been wrong in my assumption. But we'd used it before, following her brother's magic-trace to rescue him from the Conner family on Valeria. And that had been a far weaker signal. Ada's blazed like a torchlight. But there was no trace of it. Not even a whisper, even though we'd walked down the same corridor not two hours ago. At least, I didn't *think* it had been that long…

I hadn't been unconscious all day, had I? Maybe something was blocking the signal. Something on a distant world. I took the Passage fragment instead, but even amplifying it didn't work. It was dead. A lump of useless metal. I threw it at the wall, where it bounced off rather than shattering.

I left. There was nothing else I could do. This was god-awful timing of the highest order—right after I'd ditched a bunch of rules to find out what was happening on Vey-Xanetha, including sneaking off alone, using a world-key without backup, confronting an angry god without any kind of preparation. I'd expected backlash from what I'd done, but I never could have known *this* would happen less than twenty-four hours later. I didn't have an excuse, least of all for taking Ada with me. We'd run into danger without a plan and she'd paid the price for it.

People stared at me in the entrance hall to Central. My reflection in the glass doors told me why. I looked like a madman even without the blood all over my face, not to mention the Cethraxian swamp water and blood dripping from my clothes. I met wide eyes wherever I walked, including from the offworlders hanging around the door to the Complaints Division. They'd been here to gripe about the issues Earth's fluctuating magic levels had drawn up, forcing half the Alliance guards to abandon their normal duties and go chasing after griffins. Even now, a flock of rainbow-coloured birds zoomed around the entrance hall. I'd been too out of it to pay attention, but Earth's magic levels had gone back to normal. So our actions on Vey-Xanetha had been of some use. Not that it would in any way help me now.

Someone blocked my path. "Kay—I'm told you're injured." It was Saki, the nurse, and she looked about as happy to see me as a guard faced with a wyvern. Great.

"I'm fine." I glanced down at my feet, where a trail of

blood dripped from my sopping wet clothes. "Might need a change of uniform. I have to see Ms Weston. Now."

"*Not* in that state."

Seriously? Sure, I should probably make sure that blasted chalder vox hadn't broken any ribs when it hit me. I wouldn't be able to walk so fast if it had, but having a high pain threshold didn't help judgment at the best of times, especially after I'd technically died. Or close enough.

"Kay, what in the world are you doing?"

Crap. I turned slowly to face Ms Weston, who stared for a moment, then her eyes narrowed into their usual disapproval.

"I need to speak to you. It's urgent."

"I gathered, seeing as Ada Fletcher's tracker has disappeared from our system."

No.

She had no way to communicate with us now, from whichever world she was on.

"They took her," were the first, stupid words that came out of my mouth. The world tilted and swam, like through a half-formed doorway. The bright ceiling lights made my headache even worse. I had to make her believe me. "Cethrax has been using the hidden Passage to attack patrols. Ada and I went to check, and we ran into the creatures who'd been enslaving the Vox. They're not human. They took her, and I was left on Vey-Xanetha. Someone there saved my life, but I was too late. I don't know which world they're on." Ms Weston's eyebrows rose higher with every word I spoke. "Look, it's urgent. Whoever those Stoneskin people are, they're dangerous, and now they have hold of Ada. I can't find her."

A pause. Saki and Ms Weston stared at me, at the blood dripping from my hands, soaking me through to the skin. Then Ms Weston beckoned me downstairs. Not to the lifts, but to the stairs that led to the infirmary and the cells. *Oh, shit. Tell me she isn't going to lock me away.*

"Hold on," I said. "I want to speak to the council."

"Kay, you're in no fit state to speak to anyone, and I won't discuss confidential matters in the entrance hall."

I opened my mouth to protest, but I guessed she didn't want me dripping blood all over her office, either. Smothering an impatient sigh, I followed her downstairs, the nurse trailing me. Ms Weston pushed open a door to the nearest office, which was unoccupied.

"Let me get this story straight," said Ms Weston, who'd taken out her communicator. "Carl tells me you're claiming a group of non-humans have captured Ada. Not Cethrax."

"That's exactly what I'm saying."

"You saw them?"

"They killed me. Tried to," I amended, as Ms Weston's eyes landed on the blood pooling at my feet. "Someone we helped on Vey-Xanetha saved my life. Summoners with a particularly strong link to Xanet are able to heal people even close to death. Those Stoneskins—the name speaks for itself, but they're made of adamantine. Real adamantine. We had no way to fight them. We were outnumbered, and they somehow opened a door to Vey-Xanetha from the Passages."

"Speaking of Vey-Xanetha," said Ms Weston, "there are gaps in your report. The council want an explanation."

"They'll get one," I said tightly, "after I find Ada."

"Carl tells me he found no trace of Ada in the Passages, nor near Cethrax's doorways. He's searched every one of them, Kay."

"It wasn't Cethrax's doorway. They opened their own... but it closed." I could see her eyes follow every movement as I tried to rein in my desperation and keep from storming out and going into the Passages again. Losing Ada had unravelled every shred of self-control I retained, and I struggled to hold onto the pieces. "The council have made statements on less evidence. Ada's in danger, and so are the rest of us if we don't stop them."

"The most we can do is send out search patrols and put the word out within the Alliance." Ms Weston went dangerously still. "I'm sure you can guess why we can't allow word to spread about Ada beyond the Allied worlds."

Ice slid down my spine. "Enzar." Few people outside the Alliance knew who Ada was and where she'd really come from, but one of the first things her guardian had demanded when their shelter had been discovered was confirmation that nobody outside the Alliance would ever know about Ada, her magic, or her history. Even people close to her had taken advantage and almost got her killed. There were worlds outside the Alliance which would no doubt do anything to get their hands on a magic source.

"Enzar," Ms Weston repeated. "I promised her guardian I would allow no harm to come to her under my watch."

"Let me go after her. She's alive," I said, more to myself than anything. "They needed her for something. They didn't hurt her." Not that I'd seen, anyway—they'd dragged her after them while their brothers kicked me to death. *She'll think I'm dead.*

"And you saw fit to take her with you to the lower levels of the Passages without informing senior Alliance members first, knowing about the disturbance to the Balance after the stunt you pulled on Vey-Xanetha?"

My insides twisted. "You think I knew *that* would happen?"

"I think your reckless disregard for your own safety was bound to result in something like this. I warned Ada. I told her to stop you from going too far." Her voice shook with fury.

"There'll be time to apportion blame later, once she's away from those bastards."

"And what is your plan, pray tell?"

"I need a world-key. I have a tracker, I can pick up her trail. And she took her communicator. Maybe she's out of range, but I have to do *something*. I can..." I fought the hopelessness with every word. Giving up now was out of the question. It might be my fault, but if I turned my back now, I'd be condemning her. The magic that had got us into this mess in the first place *must* have a solution.

"You're not in a fit state to be trusted with a world-key," said Ms Weston. "The council are already questioning the transgressions I overlooked in your actions on Vey-Xanetha. There's no doubt you had good reason, but this... there's absolutely no reason why you shouldn't have informed myself or the council before taking action yourself. I wouldn't be doing my job if I allowed you to do any more damage."

Either she cared more about Ada than I'd thought, or I'd finally disobeyed the rules enough times to push her over the edge. Breathing heavily, ignoring the stabbing pain with every breath, I faced her. "You knew that Passage shouldn't be there. Why not close it?"

"The Passage is out of my department, and I assumed you'd have the sense to avoid it until we came to an agreement with the people who once used the escape tunnels." Her eyes flashed. "I will take charge of this myself, and you'll stay here until I can judge whether you're capable of speaking sense to the council."

"Seriously?"

"I have given you more than enough chances, Kay Walker," said Ms Weston. "Saki? Make sure he stays in here. I'm going to inform the council and ensure that they know what, exactly, we stand to face if Ada is really in the hands of our enemies."

As our gazes connected when she left the room, I caught sight of an emotion I didn't expect to see. Fear. She was afraid... not just for Ada's life, but for the whole of the Alliance. For all I knew, the Stoneskins were the Alliance's biggest enemy. They'd enslaved a god... and now they had Ada, who'd once feared she was a walking weapon. Maybe she still did.

What the hell have I done?

I didn't fault Ms Weston for pinning the blame on the one available target: me. If I'd been in her place, I'd have done the same. But none of this would help me find Ada.

"Fuck."

I lapsed into every curse I could think of, in every language I knew. As my fist struck the wall, hands grabbed my arms.

"Calm down, Kay."

"The hell I will—"

A sharp stab as a needle pierced my arm. "No," I gasped, tugging at it with my other hand, my knees already buckling. "I have to find her—please—"

But fog rose in my head, and pulled me under.

3

ADA

I stared at Aric, unable to believe my eyes. What in the Multiverse was he doing out here? I'd thought he was dead, or on another universe. His family had betrayed the Alliance and tried to steal and use a magic source on Aglaia. The centaurs had killed all of them except Aric, who'd disappeared. None of us had known whether he'd got himself stranded in centaur territory or escaped through the Passages, nor did we particularly care. Kay, least of all.

The foul-mouthed idiot former Alliance guard still wore the uniform, though the faux-leather was more grey than black, his jacket was shredded, and the metal bar he'd put through his ear had been torn out, leaving a gaping hole in his ear lobe. Our eyes met, and there was no mistaking it: somehow, Aric freaking Conner was out here in the middle of nowhere. He pushed off the rock, walking towards me. *Oh crap.* Considering I'd kicked him in the crotch last time I'd seen him, I guessed he wasn't coming over for a friendly chat.

I backed away from the others, closer to the rocks marking the division between us humans and the Stoneskin camp. He paused, a few feet away, staring at me like I was a ghost.

"You're here?" he said. "They got hold of *you?"*

I readied myself to attack if necessary. Aric practically wore a sign that said 'please punch me in the face'. Of course, it went alongside the one that read, 'touch me and I'll smash you to pieces', but I wasn't particularly fussed right now, seeing as he was one of the few creatures here who *couldn't* literally take me to pieces. Besides, if I was supposedly important to the Stoneskins, surely someone would intervene if I was in trouble. Not that I wanted to depend on them to get me out of here.

"So this is where you've been hanging out," I said.

Aric's eyes narrowed. He looked tired, but otherwise not particularly diminished for having spent the past god-knew-how-long as a prisoner. It had only been a few weeks since Aglaia. The whole Multiverse had flipped upside-down since then.

"What were you doing?" asked Aric. "Escaping? You and your family finally attacked the Alliance?"

I squinted at him. "You what?"

"Wasn't that why you joined?"

I shook my head, totally perplexed. "You've got the wrong idea. By a mile. I joined to help my homeworld. Like I was doing before. I never planned to attack the Alliance. These bastards took me from the Passages."

"Huh," he said. "I thought you and Walker were planning to..."

"Did someone hit you on the head?" I said, ignoring the painful hand that clenched around my heart at the sound of Kay's surname. "I've never plotted against the Alliance."

"Oh."

Despite everything, wild laughter bubbled in my throat. I pressed a hand to my mouth to stifle the unexpected fit of giggles. It was too much—far too many emotions crashing over me at once and the single stupid "oh" from Aric was enough to push me over the edge. Tears pricked my eyes, and I swallowed a couple of times.

"Don't you laugh at me," he snapped. "You and Walker both acted suspicious."

"Who turned out to be the traitor?" I asked. "Who sneaked off to Aglaia? Whose family almost destroyed the Multiverse?"

Aric's brows pulled inwards. "You stopped them."

"No thanks to you." I let my hand fall to my side, no longer feeling like laughing. "You're a magic-wielder, an enhanced one. You weren't born one, were you?"

A pause. "Yeah, all right," he muttered. "So I volunteered. Walker got a promotion out of being a magic-wielder and my sister had the magic implant without any bad effects, so I figured it couldn't hurt. They call it an upgrade on Klathica. It's wicked."

"Yeah, must be, now you're a prisoner," I shot at him. Childish, but I had to take it out on someone. And he was asking for it. He'd actually volunteered to be *upgraded*, enhanced, whatever they called it. I didn't know a whole lot about Klathica, only that it was one of the founding Alliance worlds and had a thing for idiotic human enhancements.

"Shut it," he said, rubbing the back of his neck. "It wasn't supposed to be like this. Wynn said—"

"Your sister," I said. "Suppose you know what happened to her? And your family?"

Aric shook his head, jaw set. "I guessed. You Alliance bastards killed them." His fists clenched so hard they shook, and I took a step back. A small part of me wanted to feel sorry for him. Evil or not, he'd lost his whole family, who, judging by the way he'd acted at Central, had probably been his only friends, too. Not that he'd done anything to deserve admiration. For all his posturing, he was a follower. He probably didn't mind being a prisoner. We stood apart from the others, but I sensed them watching us curiously.

"The centaurs killed them," I countered, omitting to mention how Kay had, in fact, killed Aric's sister, and had nearly died in the process. "Because your family tried to blow up all of Aglaia."

"Huh." Aric glared. "So you say."

"Just because they didn't tell you anything—"

He lunged for my throat, and I moved swiftly. He caught himself in time to stop from face-planting, feet apart, fists curled.

"We've played this game before, Aric," I said, circling him. Unlike the Stoneskins, he wasn't invincible, and god knew I had a whole lot of pent-up anger to take out on a walking target. He was asking for it.

"Your people killed my whole family," he said, through clenched teeth. "The Alliance are fucking hypocrites. Did they offer my dad a fair trial? No, they had him killed. Justice, my arse."

"The centaurs were the ones who killed them," I said. "Because they were violating laws on Aglaia. You know those laws. Well, you should, but you're not very bright, are you, Aric?"

"Shut the hell up, you offworlder scum."

That did it. I launched into a flying kick and caught him in the face, sending him flat on his back. Aric rolled over, but I landed on top of him, using his surprise to pin down his arms with mine. Magic rose to the surface at long last. Aric yelped as I sent the second level charge into his body, and shook all over, limbs jerking. Swearing, he clenched his hands and magic sparked from his knuckles, red and purple, but I grabbed his hands, absorbing the magic before he fired it at me. His eyes bulged as he watched his own magic join mine. *Didn't know I could do that, did you?*

"It's not the Stoneskins you should be afraid of, Aric," I said. "You should be scared of *me.*"

"You fucking freak show," spat Aric, and I zapped him again until his head fell back on the ground.

"That's not very smart of you, seeing as I have the upper hand," I said, unable to resist goading him. I hated feeling powerless, and the Stoneskins had leached away any freedom I'd had.

Except... this world was low-magic. No, I wasn't pulling it from the atmosphere. I did have magic living inside me. And I'd pulled it from him, too. That might come in handy.

Aric's eyes narrowed to slits. "Get off me," he snarled. "I'm not having those Stoneskin bastards think I'm their next target."

"I'm not moving until you promise not to attack me," I said testily. "I don't trust you."

"Huh. Fine. I won't attack you. You think I want to die out here?"

"Sensible thinking," I said, but I did shift off him, letting him sit up. "So. What kind of magic implant did you get, anyway?"

The two I knew of were lustre, which Kay had been injected with in the Alliance's experiments run by his own father—and adamantine. It wouldn't have been antimagic, though, because Kay had taken him down easily enough on Aglaia.

"I don't know, do I? It's just a boost. Obsidiate."

I relaxed slightly. Obsidiate was flashy but hardly the most dangerous, though it gave Alliance stunners a hell of a kick.

"Any other... talents?" I asked. It was a long shot, but

despite the urgency of the situation, I couldn't help the tiniest stirring of curiosity. What other magic-based substances could be injected into human beings? If it was normal on Klathica, they'd presumably pronounced it safe for public use. I vaguely remembered Kay saying some people illegally used magic as a boost—to fly, or punch through walls.

Wait. Punch through walls? It suggested super-strength... if Kay had actually said that. I was already forgetting the details.

My throat closed, and my hands trembled. *Not now,* I told myself.

"Talents? I can sense the magic level. But when those bastards grabbed me, it stopped. I couldn't sense anything. I reckon they're blocking it."

"You can't use it here? Not even this boost of yours?"

"Don't you think I'd have used it on you?" he snarled. "Or on these other suicidal idiots. Some of them want to be the Stoneskins' sacrifices, would you believe it?"

"They do?"

"Nutcases," he said. "I want out of here."

"You and me both," I said. And then blinked, startled at my own admission that we had a common objective. But right now, I was willing to do anything to get back to Earth, even team up with an enemy.

He frowned at me as though the same thought had crossed his mind.

I drew in a breath. "Don't suppose you have any ideas?" I asked, dropping my voice.

"Later," he muttered. "We have an audience."

So we did. The people nearest us were clearly awake, and more than one lay angled towards us, heads cocked. Several others had risen to their feet, lingering nearby, including the long-toothed man and the bloodstained guy. Four others accompanied them. I paused, watching, as they approached us. Like a group of wolves circling their prey.

Long-Toothed Guy bared his teeth at me, and Blood-stained Guy stared blankly ahead. I tensed, checking magic was there for me to call on—it was the only weapon I had.

"Gervene tells us something interesting about you," said a dirt-smudged teenage boy. "She says you're the one the Stoneskins were looking for."

I narrowed my eyes at him. "What's it to you?"

Long-Toothed Guy laughed. "I like her. Do we have to kill her?"

Bloodstained Guy shot him a glare, as I backed up, moving into a defensive stance.

"Four on one's unfair," I said.

"No one said anything about fair," said Long-Toothed Guy. "We kill you, we delay their plans. Gotta be worth it, right?"

"I'm sensing some faulty logic there," I said.

He hit out. I blocked his strike and kicked his knee, sweeping his legs from underneath him. I spun around to face Bloodstained Guy as he tried to hit me from behind, catching his arm in a lock. He bared his teeth at me—also bloodstained—and I was forced to let go as Long-Toothed Guy lunged at me from behind again. Big mistake. I was well-practised at dealing with being crept up on. I reached back, grabbed both his arms and took advantage of his surprise, using his own body weight to flip him over my head. He came down in a crash that probably knocked him senseless.

There was a thud as Aric threw one of the other guys into a nearby rock. I barely had a moment of surprise before Bloodstained Guy tried to hit me again. I blocked him without even turning round, slamming my elbow into his nose. As he yelped in pain, I stomped on Long-Toothed

Guy's hand. His cry was stifled as Aric grabbed him by the scruff of his neck and threw him halfway across camp.

Unsurprisingly, a dozen pairs of eyes stared at us. Nobody bothered pretending to be asleep anymore, and most had thrown their blankets down, sitting or propping on their elbows to watch the show. Gervene was with the claw-footed man and two others, all of whom looked at me like I'd fallen out of the sky. The dirt-smudged boy had fled to the other side of the camp while Aric and I had knocked the other attackers to the ground. Bloodstained Guy groaned at my feet, blood oozing from his nose.

Aric turned to me, eyes set in a glare. "You gonna thank me or what?"

"Thanks," I said grudgingly.

Maybe we really were on some bizarre reverse-world. Aric, an ally? Not beating the crap out of me?

"Huh." He slouched over to the middle of camp and kicked at Long-Toothed Guy's inert form. "Reckon this guy's out cold. It'd be nicer to kill him."

I glanced down at Bloodstained Guy, who also looked as though he wouldn't be getting up anytime soon.

"What's with the bloodstains?" I asked. "Someone attacked him?"

"He got himself stranded in the swamp," said Aric. "The Stoneskins found him on Cethrax half-mad. No idea why they didn't just leave him there."

"How long have you been here, anyway?"

Now my attackers were starting to drag themselves away—those still conscious, that is—the camp had lost interest in the fight. We hadn't drawn the attention of the Stoneskins yet, either. I didn't know whether that was a good thing or yet another reason to be wary. Maybe their pet humans trying to kill one another in the night was common.

Aric shrugged. "Couple of weeks, maybe." He eyed me with distrust. "You're not to use magic near me, you hear?"

"What do you take me for?" I said.

"I've had bloody enough of magic already. The magic-creatures chased me all over the Passages when I got out of Aglaia."

So he *had* escaped through the doorway. Those kimaros the Conners had unleashed on Aglaia must have come from the hidden Passage. They'd probably got through a door these lunatics had left open. Serve Aric right, seeing as his family had drawn the kimaros's attention to Aglaia in the first place.

"You were in the Passages," I said. "Whereabouts exactly did the Stoneskins find you?"

He ran a hand over his buzzed-short hair. "I was hiding from the magic-creatures. Found a hidden stair downstairs. I checked, figured it was safe, but then a doorway opened out of nowhere. Next thing I knew, three of those bastards dragged me through."

So they were just combing the Passages? They can track magic-wielders? A shiver ran down my spine. If I really was what they were looking for, then...

"Any idea where we're going, exactly?" I asked.

"No," he said. "No clue where those bastards came from, either."

"Does *anyone* know?"

"If they do, they won't talk," said Aric. "But I'm not dying out here. I'm a goddamned Con— magic-wielder."

"You were going to say, Conner," I said, before I could stop myself.

Aric's huge hands clenched into fists. "Stop that. You're no one."

I fought back a laugh, more anger than amusement. He was clueless. "Clearly, the Stoneskins don't think so."

"Huh." He jerked his head in their direction. "Looks like they're waking up."

I stared a moment at the shifting rock-like shapes amongst the tents, before common sense took over.

"Shit. Don't tell them what happened."

"You think I'm stupid?" he said.

Instead of laughing, which would probably have sparked another fight, I ran back to the pitiful blanket I'd been sleeping under before the Stoneskins noticed me looking. Or that I was with Aric. I didn't think they'd care for me making alliances with the others. I retrieved my water flask and refilled it at the river, and Gervene handed me another ration bar. Apparently she'd taken control of the camp supplies. What had she done to get everyone to respect her? Maybe it was the smart suit, or perhaps the fact that she was one of few people here who had a jot of sense left.

Once the camp was packed up, we set off through the wilderness again. Surprisingly, the Stoneskins didn't single me out this time but shunted us all together, even the ones having difficulty moving after the fight. I refused to feel guilty, but it was difficult. My limbs protested at being forced into marching again, my back prickling with sweat, my neck aching. The minutes blurred together with the unbroken rocky landscape. Several hours later, however, I caught sight of a shape on the horizon that formed an odd contrast to the dry ground. The leaders angled our march in that direction, and it gradually began to take shape. It wasn't rock, but marshland... but something wasn't quite right. It started and ended just as abruptly, and the air above had an odd, shimmering quality. Maybe the heat was getting to me...

No. It was a doorway.

The smell of the swampland rolled over us, trapped by the heat. It became difficult to breathe. Yet we walked *towards* the doorway, not away.

Soon, it became clear why. A stone building sat on the other side of the doorway, half-sunk into the swamp. The silent, dirty-faced boy walking alongside me muttered to himself, "Not this hellhole again, no..."

"Cethrax," I said. "This is Cethrax. They're taking us there... why?"

"Next doorway," he muttered, not looking at me. "If we don't get eaten."

"Oh, fan-bloody-tastic," I said, twisting to look at the people behind me. No one would meet my eyes. "They're okay with us getting eaten?"

No answer. Our part of the line reached the doorway. Magic rushed over me when I stepped from rocky ground to marsh—I'd thought Cethrax had barely an iota of magic to speak of, seeing as none of its natives could use it. Apparently not. Maybe I could use it here... but what use would it be? I'd had enough experience with the monsters lurking in the swamps of Cethrax. Wyverns, vox-kind and goblins were mostly magicproof. Just like the monsters that held us captive. And I didn't have any other weapons, nor any way of convincing Cethrax's monsters to help me. *Kay could probably do it.* Like when he'd talked the Vox king out of crushing us to a pulp. Kay could talk his way out of anything. He'd probably talked the entire Alliance into sending out a rescue mission. The first stop would be the hidden Passage, which led right into the swamp. *He's coming, he has to be,* I told myself, ignoring the small, insistent voice asking when I was going to give up deluding myself.

The Stoneskins led us through ankle-deep, murky water and thick mud that clung to the soles of my guard boots. Would the uniform would stand up to wear and tear? How long before the magicproof coating wore off, leaving me doubly vulnerable to an attack from one of the others?

The group halted as we drew closer to the building,

leaving us in the middle of a patch of swamp. The Stoneskins continued on their path, but several remained to stand guard around us. Apparently, they didn't want us going into the building. Flies buzzed in my ears, and the stench was worse than a sewer crossed with a slaughterhouse. Coughing, swatting at the air, we stood in a huddle of misery.

"What are they doing?" I hissed, to anyone nearby.

"Gathering supplies." Gervene inched closer to me, her feet entirely submerged in mud.

"They don't trust us?"

"They don't need us," she said. "No weapons here, I don't think. That place is just an outpost."

"For what?"

"No clue. Trade, maybe. The few times the Alliance tried to set up trade with Cethrax didn't go so well, did they?"

I might not know all the Alliance's history, but that was pretty much a given. I nodded. "So the Stoneskins hop through the nearest doorway for supplies... how do they even track the doorways?"

"I have no idea," she said. "Same way they found us. They can track magic-wielders, and doorways, too, I guess. Does it matter?"

"It might help us get out," I said in an undertone. "I'm trying to figure out how they operate."

"Don't let them find out," said Gervene. "They overheard a few people discussing wild ideas for escaping, couple of days before we found you. They took them away to their tents, and no one's seen them since."

I shivered. "Damn," I said, and quickly checked to make sure none of the Stoneskins were close enough to see us talking. Lucky we were right in the middle of the group. "Were they talking about anything in particular?"

"This one has a death wish," the dirty-faced teenage boy said.

"Just because you've given up, doesn't mean we all have," said Gervene. Gratitude rushed through me. Maybe I could pull a team together. Maybe some of us could get away.

The presence of the other people, the ones with haunted eyes and closed-off expressions, tugged at my conscience. Nell's voice repeated in my head: *You can't save everyone.*

But I had to start somewhere. "Have any of you ever eavesdropped on them?" I asked everyone closest by. There was something to be said for standing in a swamp—the Stoneskins had been forced to move several metres away otherwise they'd start to sink in the mud. Being made out of rock had its disadvantages, too.

Aric edged closer, not very subtly, knocking the dirt-stained boy headfirst into the swamp. "Hells, yeah," he said.

"Quieter," I muttered, and he glared at me again. "What did you hear? Anything about… I don't know. Where did they come from originally? Some of them speak English…"

"And other Earth languages," said Aric. "And Klathican."

"Valerian dialects, too," added Gervene. "I have… a theory. Call me crazy—they're invincible, I think, but something tells me they might have been gathered together. Like us."

"Like us," I said. "They—they were human."

"Some of them were," said Aric. "You seen those little devil-like ones? They talk like dreyverns."

I vaguely remembered some of the short, scaly creatures being amongst the ones which had attacked Kay.

Kay.

I clapped a hand to my mouth. "Oh my god," I said. "I—do you think someone… did it to them? Made them like that?"

They clearly *weren't* natural—not in the sense they'd been born that way. All looked and talked like people from at least some of the allied worlds. On some worlds, maybe it was possible—somehow—to embed adamantine into human skin. *Is that why they need me?* I'd been an experimental subject of sorts myself, after all, and the Alliance had once conducted similar experiments, injecting humans with magic-based substances. I presumed they'd been trying to create artificial magic-wielders, because on Earth, they were such a rarity.

Gervene squinted at me. "I've no idea how they'd go about doing something like that, but..."

That has to be it. If the Alliance did it, it'd explain why they held such a grudge. A former friend of mine, Skyla, had gone as far as to murder people at Central when information on the research project she'd been an unwilling part of had surfaced again.

Not just her. I swallowed hard against the lump rising in my throat, desperately trying to push back the image of Kay bleeding on the ground. *He's alive. He has to be alive.*

"Where?" I said. "Had any of you guys seen those Stone-skins before they picked you up?"

"Picked up." Long-Toothed Guy snorted. "Not kidnapped or anything."

"Well?" I said. "It might help."

Head-shakes, from a handful of people. The rest didn't look at me. Maybe they didn't understand, maybe they just didn't want to know.

"Okay," I said. "Have they mentioned any particular worlds? Where they might have come from?"

"Hmm," said Gervene. "I did think it was odd when they brought up Thairon. They can't be travelling there, it's closed off."

Huh? The name sounded vaguely familiar, but I didn't know anything about that particular world.

"That's not Alliance," I said slowly.

"It was supposed to be," said Gervene. "Before they turned on the Alliance and killed a bunch of people."

"Wait, what?" I stared at her. "What happened?"

"I don't know the details. Supposedly the Alliance sent Ambassadors in, and they'd set them a trap... there was a cover-up, but I know someone who worked at Neo Greyle's branch in Valeria at the time. Thairon used to be closely linked with Valeria and Klathica, before they withdrew from the Alliance, but they never expected them to slaughter a bunch of people. It stopped all Alliance negotiations in their tracks. Last I heard they were closed off."

"Wow," I said, because there was nothing else I *could* say. Of course, Ambassadors did a risky job, but going in to negotiate and being murdered instead? Damn. "What did they say about it? The Stoneskins?"

Gervene shook her head. "Not much. I caught a few words of a conversation. *Don't forget Thairon,* one of them said. That was it."

"Hmm." Unhelpful, or it seemed so anyway. I was willing to latch onto any information I could find. Maybe they were originally from that world. Closed off. Like this place.

"Quiet, they're coming back," hissed Long-Toothed Guy. "I'm not letting your babbling get me killed."

Aric shifted and Long-Toothed Guy pitched headfirst into the swamp. He surfaced, spluttering and cursing in what sounded like three languages mangled together.

"Is there a problem?" A voice carried over the group.

I held my breath. I hadn't realised the Stoneskins were so close—or they'd moved so quickly. Two of them had come right close to us. *Please don't let them have heard us.*

"No," Long-Toothed Guy muttered, shaking muddy water out of his hair.

Most of the others studied the ground, hardly seeming to breathe.

"Good," said the voice. "We are leaving now. It would be a shame to lose any of you."

It's okay, I told the part of my mind that wanted to start panicking. *It's okay, you're safe.*

As safe as it was possible to be in a monster-infested swamp, in the company of monsters made out of unbreakable rock, anyway.

Kay is alive. I'm going to find him. I repeated it in my head like a mantra.

He was alive. I couldn't let myself believe otherwise, or I'd fall into a darkness deeper than any chasm.

4

KAY

et up. Someone was shaking me, hands dug into my shoulders. *Get the hell up.*

Disjointed, stark images flashed before my eyes, too quickly to make sense of.

Get up. Now.

I sat bolt upright, striking out with my fist.

Saki moved out of range, glaring at me over her clipboard. "What in the Multiverse is wrong with you?"

No one had touched me. I'd imagined it. I blinked, totally disorientated. I was in one of the med-rooms, on a fold-out bed. Nobody else was in the room but her, and she was lucky I hadn't hit her. "What did you knock me out for?"

"You were acting out and causing a scene," she said, bluntly.

I blinked again, realising someone had removed my torn, bloodstained shirt, and my Ambassador's jacket hung over a nearby chair. I had one hell of a collection of bruises across my ribs.

"Ada," I said. "Dammit."

"She's out of range. Half the guard patrols are looking for her instead of keeping up our security."

"I should be looking for her," I muttered, brushing my hair out of my eyes.

"You're on probation." Saki gave me that look again. She was far from the first person to dislike me on principle because she'd had the misfortune of meeting my father, but this level of contempt was more than I wanted to deal with right now. I just wanted to get to Ada.

"You can't be serious."

"Ask your boss. You're the one who violated Alliance code."

Hell. My head wasn't in the right place. Not at all. "Yes, and one of our employees was carried off by monsters powerful enough to subdue a wild magic force *and* a Cethraxian Vox leader."

"You aren't making any sense," said Saki, tapping a pen on her clipboard.

"I'm not delirious and I'm not making this shit up," I said. "If no one acts, the whole Alliance is going to be in trouble. Whoever those Stoneskin bastards were, they almost destroyed the Multiverse already. They're the ones who knocked off the Balance." I pushed to my feet, ignoring the pain in my ribs. I could deal with pain.

I couldn't deal with the rest. Not lying down.

"I'm to keep you here until you're ready for questioning," said Saki, moving in front of the door. "You're not delirious, despite your violent and unstable behaviour. But you're clearly confused—"

"Don't," I said. "Please—don't. I'm not lying and I'm not confused. I know what I saw."

"There are no other witnesses. You might want to check how you speak to the council."

I rubbed my forehead. "My colleague just got kidnapped

EMMA L. ADAMS

right in front of me, I almost died three times, and you stabbed me with a syringe. If you wanted a friendly conversation, now's not the best time."

Saki sighed, some of the anger fading from her expression. "It's a precautionary measure. I'm sure Ada's fine. We've had guards go off-grid before. Though I have good news: nothing's broken. Those are old scars."

"Tell me something I don't know," I said. With all the blood, I must look like a wyvern had clawed me open again. Old news. "Don't suppose there's a spare change of guard uniform lying around? Mine's at my apartment, and I need to speak to the council as soon as possible."

"Yes, your boss has requested to speak to you," she said. "There's a shower through that door. And a change of clothes. I don't know what happened to you, but you don't have any serious injuries. What did you do, run into a wall?"

"A chalder vox. Amongst other things. You wouldn't believe me if I told the full story," I said, the words echoing hollowly. Even Ms Weston wouldn't, which meant I had no chance of getting through to the council.

Even showered and changed into clean uniform, I felt like hell. I wasn't in the mood to deal with the council now. I had to make a plan. But I kept getting stuck—there *was* no way to track a person from here. Even with a world-key, even with an amplifier. I needed to figure out which world it was.

Half-formed ideas weren't enough. I needed to talk to a senior Alliance member who knew the workings of the Passages. If Carl wasn't forthcoming, there must be someone else here at Central. If not...

"I want to speak to the council," I told Saki.

"Ms Weston says you're to do no such thing."

I stared. "You what?"

Saki tutted. "The council are in meetings until the end of the day. They're fielding questions from seven Alliance branches about the ruckus you caused on that other world. If you want to persuade them to put out a cross-world search warrant, it'll have to wait until tomorrow at the very least."

I leaned on the wall as dizziness made the world tilt under my feet. "You can't be serious," I said. "An Alliance member has been kidnapped by dangerous offworld creatures—ones that aren't even in the Alliance's files."

"Yes, so *you* say, but the council are well aware of your habit for rash actions. You can't walk in here dripping blood everywhere and raving about monsters and expect the council to rewrite the laws on your behalf."

"Right," I said, and my voice sounded distant, like someone else spoke. "Is that it? Can I leave now?"

"Your boss wants to speak to you once she's finished informing Ada's family of the... unfortunate accident."

Unfortunate accident.

I'd heard those words before. *It can't happen again.*

The opposite ledge of a cliff, wreathed in smoke, close but not close enough, slipping away by the second.

"Kay?"

Goddammit. I clenched my fists, breathing heavily. "Yeah." Again, my voice might have come from somewhere far away.

"I said, you can leave."

"Right."

I had no recollection either of leaving or climbing the stairs to the first floor, but I must have. Markos the centaur came out of the office and I almost collided with him.

"By the gods, human. What's happened this time?"

I shook my head. "Ask the dragon." I didn't much care if Ms Weston heard the unflattering nickname.

"I wouldn't do anything rash, human."

But I'd already knocked on her door, and opened it before she invited me in. She looked up from a stack of files on her desk, tapping at the screen of her communicator. I let the door close behind me, and saw the files were the reports myself and the three other people who'd been to Vey-Xanetha had given her. Only yesterday.

"Kay. I do hope you're prepared for a civilised discussion."

"I don't know what more I can say. I told you the truth. There's a threat to the Alliance, and they took Ada."

"Yes, I've had to relate the same story to Ada's guardian."

Once again, the floor gave way under my feet. Ada's guardian. Her brothers. Thanks to me, they'd lost her.

"You should have let me tell them."

Ms Weston gave me her iciest look. "Kay Walker, I've had quite enough of you telling me how to do my job. You're on probation, as of today, and it'll be up to me to judge when you're fit to go on missions as an Ambassador again."

Missions? I couldn't even conceive of getting on with the job without—

Panic gripped my chest, some of the shock wearing off as adrenaline kicked my heart rate into gear, but my thoughts remained as clouded as ever. Dwelling on Ada wouldn't help me think clearly. I needed someone high up in the Alliance on my side now more than ever.

"Are you not going to send anyone to the hidden Passage, at least?" I asked. "Someone has been using it. The evidence is all there. You can't deny Cethrax has taken advantage. It explains the anomalies, the unexpected attacks. That Passage goes on for miles, even I didn't see how far."

"We have enough on our hands keeping up with regular patrols," said Ms Weston. "I'm in charge of the investigation, and I've put out a message to Valeria and Alvienne. The other Allied worlds are considerably displeased with the chaos they experienced while you were on Vey-Xanetha. Your profile's plastered all over it, unfortunately, and considering the stories of you raving in the Passages have spread already, they're demanding more evidence. The hidden Passage will be under guard until further notice, but nobody has found so much as a trace of these *Stoneskins* you speak of."

Oh, crap. Our battle with the mad god was bound to have caused a major disturbance, but I hadn't expected half the Multiverse to back out of searching for Ada.

"And the Stoneskins?" I asked.

"As I said, with no evidence—"

"I can find evidence," I said. "If you'd let me."

"You, Kay Walker, are going to stay here, on Earth. Your past behaviour does you no credit."

"I acted in the way I saw fit to protect the Alliance and my fellow Ambassadors. To save human lives," I said. "I've never violated our mandate. Every time, I put the Alliance above everything else. If you think I'd ever do anything like that on purpose, you promoted the wrong person to Ambassador."

I braced myself for her to hit me with everything. She couldn't punish me any more than I could myself.

"So that's where you stand, Kay? You'd defend your own actions to the last, even though you've put one of our members in enemy hands?"

"Enough," I said quietly. "Don't think for a minute I don't regret what happened. And don't think for a minute I won't try to save her."

Silence. Ms Weston looked at me with... I couldn't tell what emotion she was trying to keep out of her eyes.

"You're in shock," she said, quietly. "I can't control your choices, Kay, but I have a responsibility towards all my employees. I thought you of all people would understand the futility of throwing your life towards a lost cause."

A thousand knives stabbed me at once.

She knows. In the forefront of my mind, Ada's face was replaced by another, one I'd tried to forget.

Elizabeth Walker. Alliance Ambassador, who'd given her life for what Ms Weston called a lost cause. Thirteen years ago, she'd tried to rescue a world the Alliance had labelled as beyond help. An idiotic suicide mission, as my father put it. It made no difference—suicide mission or not, she was dead.

And Ms Weston thought I'd do the same, given the chance.

"I'm glad you think so highly of me," I said, icy-cold. "I have no intention of involving anyone else in this. And I have absolutely no intention of throwing away my life in the name of a hopeless cause. Ada is alive. Those creatures are a legitimate threat both to the Alliance and to the Balance. And if no one else will do anything, then yes, I'm going to break Alliance code."

And I turned heel and left.

∿

I'd pay later. I had no doubt. But there was something more important I had to do, and I refused to think about the rest until I had to.

"Kay." Markos crossed my path, looking unusually concerned. "Ada's missing?"

"Yeah," I said. "I know. I'm going to talk to her family."

The centaur's eyebrows shot up. "Are you sure?"

"Her brother works in tech. He'll be—" I checked the time. It was early afternoon; I'd been knocked out for hours. But if he'd heard the news, he'd have gone home. They'd be... planning to leave? To mount their own rescue initiative using their old contacts? I didn't know her family, not really. Except one thing: they'd die to protect her, and they would never forgive the Alliance.

"You're going after her."

"I have to," I said, and all but ran into the corridor before he could respond. From the shouting coming from Ms Weston's office, someone was in trouble. Hopefully not Ada's family. I backed up, and walked into Amanda.

"Shit. Sorry."

"I heard." She brushed a strand of hair from her eyes. "I was looking for you."

Oh, shit. She and Ada had been friends, for the brief time Ada had been at the Alliance.

"Sorry," I said, like that made a blind bit of difference.

"I know it wasn't your fault," she said. Her concerned expression ought to have been a relief after the crap I'd faced, but it wasn't. It *was* my fault Ada had been in the Passages in the first place.

"You're the only person who seems to think so." I edged past her. "I have to go and talk to her family."

"Kay…" Her voice followed me. "Was there really no trace? From the tracker?"

How much did she know? She was Ms Weston's sister, so she was more aware than others in the Alliance about certain things. Like…

Sources.

"None." I turned back to face her. "Did your sister tell you what they were made of? The people who took her? They weren't human. But apparently I'm not in my right mind."

"She said you were raving about adamantine."

Something inside me clenched at the word. "Yeah. That's what they were made out of, like solid unbreakable rock. They beat the hell out of me and took her through a doorway." I ran a hand through my hair. "If you know anywhere I can get more information, it might stop me from getting killed when I go after them."

"You'll die," said Markos from the office doorway, unhelpfully.

"Yeah, already did," I said. "Hell didn't care for me, so here I am. And there has to be a way. For those creatures to even exist…" The only adamantine on Earth was the outside of this building, and parts of the inside, too. And the other Alliance branches. And…

I automatically reached into the pocket of my coat, before remembering my dagger had shattered when it made contact with the Stoneskin.

"What's stronger than adamantine?" I said, aware both Markos and Amanda were staring at me like I was crazy. Again. "My dagger's made of the same material as them, it shouldn't have broken so easily."

"If they had a higher concentration of antimagic in their skin than the dagger, then it's possible," said Amanda. "Novices have shattered those blades when fighting in the Passages. It's why we have so many in storage."

"Fighting Cethrax," I said, another possibility striking me. "The vox-kind have magicproof armour, but it isn't adamantine. What is it?"

"Kay, if you're thinking of recruiting a wyvern to go after Ada, you're digging yourself an early grave," said Markos.

"No," I said. "Adamantine isn't unbreakable—evidently. And there are ways to enhance it." Like the coat I wore. It had antimagic woven into the fabric. Not that it made any difference when faced with extra-powered magic, like a boost…

A power-boost.

I looked at Amanda. "I don't suppose you happen to know what Klathica puts into those super-strength enhancer implants?"

When the magic level had gone up, people had even caused damage in the Passages with those temporary magic-boosts. With some kind of *magic source*.

"I… I don't know. I'll look it up." Ignoring Markos's snorts, she turned back to the elevators. Two of them were out of order courtesy of a griffin which had got loose in here a few days ago. And to think I'd thought *that* was as messed-up as Central could get.

"You'll have better luck searching in here than the archives," said the centaur. "Your sister's got me re-organising half of them, looking for obscure information."

So that was why the office was in such a mess. It had been in the same state for a week. Not that I particularly cared what Ms Weston was preoccupied with at the moment.

"I'll have to talk to Ada's family," I said. "But if you find anything, can you message me? If there's a source that can match adamantine..."

"I'll try," said Amanda.

"Dragon incoming," said Markos, as Ms Weston's office door opened. Amanda stepped past me and I carried on downstairs, hoping she hadn't overheard. Everyone stayed out of my way in the entrance hall. I wasn't sure if Carl, Ms Weston or Saki had told everyone I was a lunatic, or if I looked like one anyway.

I didn't have my motorcycle with me, so I walked to Ada's house as fast as possible. The crowded roads were even more alien than the Passages. The roar of traffic echoed as if from a distance, and the crowds grated on my nerves even more than usual. I was on the verge of using magic to shove people out of my way, but I couldn't use it on Earth anymore now the levels were stable again. Plus that would definitely get me listed under *unhinged.*

Ada's family might have left already. I had to make a plan. I had all the Alliance's information on sources already on my communicator, from when I'd been trying to figure out what lustre could do. But Earth wasn't exactly the first stop for information on magic. I could gain access to all Alliance branches across the Multiverse as an Ambassador and logically, that should have been my first step. Except Carl wasn't allowed to let me into the Passages anymore, and to be honest, I didn't even know what I was looking for. I could steal another world-key, but I'd lost Ada's signal, and even if I did find her, there might be a million of those stone monsters guarding her. Every idea I contemplated was a dead end.

I stopped short as I reached Ada's house. The curtains were drawn. Had they left already?

Get on with it, Kay. I knocked, twice, and the door opened. I had a glimpse of a short figure through the gap before a fist slammed into the side of my face. I could have blocked it but I didn't, letting the pain ring through me.

Nell's elbow caught me in the ribs, right on the bruises. *Damn.* I clenched my teeth together, fighting the instinct to hit back. I held still, hands clenched, as she hammered strike after strike at me. My head snapped back as her fist connected with my jaw. She could have knocked me out or even killed me if she'd wanted. My vision clouded, sudden weakness threatening to drag me to the ground and leave me there.

Another kick knocked the breath from my lungs and sent me sideways into the fence, my head striking the wood. I leaned on it, blinking at her furious face. Blood dripped into my eyes from a cut on my forehead.

"What's going on? Nell?"

Great, Ada's older brother had arrived to join in the fun.

"You'll have to get in line," I said.

"Holy crap," said Jeth. "Nell, that's enough."

Nell breathed in and out, but the rage left her eyes. Beating the hell out of me wouldn't bring her daughter back.

I pushed back from the fence, ignoring the pain of a dozen new bruises, and faced Jeth. "She's not dead," I said, my voice hoarse. "I need your help."

The Fletcher family stared at me. As I expected.

"I have a tracker." I coughed, my ribs aching. "I can trace

her even if the Alliance can't. They... won't help me. You know how important this is."

A long pause. I mentally braced myself for another blow. Nell watched me for a moment.

"If you're lying," she said. "I'll kill you next time." And she turned her back and went into the house.

Jeth blinked a couple of times.

"Guess that wasn't an invite?" I said, coughing again. I wiped blood from my eyes with my left hand.

"Come on in, you need to clean up," said Jeth, turning his back.

I was acutely aware of intruding in their home, even as I pressed a damp cloth to my forehead to stem the bleeding. Ada's family were my last hope, short of involving others at the Alliance in illegal activity—but I was on my way to doing that already. I braced one hand on the kitchen table. Maybe Ms Weston was right, maybe I was still in shock. But no way would I sit on the side lines while the Alliance ignored Ada's plight.

I looked up as a person entered my peripheral vision. Jeth watched me from the doorway. Wary, like he expected me to light the house on fire.

"You have computers with offworld tech, right?" I pulled the tracker from my pocket, which was crusted in dried blood.

Jeth stared at it. "That's a tracker, right? Whose blood is that?"

"Mine."

"Jesus Christ."

I'd forgotten about that. I wiped the tracker on the outside of my coat as Ada's brother shook his head.

"Was it the same people who took Ada?" he asked.

"Yeah. Someone saved me. But the door closed." I pressed the cloth to my temples, and told him about our final fight on

Vey-Xanetha, the Vox, and the stone-skinned people who'd attacked us and taken Ada. "I was stranded there," I said. "The world-key is back at Central, and it was only linked to one world."

Not that it would do any good if I had no idea which world she was on. Each world required a certain symbol. I knew the base set, but not the individual ones for each world —except Vey-Xanetha, seeing as I'd been there. And I was willing to bet even Ambassadors weren't allowed to see all of them. The council probably had even the darkest corners of the Multiverse on record. Just in case.

Nell and Alber both stood behind Jeth. They'd come to listen in.

"You know how to find her?" asked Alber. He and Ada could easily have been blood relations. Nell, too. They had the same soft facial features, the same shade of tan. Alber's eyes were purple, with the tell-tale glint of a magic-wielder. Nell's were blue, but they might have been contacts. Like Ada's.

I couldn't say, *I don't know.* "I think so."

"Whoa, slow down," said Alber. "You took her into the Passages, right?" I didn't miss the accusation in his voice.

"Ada and I decided to check out the hidden Passage after the mission. On Vey-Xanetha, we found out someone was creating doorways to Cethrax, and we realised the hidden Passage was the one place we hadn't checked. And we found a doorway that shouldn't be there. Those Stoneskin creatures were using it as a shortcut. I don't know if they're on Cethrax or where, and anyway, it's swarming with vox-kind and wyverns—I can't go there unarmed and alone, without knowing her location." I looked at Jeth, who nodded, slowly. "I need to make another world-key. And I need to hack into the offworld communications to send out a signal to her, let her know I'm coming. Most worlds have some kind of base point." Even Cethrax did, from the days before missions into the swamp had been stopped on the basis of safety. And bases were close to the Passages.

"I've no clue about world-keys," said Jeth. "But cross-world communications—maybe. I'll have to think. She has a standard communicator, right?"

"Yeah. We didn't think. The earpieces are back at Central. They ran out of battery. I have the tracker, and I lost her trace when they closed the doorway." But a trace would be here, in Ada's house. It had to be.

"Trace?" asked Alber, blankly.

"When a person uses magic, they leave a kind of echo. I can pick up on it and follow it, using a tracker. If I found her signal and I had a key that opened any world, then in theory, I could find her." I couldn't tell them that if I'd lost her signal for good, that was it. Not to mention the sheer unlikelihood of opening a door to the exact right place. I didn't know nearly enough about the source the world-keys were made of. The source I'd tapped into on Vey-Xanetha.

"That's... not right." Jeth shook his head, frowning. "Trackers can't trace a person offworld. They usually only work on low-magic worlds where there isn't as much inter-ference. Ada told me that's how she found Al, when..."

"When those Conners took me prisoner," said Alber, his jaw clenching. "They didn't have anything to do with this, did they?"

"No, they're dead," I said. "Did Ada not tell you...?" It didn't matter if her family knew now, anyway. Somehow, saying the words aloud was nothing compared to the shit I'd been through already. "The experiment. I was a part of it. I have... lustre in my blood. I'm an amplifier."

I paused. The Fletcher family gaped at me like I'd declared I could teleport between universes.

Jeth was first to speak. "You... you were part of it?" He turned to Nell. "Did you know?"

"I suspected," she said, "but I've never heard of *lustre*."

"You haven't?" So Enzar didn't have access to amplifying sources. I stored that information away. Right now, all that mattered was finding Ada. "I can only amplify certain magic-fuelled devices, like the Chameleon—or bloodrock, I guess."

Jeth shook his head. "That's... insane. Ada didn't tell us." A note of suspicion crept into his voice.

"It's not like I've been telling everyone across the Multi-verse," I said. "Even my boss doesn't know."

"That so?" Jeth looked at me with definite suspicion. "Wasn't your father the one who spearheaded the whole thing? Skyla said, right?"

For god's sake. "That's irrelevant," I said tightly. "I didn't volunteer to get shot up with an unknown magic source." I looked away from their stares, fists clenching. "If I knew how to find Ada, I would. But I don't."

"You can turn invisible," said Nell. "You can go anywhere, unseen. Why not use it to go after these creatures?"

"I need to be touching a Chameleon," I said. "We handed them in at Central because the batteries had run out. I don't need it to actually be switched on, though. I can draw on the source even if it's dormant. Chameleons are made out of bloodrock, right?" I directed the question at Jeth.

"The coating's bloodrock," he said. "The inside is a mixture of Valerian and Klathican tech—you know their enhancement drugs? They give people a temporary boost. I figured I could create a one-use only device that did the same. Most didn't work, but for some reason, bloodrock did. It's more efficient than bloodrock solution because it doesn't rely on being constantly applied. But I'd never—I'd never have thought of injecting it inside a person." He cleared his throat, not looking me in the eyes. "If you found Ada, you'd have to hand her the device, and make sure the battery was charged."

"I can transfer my abilities to her," I said. "She has an absorbent in her blood."

"She does?" Jeth glanced at Nell.

"Don't you claim to know more about my daughter than I do," said Nell, her mouth tight with anger. "You've done nothing but stir up trouble."

"Nell," said Alber, placing a hand on her shoulder. "Right now, he's our only chance to find her. I can do magic, but she was always a million times better at it than me." His eyes glittered.

Jeth sighed. "The Chameleons are charging at Central. There are two left, under lock and key at the moment."

"There were three," I said.

"Yeah, I gave one to someone who wanted to have a look at it. Ms Weston."

Great. What did my boss want with the Chameleon? She distrusted most offworld tech, and camouflage tech was tricky at best, blowing up even if you knew what you were doing. I'd surmised that was why no one in the Alliance had made them until Ada's family had come along.

"Okay. Aside from those, I can also amplify the tracker," I said. "That means I can up the effect and follow the trace wherever it leads. I can use it to locate Ada, but I'll need to be able to open a doorway. I tried it before and the trace had just vanished. I don't think she's in a world linked to the Passages."

Jeth's eyes widened. "Is that even possible?"

"God knows," I said. "Maybe I can only track places directly behind the doorways. It's not exactly practical to search every inch of the Passages, especially with Cethrax's monsters using it as a stomping-ground—not to mention those kimaros. Magic-creatures," I added in explanation.

"They're like living magical energy. Veyak, the living god on Vey-Xanetha, was like a supercharged version."

"That's what took my daughter?" asked Nell.

I shook my head. "No. Something worse. Whatever they are, they're powerful enough to control a sentient magic force and Cethrax. But my supervisor told me the council won't listen. Vey-Xanetha has caused enough trouble already."

"They won't search for her," said Nell, in a low, cold voice. "They abandoned her."

"They're putting out a search warrant," I said ineffectually. "I know it's not enough. They don't have the resources we do."

I hadn't known how completely I'd been sliding away from the Alliance's rules. Before, I couldn't to afford to second-guess the system, not when it had been all I'd had. But now Ada had gone, I'd turn my back on the Alliance to save her.

"I'm going after her," said Alber, his jaw set. "No matter what."

"It'll be dangerous," I said. "Even if I get hold of a working world-key, we'd have to shortcut through Cethrax. You can fight?"

"We can all fight," said Jeth. "But if she has a communicator, I can send out a message across the Multiverse. I can write it in a code we made up when we were kids so only she'll understand. She'd have to be within range, but I can keep doing it while you work on your plan—the thing is, the Alliance communication signals only go so far." He looked directly at me. "We need a source."

5

KAY

I f ever anything proved the break of my faith in Central, it was sneaking into the storerooms, invisible, to raid their supplies of dangerous offworld substances.

It was early evening when I left the Fletcher family's house, detouring back to my own flat to wait for the guards to switch to the less stringent evening patrols. I ditched my Ambassador's jacket, figuring my regular guard coat would draw less attention, and ran over the plan in my mind while I heated up a microwaveable meal. I had no appetite to speak of, but the energy crash coupled with all the blood I'd lost was starting to hit me hard. I needed to be at the top of my game if I wanted to pull off this bout of breaking and entering. I also needed to get hold of a new communicator, but that could wait.

Alber wanted to come with me, and only his older brother's warnings kept him at home. Jeth and I both had plausible alibis for being at Central, though mine was precarious at best.

The problem, of course, was they'd reinforced the back windows after Ada had broken in to steal bloodrock, so long ago. But I didn't have to worry about a time-limit on invisibility. Once I had a Chameleon, I was set. Except I needed to get hold of one in the first place. Two were in the tech department, locked up and charging after the batteries had been drained… and the third was in Office Fifteen. To be precise, in Ms Weston's office.

Thanks, universe. I left my flat and walked casually towards Central. Once I had the Chameleon, I'd have the run of the Multiverse. I'd be able to get anywhere, unseen. I'd be able to find Ada.

I hid outside until the latest patrol came back from the Passages, and I managed to slip in through the front doors alongside another group of guards. The doors had been enhanced so magic-based effects like bloodrock solution didn't work anymore. I wasn't sure if the same applied to invisibility, but I'd think about it later.

A couple of heads turned in my direction, but I'd already strode off. Now I wasn't covered in blood, I could blend in with other people easily if I wanted to, especially here, where all the guards wore the same uniform and most of the new novices didn't know me.

I headed for the first floor. Office Fifteen was a ghost town, as per usual. But I had no doubt Ms Weston was around somewhere. She practically lived here.

Her office was empty. I paused outside the door for an instant, checking for intruders. No signs. Not so much as the faint sound of a footstep. Even the open booths where the staff usually worked were empty, but there hadn't been many people around since the murders—only Markos had stuck around in Office Fifteen, and Evan the wannabe-assistant. No way he'd be here after hours. Everyone else thought it was haunted. Still, paranoia sat on my shoulder as I eased the door to the boss's office open, careful not to leave fresh fingerprints in case she went to extreme measures to catch the intruder. I wouldn't put it past her, considering we'd had a traitor in the office before.

Technically, *I* was a traitor, but I pushed that thought to the back of my mind as I scanned the room for likely hiding places. All the filing cabinets were closed, but they contained only papers—I'd seen them open when I'd been in her office earlier. But I'd never seen her open the desk drawer on the left.

I manoeuvred it open with my jacket sleeve pulled over my hand, and sure enough, there were several pieces of magi-tech in there. I picked up the Chameleon—and stopped short as I read the name on the file underneath it. *Adamantine.*

I froze. *Don't touch it. Don't leave evidence.*

I couldn't move.

Slam. I jumped at the sound of footsteps. I slid the drawer closed but knew it was too late to move.

An ear-splitting crash rang through the empty office. I remained frozen in a crouch, convinced I'd be caught any second.

"Oh, for crying out loud, Markos!" shouted Ms Weston.

Holy shit. The centaur had distracted the dragon. I grabbed the Chameleon and turned invisible, cursing myself for not doing so the instant I'd picked it up. I really was losing it, forgetting something so bloody simple.

As I slipped through the partly-opened office door and closed it quietly, I caught sight of Markos standing near a row of toppled filing cabinets, and an absurd smile on his face. Maybe there was one person left here who didn't think I was crazy, after all.

Still invisible, I went back downstairs. Next stop: the storerooms.

Of course, the door was locked and guarded by two senior guards—no novices would be entrusted with that job after both Central *and* West Office had been robbed recently. The last thing I wanted was to raise suspicion any further, so I went down the corridor to the back door and paused, checking for any extra security measures I'd forgotten. I tapped the earpiece I'd clipped on.

Jeth had gone to the second floor tech office, "borrowed" the store-room key and taken one of the other Chameleons. As only he knew how to fix them when they broke, no one would get suspicious. He'd also stolen spare batteries from the stores, but no magi-tech lasted long on Earth unless it was hooked up to an offworld-based energy source. It had taken more nerve than I'd have expected of him, creating those Chameleon devices while running the risk of the offworld tech severely backfiring—but there was no denying they were bloody useful.

"Okay, I'm ready," Jeth's voice said in my ear. A moment's pause, then a *crash* made the earpiece vibrate so hard, I ducked around a corner in case someone heard. Except it was masked by the real noise coming from the second floor, which sounded like steel dominoes toppling over.

The guards ran forward, alarmed, and I took my chance. I'd already swiped the spare key from Carl's office, and it took all of five seconds to unlock the door and slip into the dark crate-filled room.

I'd never been in here before, but I'd seen Carl setting up magic-based tripwires at certain corners. The cameras would be no problem, of course. But I wouldn't have long before the guards came back. The crates were organised according to world of origin, but in no particular order. I walked as fast as I dared, searching for something familiar.

Bloodrock. I picked the lock on the crate, and found a heap of small canvas bags. They wouldn't miss one, and only a small amount would be needed for Nell to use.

The samples were from Enzar, so the contents of the

nearby crates must be, too. I opened them one at a time, checking for anything with the properties I needed.

There it was. Adamantine. Central would have some spare in storage, because it was what they made the entire facade of the building out of. In its pure form, it was glossy black, like coal coated in plastic. Most magic sources looked the same, including lustre—only magic-wielders could tell the difference, close up. But there were files with their properties listed, and Amanda had sent me an image of the source Klathica used in their super-strength implants. Not adamantine, but something called sciras—adamantine with its antimagic properties stripped away. It was used to reinforce buildings but didn't react to magic. And of course, someone had had the bright idea of turning it into a super-strength booster.

I had absolutely no intention of messing with magic implants, but if I could amplify a pure source, I fully intended on getting my hands on some of that sciras. It was a rare source, but then, so was adamantine, and Earth had no shortage of that.

I searched all the boxes until I found the right crate, removed a small sample of the sciras, and pocketed it.

I had to do it, I told the warning voice in my head. If nothing else, at least we'd be prepared if the Stoneskin people declared war on us. If the implants worked the way I thought they did, I could amplify sciras like any other source, and it would turn *me* into a temporary shield. I'd be able to face those Stoneskin bastards head-on, long enough to take Ada back before they realised what she could do.

Ada's magic was so dangerous, it would only take one mistake to knock out the Balance, and the Multiverse along with it. Ada knew that, but the Stoneskins might not.

Or they might be counting on it.

I closed the crate and moved swiftly around the rest of

the storage room. Most offworld substances were volatile as gunpowder in the Passages, and even attempting to use them on Earth or in the between-world would be worse than running headlong into a group of those Stoneskins again. No, sciras was the best I could get. And bloodrock. I backed out of the stores and found the place where the spare weapons were kept, swiping a couple of daggers.

I tapped the earpiece. "All clear?"

Jeth's voice was a whisper. "Yeah. Be quick, though, Carl's headed over that way."

That figured. I'd deliberately chosen a time when he'd be out dealing with novices, but as head guard, it was his responsibility to make sure no trespassers got in again. I eased the door open, slipped out, and let it close behind me. After a few seconds, when I'd checked no one was nearby, I re-inserted the key and locked it again. The guard office was doubly locked, so I had no chance of getting hold of a new communicator yet.

I ran for the back door to Central and circled the building to the car park. At least Central's front gates were open. I wasn't stupid enough to meet Jeth in a place the Alliance might see us, so I walked halfway back to his house, losing myself in a crowd. The roads were packed with early-evening traffic and commuters walking to the Tube station. Everyone was in too much of a rush to notice someone invisible knocking into them.

I ducked into an alley and switched off the camouflage once I'd put a good distance between myself and Central, and power-walked back to Ada's house. I knocked, and the door opened in an instant.

"Where's my son?" Nell demanded, her hair straggling down, eyes blazing.

"Behind me." I tapped the earpiece. "I figured we

shouldn't draw attention. Here." I passed her the bloodrock, and her eyes narrowed.

"The accursed stuff has caused us enough trouble," she muttered.

I said nothing. There was no arguing with that.

She took the bloodrock into the kitchen and tipped one bag of powdered transparent substance onto the table. "How much do you need?"

"Enough for everything we're using, just in case. It's partly a precaution. I don't think the Alliance will check up on you yet, but—"

"It's better to be safe," Nell said, cutting me off. "Pity you didn't remember that before, Walker."

It took a great deal of self-control not to snap at her for not preparing for this eventuality, or to direct some of the guilt eating at me in the direction of the person who'd signed her life away to protecting Ada.

Who are you kidding, Kay? You've lost it. And you're going to drag Ada's family down with you, just like you did to her.

Shut it, I told the unwelcome voice, and pulled out the bag of adamantine. "I have this, too, but I don't know the details on breaking it down to make a protective covering," I said. "Nor, to be honest, exactly how it's used." I'd only known the name. It wasn't like the Academy had taught Dangerous Offworld Substances 101. And as for the sciras, I hadn't even known it existed until a few hours earlier. Like lustre. What a goddamned mess.

"What's in there?" Nell's head snapped up from where she was dividing the bloodrock into heaps, and fixated on the bag of adamantine. Our eyes met, and I couldn't say the word. It was like looking into an abyss of such pain and loss, I jumped when the door opened, breaking the silence.

"Jeth," said Nell, recovering in a second. "I hope you have a better explanation for this plan."

"I have one," I said, "if you'd give me the chance to explain." Seeing that look in her eyes had unnerved me beyond measure. Too close to what I saw in my own eyes whenever I looked in the mirror.

There was no trace of it now. "Fine."

"I got everything we need. You?" I said this to Jeth, who nodded.

"Yeah. Got all the spare parts. They leave all kinds of junk in the storerooms. I reckon I can adapt one of my computers to set up the communication channel."

Jeth hitched his rucksack off and opened it to show gleaming bar-like contraptions which appeared pretty similar to Valerian hover-car engines. "It'll give it a boost beyond Earth levels. What's your plan?"

"Go back to the Passages and try to find her signal. It's all I can think of." I had the tracker and the world-key, just in case. "But first, I'll need protection." I pulled out the sciras. "This is a source. Is there any way you can make it into a device like the Chameleon?"

Jeth frowned. "What is that?"

"Sciras," I said. "It's a power source, one which can turn you into a human shield. Klathica uses it in their magic-boost implants, and if it can punch through concrete, it can take down a Stoneskin. I can't amplify adamantine—it's the best we've got."

"I can try," said Jeth, looking doubtful. "Punch through concrete?" But he took the sciras from me.

"It's logical," I said. "There's some kind of rule behind what I can and can't amplify, but if I'm touching something in pure form, like the bloodrock on the outside of a Chameleon, it works. Why should sciras be any different?"

Nell tutted. "It sounds like you're making theories up just to suit yourself. *Nobody* is invincible."

"Nell," said Jeth warningly. "Cut it out. This is our plan,

and it's all we've got."

"How long will the communication take to set up?" I asked him.

"I'll go as fast as I can, but probably twelve hours—or more. It's a tricky one. I've never done it before. I'll keep you updated." Jeth handed me a battery. "That thing has an hour's life in it, but if you can amplify it, it'll last longer."

"Thanks," I said, taking it. "Keep me updated. I'm going into the Passages, and if you aren't done by morning, I'll go to Valeria and see if there's anything I can bring back with me. I've got a hover bike, they aren't going to kick up a fuss if I remove any parts you need."

"Screw offworld security," said Alber, appearing in the doorway. "You're going to try and find her tonight? Can I come?"

I shook my head. "I can't transfer the invisibility to just anyone. Not even most magic-wielders. It's too dangerous in there at the moment."

"Come and help me," Nell told Alber. "You, Walker, had better keep your word."

"I will."

Sure, finding the right world was a long shot. But it was better than doing nothing. Better than letting her slip away again.

The Passages were a bust. Hours later and I hadn't picked up so much as a trace of Ada's signal. All I'd managed to do was get lost in the hidden Passage, and had to sneak around a prowling chalder vox. At least it was too stupid to notice an invisible presence. But there was no sign of any unknown doorway, Cethraxian or otherwise, and none of Ada's trace. Even if I had found a doorway, wandering into the swampland without a plan would be a stupid move. I'd made enough of those already.

Even walking around the areas of the Passages not in the UK time zone was precarious, with the number of new patrols. Whenever I reached a deserted stretch of corridor, a patrol would appear a minute later, and I'd have to move. Even amplified, all the world-key did was open the in-between place, the endless void, and I couldn't get a handle on any particular world from there. It was like being thrown into empty space without gravity to anchor me. Not even magic could reach me there.

Frustrated, I went downstairs to the hidden Passage again. There were three different stairs to the first level, and I ran into several doorways to Cethrax. Despite everything, I hovered on the threshold of one doorway, looking out into the swampland. Typical Cethrax. Dull purple sky, bleached-white trees like shattered human bones—for all I knew, that's what they were. And mile after mile of swamp. The Cethrax-ians were predators one and all, because no plant life grew out there. I had no idea why the air was even breathable to humans, if you discounted the stench of decay, like their whole planet was rotting from the inside out.

The Stoneskins *had* been using Cethrax as a transit point.

I tapped the earpiece. "You there?" I said, in a low voice.

"What?" said a sleepy voice on the other end. Then, more urgently, "What happened?"

"Just had an idea. I'm in the hidden Passage, and there's an overlap with Cethrax. I know it's unlikely, but suppose the Stoneskins pass through Cethrax again. I can leave a message here. In that code you mentioned."

I thought he'd argue, but he said, "All right. This commu-nications thing's being a pain, but I reckon I can sort it by morning. I can't believe you're in that place at night."

"It's only night time in the UK's time zone area, isn't it?

What's this code?"

I found a nearby rock and used the side of one of the daggers to carve the code into it, at Jeth's dictation. Then, with a last look around, I backed through the doorway.

I left the same message at a half-dozen sites, having to stop once I reached the apparent dead end of the Passage. No more doorways here, but they moved around frequently. Cethrax refused to acknowledge not only the Alliance's rules but also the rules of nature in general—at least in the Passages. It had confounded the Alliance from the start, because it seemed at first glance to be a habitable planet… were it not for the monsters. The air had the right levels of oxygen to support human life, gravity worked the same way it did on Earth—but the inhabitants were half-corporeal, half-shadow, and doorways seemed to open at random. Nobody knew why. Unsurprisingly, the Academy was more concerned with teaching us how to kill the monsters in the lower levels of the Passages rather than pondering the philosophy of doorways.

Possibly, it was the sleep deprivation talking. There was one more thing I needed to try. I'd taken one small piece each of sciras and adamantine, and now there didn't seem to be any patrols around, I let the invisibility drop. I searched for a signal, but the adamantine remained a cold, lifeless piece of metal-rock.

Dammit, Kay, you idiot. Adamantine must be so resistant to magic it even blocked my amplifying abilities. I'd never been able to absorb Ada's powers, though she could project hers onto me. That was how she'd saved my life from the mad god on Vey-Xanetha by grabbing my hand. But pure adamantine didn't seem to work. Not that I had any way to test it unless I zapped myself with a stunner or walked into a magic-creature, and I wasn't overly keen on the idea of being taken out by amplified magic burn again.

So adamantine wouldn't work. At the same time, though… it was magic in itself, even if it blocked or absorbed all other magic. It ought by rights to have had some kind of signal—Ada did. Those Stoneskins…

They were made of adamantine. It was hammered into their skin. Could it be blocking Ada's signal? Even if she was *dead,* her signal would remain, for a while at least. And it shouldn't have disappeared from the Passages so quickly.

I pocketed the piece of adamantine. Once the skin contact disappeared, awareness of magic flooded me again. I hadn't even noticed the buzzing sensation was missing. Like it had never existed in the first place.

Bloody magic. Ada herself had a signal despite the adamantine in her blood, but maybe it was different if it was somehow melded into the skin like those Stoneskins. Or maybe magic was just goddamned incomprehensible.

I took the sciras in one hand, sensing its faint signal. It wasn't a powerful source. But it *was* harder than diamond.

I clenched my fist around it. Magic flooded me, but for an instant, I hesitated. *If it doesn't work, this is really gonna hurt.*

I punched the wall.

My fist bounced painlessly off the rock. I stared at the unbroken skin on my knuckles, then hit it again. A buzzing static pulsed against me, and I took a swing with the other hand.

No pain. Nothing. The wall was undamaged, but so was I. My skin buzzed, and I ran into the next chamber, where the wall was stone, not metal. The hidden Passages were a mixture of both, suggesting they'd been man-made, or perhaps built in a hurry. The Alliance couldn't have a never-ending supply of whatever metal made up most of the Passages on the first and second floors.

I drew back and punched the stone wall. This time, I left a fist-shaped hole, and it didn't even leave a mark on me. I stared at the gap in the stone. Better not try again in case I brought the wall down. But with my new weapon, I could go up against a Stoneskin.

I tapped into the Chameleon again, becoming invisible. Could I hold onto both signals at once? It'd make it easier to sneak up on those bastards. But I could only amplify one source at a time.

"This is the one?" A voice echoed down the stairs. I stopped, glad to be invisible.

"Yeah... looks like any lower level Passage, but it's unmapped. Seems suspicious to me." That was Carl. So someone had come to investigate the tunnel? About bloody time. Admittedly, the past few weeks the main Passages had been plagued by magic-creatures and Cethraxian vermin, but it was a pretty major oversight. At the very least, the doorway to Earth near where Ada used to live ought to be permanently closed.

I kept still and silent until the guards were downstairs. A patrol of four led by Carl. These were more experienced guards, including Amanda.

Yeah. I definitely didn't want to be seen here. I crept to the stairs and climbed swiftly, hardly breathing until I reached the first-floor corridor.

I left the Passages, half-forming a plan. I needed to get my hands on a new communicator, ideally, but that would put me back under Ms Weston's watch. I returned to my apartment instead. A buzzing sounded as soon as I opened the door, and I went for my weapon, wondering if it was possible someone had broken in—*why*, I had no idea.

I paused for a couple of seconds, my dagger in hand. The buzzing noise went off again.

I tracked the sound to the drawer containing old junk I hadn't bothered to throw away. Someone was calling my mobile phone. I'd forgotten I'd even left it switched on, but only one person would call that number.

"Simon?"

"About time," said Simon. "I've been trying your communicator for hours."

"It's broken."

"Thought so. Kay, the Alliance here just got a notice that confused the hell out of me. It said something about hidden Passages? We're banned from going to certain areas. Is it the same for you?"

So they did listen.

"Yeah," I said. "You can't go offworld at all?"

"Yeah, we can, but I'm guessing security's extra-strict on your end, right?"

My hand clenched around the phone. "I can go offworld. I need to, actually."

"Whereabouts? I was going to Valeria. Next chance I get."

"Today?"

"You want to show me that hover bike? Wait, isn't it like four in the morning where you are?"

"Suppose it is." I hadn't had any way of checking the time in the Passages, and panic had wiped out all exhaustion. Yet another thing that would no doubt come back to hit me later, but Ada's plight was a raging storm in my head.

I closed my eyes. Maybe I did need more people on my team. If my own Alliance didn't believe me, maybe Simon would.

"Sure thing. I'll give you a tour of offworld district."

"Man, I've been waiting. Can't believe how long the permit process takes."

"Yeah." Had I ever worried about that? Simon didn't have a clue just how batshit the world had gone in the past day. I'd be doing him a favour by keeping him out of this. But I had a suspicion the Stoneskins were up to something bigger than a random attack in the Passages. Someone had to warn the rest of the Alliance branches. Someone who hadn't been discredited.

"Wicked. I'll meet you by the west-city-side Passage, okay? That's like the halfway point for both of us."

"Sure." In Valeria, all Passage doors there tended to lead to the same city, Neo Greyle, even the ones in places that logically should have been on the other side of the world. But then again, in the Passages, logic was optional.

Even an hour was too long to wait, but I was crashing hard by that point. I chewed on a protein bar that tasted of nothing while skimming my communicator feed in the hope something would come up. It didn't. The Alliance must be keeping Ada's disappearance confidential. I'd suspected as much, but a fresh wave of dread took hold of me all the same. Would anyone ask questions, or would it be swept under the carpet in the name of confidentiality?

Wouldn't be the first time.

Sleep was out of the question, so I ran a shower in the hope I'd feel less like crap. I hit the punch bag a couple of times, but I didn't want to try my luck with the sciras-booster in here. With the way my luck was going, I'd knock a hole in the wall or ceiling.

My phone buzzed. Time to break the law. Again.

There were no guards around when I reached the Passages, but I kept an eye out, invisible, while I eased the door open. As it slid closed, I was already moving. Simon was using the second level Passage, so there were fewer patrols that way. I climbed the nearest stairway and hurried along the corridor. When I spotted a person ahead, I tensed even though I was invisible—but it was Simon. I switched off the camouflage and approached him. He jumped a foot in the air when he saw me.

"Christ, Kay," he said, staring. Oh, right. The bruises on my face. "What happened?"

"Long story," I said. "Starting with how I'm not supposed to be here. Let's move."

I tried not to think about the fact that the entrance to Valeria I'd picked happened to be the same one we'd escaped the Campbell family through. After we'd both killed. The first time she'd looked at me like—

Stop that.

"You go through the door," I said to Simon, halting one corridor before. "I'll catch up."

Simon peered around the corner, frowning. "What's this about? You said you're not supposed to be here. You're not sneaking in, are you?"

"Kind of. They won't catch me, don't worry." I paused. "You won't get into trouble. It's all on me."

He didn't move. "Kay, are you... all right?"

Great. Now Simon would think I was a nut-job, too. "I'll explain when we get there," I said. "Don't freak out. It's just magic."

And I switched on the invisibility.

Simon's eyes bugged out. He blinked repeatedly. "Uh... Kay?"

I switched it off. "See? I can sneak in just fine. I'll explain how when we get there."

"You'd better," said Simon. "Holy hell, Kay."

"You don't have to do this," I said. "Just believe me when I say I'm in a world of trouble, and so's Ada—and Central's staff won't believe me when I tell them there's a threat to the Balance. To the Multiverse, even. I can prove it, once we get out of here."

Simon glanced over his shoulder. "All right, man. You'd

better tell me."

"I'll be right behind you," I said.

He kept looking over his shoulder as he approached the guarded entrance to Valeria, when the guards scanned his Alliance ID.

"You coming here alone?"

"Yeah, figured I'd check out the district. My first trip offworld," he said. Pretty decent attempt at being casual. I'd really freaked him out.

Through the doors. I followed, doing my best not to make a sound, but nobody looked in my direction. I switched off the camouflage once we reached a crowded street in the shopping district. Not too far from here was the place I'd once hijacked a hover bike a goblin had stolen.

"Damn, Kay," he said. "This place really is as big as they say."

"Yeah." The back of my neck prickled like I was being watched, though that might have been down to the number of Enforcement Officers wandering around. Neo Greyle had upped security after the whole invisible-goblin fiasco and the stunt the Conners had pulled.

The roads and skyways were packed with traffic as usual, rows of gleaming hover cars and sleek hover bikes reflecting the cloudless sky. Neo Greyle was more of a country than a city, and appeared even bigger because it was so uniform—silver skyscrapers, reflective-metal flooring on both road and pavement, glass-fronted open shopping centres, hover-ports and a never-ending stream of people. Above, skyways curved around the buildings, lit up in a stream of blue lights over our heads.

I'd learned my way around this part of the city, yet it seemed alien in a way it never had before. I shook my head. "I need a caffeine hit." I turned in the direction of the offworld district, Simon behind me.

"Did you even sleep last night?"

I half-shrugged. "Never mind that."

"Kay, I know when you're freaking out over something. What in the world happened?"

"Ada," I said, quietly. "She's gone. There were these—" I sidestepped a group of tourists. "We were attacked. Central don't believe me because we weren't meant to be in the Passages in the first place. It's to do with what we were dealing with on Vey-Xanetha." I stopped as we reached a crossing, tapping my foot impatiently, waiting for the traffic to stop.

"You went where in the Passages?" asked Simon. "Wait— what they told me. The area closed off…"

"Apparently that part got through to them," I said, taking off once the blue light fastened to the side of the building signalled the traffic to stop. "They don't believe the rest. It's too outlandish, I guess, but these creatures are using Cethrax as a Passage and they took Ada."

"I believe you," said Simon breathlessly, hurrying to catch up. "I think. What're you doing?"

"I'm working on it. She could be in any world, anywhere…"

The sheer hopelessness of it all hit me again, just as hard as before. I strode through a group of businessmen and women, not caring when I knocked them aside.

"Jesus, Kay," said Simon. "Okay, I'm not riding a hover bike with you in this state." We'd just passed by the depot where I'd parked my own bike, which I'd bought what felt like a century ago.

"I don't need a goddamn babysitter," I muttered, looking out at the skyscrapers, the traffic, the millions of people out there who had no idea the whole Multiverse was under threat. Restlessness burned deep in my core, urging me to *do something.* But what, I couldn't say. If I went to every world's

Alliance headquarters, most wouldn't believe me. I'd be ousted as a nuisance at best, a threat at worst.

"Looks like you do," he said. "Where are you even going?"

"Somewhere to talk without being overheard." I led the way to the nearest rooftop cafe, hoping I didn't run into any other Ambassadors. At least the noise of the hover bike race-track nearby would drown out our conversation.

"Okay, this place is pretty cool," said Simon, peering over the edge of the roof as we sat at a booth as far away from everyone else as possible. From a distance, we'd look like ordinary off-duty Alliance guards. "But seriously—tell me what happened. All of it."

I told him. Even as his eyes widened and he tried to inter-rupt multiple times, I kept talking. Everything, from my own magic to what really happened at Central—only pausing to check for the thousandth time we weren't being overheard, and to order double-espressos when a barista came over.

I left nothing out of the explanation. If I died, there'd be no evidence anyone in the Alliance trusted to prove they had a dangerous enemy out there. I knew better than to expect them to accept the testimony of Ada's family. Even Markos, as an offworlder and non-human, wouldn't be trusted by some of the higher-ups. Simon, on the other hand, had a perfect record, even if he did work on the other side of the world. I'd never have placed the burden on him if I didn't feel I had no choice.

"Well, that explains why you look like hell chewed you up and spat you out again," he said. "Of course I believe you, man, but you've got to be careful with the Alliance. If you're locked up…"

"Then no one will be able to do a thing. I know." I shook my head, sipping coffee. "I don't have a lot of options, though. Earth has no information on magic-based sources. Besides, if this communication device works…"

Simon was staring at me. "I can't believe you're really… you can amplify any source?"

"Only certain ones. I can turn invisible when I amplify bloodrock. And there's the world-key and the tracker, but I've no clue what's in those. I'm taking a wild guess it's like the material that makes up the Passages. If I knew what it was, I'd know where to get hold of it. Not like they covered it at the Academy."

That was the problem. Even if I found Ada's signal, even if I used the world-key, there was no guarantee it would work, because I didn't know all the consequences of messing with an offworld substance. And when I used magic without knowing the outcome, things rarely worked out well.

"I'm not sure you *should*," said Simon. "Remember the lecture old Mr Helm gave us when people started asking why there weren't Passage-shortcuts to different places on Earth?"

"Oh, yeah," I said, suddenly sharply awake again—though some of that might have been down to the double-espresso shots. "He works at Valeria's Alliance now, right?"

Simon shrugged. "He was a researcher, he might be anywhere. Why? I couldn't make heads or tails of that lecture on the metaphysics of the Passages. And didn't you fall asleep in the lecture theatre?"

"That figures," I muttered. "Actually, it's just the kind of thing I need to know." *I think.* "He wrote a thesis on sources, right? It makes sense to check if I'm going to accidentally tear apart the fabric of reality by using the improvised world-key."

Simon's jaw dropped. "Is that possible? Kay, I like reality the way it is. I'd prefer you didn't tear it to pieces."

"Not gonna happen," I said. "But I do happen to know where Valeria's research lab is…"

6

ADA

Trekking across the swamp was even less fun than I'd imagined. With the Stoneskins close by, I had no chance to talk to the others, and I didn't dare risk it in case one of them turned on me. The likelihood of a human surviving the swamps of Cethrax was precarious under normal circumstances, let alone in the company of monsters which didn't care if we lived or died.

Reassuring, Ada.

The one consolation was the swamp seemed to annoy the Stoneskins almost as much as us humans. Though they didn't have to worry about the flies buzzing around our heads and biting any exposed skin, their stone-coated feet stuck in the thicker patches of mud as much as our human feet did. I didn't have too much trouble with my waterproof guard boots—though they were unrecognisable coated in mud—but more than a few people lost shoes or sank to their knees in swamp water. The Stoneskin guards were the only people complaining, in low mutters, as they were forced to help each other along the murkier stretches of ground.

If anything, though, that made it worse, because it was so... human.

Were they experimented on? Or created? My thoughts kept circling back to that. But any attempt to talk to them had met with stony—*very funny, Ada*—silence.

The heat, the stench of the swamp and the buzzing flies got to me so much I almost forgot to be afraid. When we halted at a shallow lake with stepping-stones made entirely of mud, I turned to glare at the nearest Stoneskin.

"Couldn't your boss take us *around* the swamp?"

A sharp intake of breath: Gervene. The other humans looked away from me and began to cross the swamp without complaint.

"It is not for us to question," said the Stoneskin. "Nor you, Adamantine."

"Quit calling me that," I muttered. Only Nell got to call me by my real name.

"You're an interesting human." The Stoneskin tilted his head on one side. I paused, studying him for an instant. His ragged clothes barely contained six feet of stone-like skin, marbled black and grey. But he spoke with an unmistakeable American accent.

"You're from Earth," I said, taking my first step onto a 'stepping stone' and thankfully not sinking.

By now, the other humans had moved far away from me. Even Aric and Gervene.

I thought I wasn't going to get an answer, so I concentrated on not falling into the lake. Mud sucked at my shoes, my shirt clung to my back, and I was tempted to take off my jacket, were it not for it being the only thing keeping the flies off me. Not to mention I had my communicator in the pocket. By some miracle, no one had searched me. As long as I had it, I could contact the Alliance... if we ever got within range of a signal.

On the other side of the lake, I shook the mud off my shoes. The Stoneskin man remained alongside me, presumably to stop me running off.

"You're not going to answer my question? Were you from Earth?"

His cliff-like face was impassive. "A long time ago, it was my homeworld. You, however, aren't from Earth at all."

"I've lived on Earth all my life."

"Not *all* your life, if the StoneKing is telling the truth."

Interesting. So he doesn't take the leader's word for it?

"That's for me to know," I said. "Not you, or any of your kind. You're kidnappers, and murderers too, I'm told."

"We obey the StoneKing."

"Sounds like tyranny to me," I said. "Who *is* the StoneK-ing? Which world is he from? And where are we going?" I clamped my mouth shut before more questions spilled out.

For a moment, I expected him to hit me. His head tilted as a scream tore through the air. It came from up ahead, near the humans at the front of our group.

"What was that?"

The Stoneskin didn't answer, but the swampy water ahead was rippling oddly, a dark shape shifting under the surface.

My heart sank. I had too much close-up experience with the monsters from Cethrax's swamp, and none of us were armed except for magic.

A wave of filthy water rose, higher than our heads, higher than a house. I backed up, stumbling in the mud. The wave crashed down, drenching everyone within a ten-metre radius. Spitting out filthy water, I caught glimpses of the others struggling in knee-deep water before agonising pain pierced my eyes.

I bit down to keep from crying out. The water must have got behind my contact lenses. Blinking rapidly, eyes streaming, I half-crawled out of water that suddenly came up to my chest to find the Stoneskins had moved, and there were at least ten of them barring the way between me and the other humans. As I crawled onto the marshy ground, they surrounded me.

They're going to kill me? My eyes were a roar of agony, and the world kept breaking up into fragments. Red. White.

Cethrax had a higher magic level than Earth. I couldn't remove the lenses here in case my magic went haywire and the Stoneskins took advantage.

Water crashed down again, choking me, throwing me against a wall of... rock? No—the Stoneskins had formed a wall from their own bodies, moving close together, leaving no gaps.

And on the other side, a shadowy, lithe shape struck the nearest human. Bloodstained Guy disappeared into the swamp with a choked-off scream.

Dread pulsed through me. That was a selver, a swamp predator. The Stoneskins were protecting *me*, but they'd left the other humans alone and undefended.

"Kill it!" I shouted at them, over the Stoneskins' heads.

No response. I looked desperately from one marbled face to the next, willing my vision to stop breaking up. Cursing, I dragged my feet away from the wall of Stoneskins, to a twisted husk of a white tree trunk. I climbed onto it, fingers scraping against bark. It was as sturdy as it looked, easily supporting my body weight. I climbed as high as possible, aimed, and shot magic into the air.

My vision broke into flashes of red. I didn't even see where the magic struck, but a stone-like hand clamped around my arm and lifted me before I fell. I blinked franti-cally, the world reappearing in segments—the Stoneskins had closed around me again, and behind them, the humans had gathered together, too. The snakelike shadow appeared on the water again, lunging for feet and ankles. I swore, grabbing for magic, but the Stoneskin's adamantine hand moved to my palm. I couldn't use magic when he was touching me—when any of them were touching me.

"Stop that," I said. "I'm not gonna let them die out here."

"You are valuable to us," said the Stoneskin. "We would not have you waste your magic here."

"What do you mean, 'waste' it?" I said, trying to tug my hand free.

The selver's shadowy head lunged, and a burst of magic exploded from somewhere in the group. Everyone ducked as sparks flew, but the wall of Stoneskins stopped any from reaching me. The magic fizzled out as it touched them. Like when I'd been hit by high level magic. They absorbed all of it.

A final flash of magic, and the selver lay face-down in the water, unmoving. The others had killed it.

I breathed out. *I need to get rid of these lenses.* I had a spare pair in my pocket for emergencies, but the filthy swamp water stung like a bitch. And like hell was I letting these bastards see my real eyes.

The Stoneskin let go of me. My fist automatically clenched, but hitting him would do more harm to me than him. "Thanks for nothing," I snarled. "Can I have some space now?"

The Stoneskin soldiers were already moving to allow me to walk forward, forming a guard either side of me. None of them said a word to me, though the one I'd been speaking to shot me a glare. So much for allies.

We'd walked ten more minutes before they moved completely away from me, letting me re-join the other human prisoners. I didn't know what to say to them. There was no way I could have saved all of them even if I hadn't had a wall of Stoneskin warriors between me and the enemy. At least Gervene was still alive. And Aric, though his fists were clenched with anger. My heart sank as he cast a furious look at me, but he didn't speak.

My eyes burned with pain by now. I had to bite the inside of my cheek, hoping the swamp water hadn't given me an infection or damaged my eyesight permanently. White flashes kept permeating my vision, and I didn't know if it was down to magic or not. For once, I hoped it was.

Then came a sight I'd both hoped for and dreaded: a slice of the world had been cut away. On the other side was a familiar blue-lit tunnel. The Stoneskins ahead of the group had already passed through it.

But the Passage wasn't a tunnel but more of a small corridor, bordered either side by shimmering walls. Nowhere to run either side. I stopped, letting the other humans pass in front of me. Three Stoneskins walked at the back of the group, to make sure no one ran away. I looked wildly from side to side, the impulse to run stronger than ever.

My heart stopped in my chest.

At the edge of the doorway, on Cethrax's side, a line of symbols had been cut into a large rock.

A familiar group of symbols. But that was *impossible.* The code my brothers and I had invented couldn't be here—not in the middle of nowhere, in another world entirely.

But the words read: *I'm coming, Ada. I promise.*

"What are you doing, Adamantine?" I recognised the speaker as the Stoneskin who'd confronted me at first, in the Passages. Who'd kidnapped me.

"Are we in the Passages?" I demanded.

"This is our area," said the Stoneskin, "and you shouldn't stay here." He took my arm and steered me alongside him. I dragged my gaze away from the code and forced myself to follow the Stoneskins through the doorway. As I turned back, the last Stoneskin held out some kind of device, and the walls either side of the Passage fell away.

That was the hidden Passage. They'd somehow sealed an area of it to use as a tunnel… but so no one could get away.

I glanced sideways at the Stoneskin to make sure he wasn't looking, dug in the pocket of my now-swamp-water-soaked guard trousers, wishing I'd left a trail of breadcrumbs or something. As it was, all I had was a Valerian bottle cap. But it would do. I dropped it on the floor, kicking it into the Passage. If I couldn't run, I could leave a clue… if anyone even came this way.

The Stoneskin pulled me over the opposite threshold, onto scorched ground under a dark red sky. Another waste-land. The Stoneskin let go as the other two used the devices in their hands to seal the doorway behind us. Nothing remained but unbroken, burnt ground, and a crescent moon in the sky like a curved claw.

But my mind raced. Someone had left a message. Only Jeth and Alber knew that code, but they couldn't have known I might possibly be on Cethrax. One person might have guessed. Someone who thought of everything.

My heart lifted, and even the dark sky seemed to brighten.

Kay was alive.

7

KAY

"You sure about this?" said Simon, as we climbed off the locomotive on the city's west side. I'd been here before, though not for a while, and it was close to one of the doorways to Earth. There were also a ton of Alliance guards around, but at least none of them knew me.

"Positive," I said. "I can get us both into the building. It's not high-security."

If it was, I'd use the invisibility, though that would mean Simon waiting outside. But Mr Helm wouldn't be particularly enthused to talk to me if I broke into the lab through the window. Better to use the front door if possible.

A silver sign made up of foot-high letters proclaimed the building to be the "KimaroTech Research Centre." The building itself was relatively small for Valeria, but ten storeys high and made of the same reflective metal as its neighbours, so I couldn't see in through any of the windows.

"Wait," said Simon. "Doesn't your family own this building?"

Damn. I'd hoped he wouldn't remember that particular detail from our Academy classes on Valeria's landmarks.

"Yeah, but I've never been here." Neither had my father, as far as I knew. The Walker family had ties in so many industries in so many universes even I didn't know all of them. The lab was an outpost of the KimaroTech Institute on Klathica, a company my grandfather had founded. Unifying Klathica and Valeria, two worlds which had nearly ended up on opposite sides of a war. His shining achievement. Not that Lawrence Walker gave a crap, since it didn't involve him directly.

Two security guys dressed in the same shell-like gear as the Enforcement Squads confronted us at the doors. The whole building was far more guarded than I expected, considering—the Campbells' place had hardly been under guard at all, but here, every inch was covered by men and women wielding Valerian-style laser guns, the sort only law enforcement were allowed to carry. Simon shifted uneasily.

"And you are…?"

Looked like I'd have to play that card after all. "I'm Kay Walker, Alliance Ambassador for Earth. I believe my family owns this building?"

That got their attention.

"Robert Walker's grandson?" The guards exchanged glances. *So* he *didn't come here,* I thought, with some relief. My father left an impression few people forgot.

"Yes. I need research for a project I'm working on, and Central isn't being very accommodating. I'm sure you understand."

"Yes… of course." They wore awed expressions. *Yeah. They've definitely never met Lawrence Walker.*

And there probably wasn't anyone here who'd met Robert Walker, either. He was commonly known as the Alliance's founder on Earth, though in truth, he was just the council's leader and the one who all the media attention had focused on. He'd been the first to take advantage of the possibilities

EMMA L. ADAMS

offworld offered to Earth, and had an uncanny knack for finding the best opportunities before anyone else did. On Klathica, for example, he'd pioneered the first magic-based human enhancement drugs, and on Alvienne, it had been a Walker-owned company who'd funded the cure for a plague that had wiped out a fifth of the population.

Robert Walker had been an opportunist and a clever one, too. Not that I knew what he'd been like in person, seeing as he'd died before I was born. But he'd left a rather more impressive legacy than my father, who occasionally showed up at the various factories, laboratories and Alliance branches once every decade or so just to maintain the Walker reputation. As for me, I'd rather walk unarmed into Cethrax.

"Damn," said Simon, staring around at the glass-and-chrome reception area. We followed the guard who'd met us outside into an equally bright hallway, lit with fluorescent ceiling lights. The walls were see-through on either side, showing labs containing gleaming Valerian tech.

"What even is this stuff?" Simon openly stared through the nearest window.

"Supposedly research into the fundamental forces of the Multiverse," I said. "It works better on a world with magic, that's why he didn't set it up on Earth."

"Your grandfather?" I heard a dozen questions behind the words, and sighed inwardly. The guard leading the way seemed to be listening, too.

"Yeah, I've never been here, though. He died four years before I was born. The main branch is on Klathica."

"What the hell is that?"

We'd passed through a pair of open blacked-out sliding doors not unlike the doors to the front of Central—glass reinforced with adamantine—and into another lab. Each corner of the room was taken up with a strange device consisting of two contained black-walled metal cage-like

96

things. One contained an odd-looking dark blue cube covered with dials, and the other contained a hover car, caught in the middle of a metal ring. As we watched, it faded out, becoming transparent, then faded back in just as quickly.

Bloodrock. Someone was using magic-based sources here, all right. Was this even legal? I watched, slightly mesmerised, as the car faded and became an outline, rotating on the spot.

"Kay Walker?"

I spun around. Mr Helm's face poked out from the top of a thick layer of shell-like, magic-reinforced black clothing that covered him from head to toe. Like a mad scientist's version of a suit of armour. Given the volatile substances he was experimenting with, he probably needed it.

"Hey, Mr Helm," said Simon. "You remember us?"

"I never expected to see you two again," said Mr Helm. "I suppose the Walkers *did* sponsor our laboratory from the start... any donations would be most welcome."

I wasn't sure if he was joking or not, and I was less convinced whatever in the Multiverse he was doing to the car was legal by the second.

"We came here to ask you a couple of questions," I said. "About your research... what you lectured us on in our fourth year at the Academy."

"So you do remember." Mr Helm's eyes gleamed. "I didn't detect a great deal of enthusiasm, I admit... Academy graduates rarely show an interest in the metaphysical components of the Multiverse."

"That's because you need a PhD to read the textbook," said Simon. "What's that?" He indicated the floating, half visible car.

"My current project," said Mr Helm. "A means of transportation through the Passages... or otherwise."

"Invisible?" asked Simon, with a not-so-subtle glance at me.

"Camouflage is the technical term," said Mr Helm. "But yes—it is a precautionary feature, due to the unsafe nature of the Passages. The problem we're having is the effect transfer —the person *in* the car would have to be in a certain position for the chameleon effect to pass over to them, too. With the help of some new research, we've certainly managed to make progress… thanks in no small part to the Alliance."

Well, crap. Could he have got the idea from *Earth's* Alliance, and the Chameleons? Word did tend to spread quickly, and Valeria's Alliance had confiscated all the blood-rock those Cethraxian goblins had been carrying around.

What does that matter now? "Not that it isn't interesting," I said. "But I had a question about something else. You said in your lecture—something about the substance the Passages are made of, and the reasons why it's not possible to create a direct shortcut across Earth—or any world."

"Any particular reason for that?" His discerning eyes searched me. Lying might work, but wouldn't get me answers.

"Cethrax," I said, and Simon turned to stare at me. "Their Passage doorways aren't constant, like the others. You've probably heard the trouble the Alliance has had recently with Cethraxian foot-soldiers running havoc across the worlds. Why is their world an exception?"

Mr Helm blinked. "I suppose that's a valid concern for an Ambassador… have they been giving you a lot of trouble?"

"You have no idea," I said. "So why do doorways randomly appear to that world? It has something to do with their semi-corporeality, right?"

"You clearly know *some* things," said Mr Helm. "The Valerian term for the material the Passages are made of is 'auros'—that's the standard one, anyway. I am no magic-wielder, but I have heard from certain people gifted with magic that every world has a slightly different... the terms vary, but the Earth equivalent is a radio wave, is it not?"

I nodded. "Radio signals. And when there's more than one world, you can sense them both, overlapping... that's what I heard," I added, figuring telling the guy I was a magic-wielding amplifier was a bad move. He'd probably want to lock me up and study me.

"Yes... a doorway can be created by a magic-wielder with awareness of those *signals,* because only they can sense exactly the right world they want the auros to connect to. The same goes for those world-keys the Alliance has. There are so few of them precisely because there are so few magic-wielders with the gift. But it *is* possible. The problem that arises when creating pathways across the *same* world is that the signals are usually muddled. The doorway will be stuck in an endless loop—or, depending on the strength of the source used to power the world-key, self-destruct. The exception is Valeria, because our world has a stable level of magic."

I can create a world-key with this auros. Because I can sense the signals. "But it doesn't explain why an open doorway can't be created on Earth directly into another world, rather than through the Passages."

"Because Earth is low-magic," said Mr Helm. "You'd need two worlds at second level or higher, and a suitable source on either side of the doorway before you could even begin. The Passages also works as a safety net. Most magic disperses into there. If you link two worlds directly, and one is at a higher level than the other, the Balance tips and both are adversely affected."

That's what happened on Vey-Xanetha. Cethrax is second level... and the two were linked before. Across the chasm.

"Cethrax is an exception," I said. "Why?"

"That," said Mr Helm, "is a mystery even I don't have the answer to. Cethrax is known to be magically unstable, though the actual inhabitants are mostly magicproof. I would hazard a guess something happened there a long time ago—perhaps one doorway was opened, or several, and the change in the magic level adversely affected the whole world until the doorways became a permanent fixture. Magic always has a counter-reaction."

Too true. I'd figured from what we'd seen on Vey-Xanetha that humans had once lived there, and had probably been the monsters' playthings. No other species could use magic, at least according to the Alliance's records. Maybe opening the door to Vey-Xanetha was what had wrecked Cethrax. No wonder they didn't like humans.

"I hope that was helpful," said Mr Helm.

"Yeah, it was," I said. So I could create a doorway myself, if I picked up on the right signal...

"Do doorways always open at random?" I asked. "Because I've been on offworld missions before, and it always struck me as odd how it rarely opens into the middle of the ocean, say. It always seems to link to inhabited areas. On some worlds, anyway."

"That," said Mr Helm, "is because auros is drawn to other magic sources. If there's one source in a whole world, any doorways will tend to cluster around it—or within a few miles of it, at least. It's not an exact art."

So that was it. If Passages were drawn to sources, no wonder there were so many here in the city. Neo Greyle's hover-tech practically shone with magic.

"Art?" said Simon, walking around to the other side of the car. "Thought it was nature. Or wacky Multiverse nature, anyway."

"On some worlds, magic is seen as an art form," said Mr Helm. "There are patterns, as there are in nature."

"Don't suppose you've ever spoken to the Klathican branch?" If anyone knew about sources, it was that place.

"I cannot say I find their Embassy staff particularly accommodating," said Mr Helm. "I do know they speak highly of your grandfather there."

I bet they do. He gave them a crap-ton of funding.

"I'm interested in magic sources," I said. "Off the record, mind." Maybe I was deluded to think the guy wouldn't rat me out to the Alliance, but the constant hum of the hover car reminded me he was playing fast and loose with their rules himself. Once, I'd have said the last thing I wanted was my name getting out on Klathica, the world my family's name wrought the most influence on. But that was before.

"Sources... even the definitions aren't consistent," said Mr Helm. "It was at first thought there were three—antimagic, enhancement-magic, and base magic—auros, that is. Then scientists began to realise there were subtle differences in sources, depending on which world they were found on. In high-magic worlds, antimagic thrived. Mid-range worlds were the source of new discoveries—sciras, for instance, and lustre. I did write a paper on the subject," he added.

Yeah. I should have known he'd have all the names memorised if he knew auros, the rarest of them all. But it still came as a shock to hear them spoken so casually by a stranger.

"What's bloodrock, an enhancer?" I asked, watching the car rotate out of the corner of my eye. Simon didn't seem to be able to look away from it.

"Yes, that's what it would be under the old classification. The name is translated from the ancient language of Klathica, where it was the first source to be discovered..."

Simon cleared his throat loudly. "That's interesting and everything, but the point is, we need to know about this arros—"

"Auros," I said. "It's called base magic—why?"

"Because there's nothing else like it in the Multiverse," he said, "and on some worlds, it's caused conflict beyond imagining. Thairon, for instance."

I nodded. I didn't particularly want to get into a conversation about the world my father had spent the past five years on. *It had auros?* It couldn't have anymore, because all doorways had been closed off. That was the only reason I wasn't wrapped in constant paranoia he'd make a sudden reappearance.

"I apologise, I'm boring you. I did write my thesis on the improbability factor of Passage doorways."

"Sounds fascinating," said Simon, walking around the car's other side to inspect the rest of the lab. "What're the cages for? Human lab rats?"

"Of course not." Mr Helm looked affronted. "We've never actually locked anyone in there... not without their permission, anyway. It's an experiment into unbreakable cages. Seeing as Valeria has had a lot of trouble with criminals lately, the Enforcement Squads are hoping to make these bars mainstream in containment facilities."

"Yeah," said Simon, tapping the side of the cage. "Isn't that just reinforced adamantine?"

Even coming from Simon, the word triggered a reaction. My fist clenched. "We should go," I said. "Thanks for your help," I added to Mr Helm. "I might have to check out your thesis."

"As a matter of fact, I uploaded it to the Alliance's database to read online—you can find it on your communicator."

I nodded. I needed to replace mine, but that could wait. My mind was racing. Doorways were drawn to sources... and Ada had a source *inside* her. But maybe I was making connections which weren't actually there out of sheer desperation.

"I'm glad to have helped," said Mr Helm. "Our laboratory has greatly benefited from the generosity of your grandfather…"

"Yes," I interrupted before he started rambling again. "I have one last question. Do the trackers used by the Alliance to pinpoint magic-wielders work with doorways? Could the Alliance track a magic-wielder to another world?"

"Why… no, that's impossible," said Mr Helm. "You must know in any world where magic is above the second level, it's impossible to track an *individual* signal."

Unless you can amplify a tracker. It'd be a long-shot to figure out why Ada's signal disappeared. Only a magic-wielder able to sense the 'radio signals' of each world could create doorways, if they had a world-key or auros. But that didn't mean I could find Ada, if I still couldn't pick up on *her* signal.

Like I'm giving up now. "Good luck with the car," I said. "We should go."

"You gonna tell me what all that was about?" asked Simon, once we'd left the building and were past the guards outside. "Kay, it sounds like you can do what no one else—"

"Yes," I said, in a low voice. "But don't tell anyone. Even I don't know why."

I hadn't told him about the experiment—that was the one piece of information I'd omitted. It seemed irrelevant now, and would lead to questions I didn't want to get into. Finding Ada was paramount.

"What's the plan?" he asked as we boarded the train again. The hover locomotive barely paused before zooming off at top speed, the wind through the wide open windows bitingly cold.

"Ada's brother's setting up communications. I'm supposed to track her, but I can't… so I'll just have to keep opening doorways until I find some sign of Ada."

"That's… risky," said Simon. "Really risky."

"You think I don't know?" I ran a hand through my hair, frustrated beyond measure. "I couldn't convince Ms Weston Cethrax was under the control of those—*things*. Not to mention what happened on Vey-Xanetha, because Ada and I were the ones who fell through the doorway and saw the Vox. And—damn, I should have asked. I don't like that the lab's named after those magic-creatures." *KimaroTech.* Had my grandfather named it?

"Didn't look shady to me," said Simon. "A bit overly-secure, maybe, but I suppose that's normal for this place…"

He paused, looking around the almost-empty carriage. Through the open window, Valeria's capital shot past in a blur of silver-grey. Three teenage guys wearing hover boots flew by, waving at the passengers.

"I kind of expected him to give us a lecture on the meaning of existence. The answer to the big questions."

"Nah, he seems more of the practical type," I said. "That car would save on hours wandering the Passages, if it works. Only problem is, you run the risk of hitting patrols with an invisible car. And engines and the Passages don't exactly go together if it gets overheated." I remembered the story that had done the rounds at the Academy of the idiot who'd tried to drive an Earth car into one of the main Passage entrances. It hadn't ended well.

"He's the expert," said Simon. "What now? Want to tell Valeria's Alliance about it all? They might listen."

"I'm not supposed to be here," I reminded him. "They'd have me sent back to Central in a heartbeat. I'll bet Ms Weston's already got people looking for me, seeing as I swiped the Chameleon and world-key from her office and I don't have a communicator."

"Damn, Kay," said Simon. "I can't believe this is happening. I mean, no offence, but you've always had a knack for trouble..."

"Tell me about it," I said. "This is on a whole new level. But Ada's out there. She's alive."

"I get it," said Simon. "She—she's not like you, is she? That kind of magic-wielder?" He spoke in an undertone, but I scanned the carriage all the same.

"Not exactly," I said. "It has to do with her homeworld. That's what I'm afraid of—the Stoneskins were planning to use her for something. Her magic's not like anyone else's, as far as I know."

"Hell." Simon looked thoroughly spooked. "Is there no one—? Look, man, I'll vouch for you. Spread the word. Whatever I can."

Even through the numb horror of Ada's absence, a small measure of relief came through. "Thanks, mate," I said. "Not sure if they'll take your word for it, but if I had proof they exist, without a doubt... I need to get Ada away from them. Never mind the damned rules."

"I'll look for proof," said Simon. "You concentrate on Ada. There has to be evidence something's not right on Cethrax, right?

"Is anything ever right there?" I said. "No—tell them you saw something around the hidden Passage. Does New York even know about that?"

"Huh. You know, I've not heard it mentioned..."

"Typical of bloody Central, keeping it secret," I muttered. "Okay. Tell them. I know it's not in your area, but there are a bunch of hidden staircases down there and there's probably one up near where you patrol. Tell them you heard a noise and followed it."

It seemed a flimsy lie. But plausible enough for what we needed. I didn't think Earth's other Alliances would be too pleased Central had been keeping something like that a secret. Let alone the other allied worlds.

"Cool. I'll do that. You find Ada, and try not to get yourself killed."

There was something else I needed to mention. Something I should have done when I'd joined the Alliance.

"If I do die," I said, "can you make sure everything I own is donated to the shelter in London?"

Simon blinked. "Shit, man, I didn't mean—you really don't think—?"

"Just in case," I said. "I wrote it down, it's saved on my communicator backup." One of the first things I'd had to do on joining the Alliance was their formal last will and testament. You'd think it would have put off some of the idiotic new recruits.

Simon stared at me with questions in his eyes. But there were some things I'd take with me even to the grave.

I checked the view from the window again. "It's our stop."

Simon shook his head, looking dazed. I'd never meant for him to be dragged into the insanity my life had turned into since I'd joined the Alliance. But maybe, if we warned the Alliance branches, they'd be prepared for whatever was coming.

I always thought I was prepared for anything. The worst-case scenario was usually my first thought. But I'd never imagined Ada and I could possibly end up at the centre of a war the Alliance might not be able to win.

8

KAY

Once Simon had gone, I turned invisible to go back through the entrance to London near Central. Luckily, there weren't any patrols about as I slipped through the door, tapping the earpiece as I did so.

"Any progress?" I asked Jeth, walking down the paved side of the street rather than alongside the Alliance's gate. The buildings were covered with claw-marks from the time a wyvern had escaped here.

"I've set up a signal. I can't guarantee it'll reach every world, but it's like a boosted communicator. Where are you?"

"Just got out of the Passages. I've been asking around about opening doorways, and I *think* I can create a world-key to anywhere. I worked something else out. But I'd rather not be overheard."

"Come over here, then. And watch out for Nell, she's not happy."

"Figures," I said.

Ada's younger brother answered the door. "You're back," he said. "You left the message for Ada, right?"

"Yeah."

He moved back to let me into the hallway. "How do you know she's even there?" We went into the kitchen where the bloodrock and adamantine was heaped on the table. Nell, who was fiddling with the stove, looked up to give me a glare.

"I don't," I said. "But just in case. I think I know what's blocking the signal."

"What signal?"

"Every magic-wielder has one. I can usually pick it out and track it, but I haven't been able to sense Ada's since they took her, even though we were in the Passages not long before. But I tried to amplify this—" I pulled out the piece of adamantine—"and it blocked me. I think it repels magic altogether, and it's what those Stoneskins were made of."

Nell finally looked at me. "I see."

Now I saw she had a heap of bloodrock in a pan. Melting it? Was that how she made the solution?

"It explains some things," I said. "But the sciras worked. I should be able to stall them, at least, but I'd rather get Ada out first."

"I can deal with that myself," said Nell. "We do have more than one Chameleon, you know."

"Yes, but you're unprotected. I don't know how many of them there are. Not to mention, if they're using Cethrax, we'll have to contend with whatever the swamp throws at us." At best, goblins. At worst, wyverns.

"I will not abandon my daughter," snarled Nell. "Never. You have no idea what I sacrificed for her. I was the Royals' slave. My family was slaughtered before my eyes—" She choked off. "And I saw them *change* her, and I couldn't watch anymore. I took her during the night, and against all the odds, we both survived to start a new life. I never wanted anything else for her. I *am* her parent, in all the ways that matter."

"I know," I said, quietly.

Her sharp gaze missed nothing, and I didn't want to bring up the truth she'd seen in my eyes. I could imagine the horrors she'd seen all too clearly.

"All right," I said. "You can come, but I can't promise anything. As long as the signal's blocked, I won't be able to track her accurately unless she contacts us another way. She's quick-thinking and a good improviser. If we send out the signal, she'll think of a way. Just like when she broke out of Central." *I hope. God, I hope.*

It wasn't that I didn't believe in Ada—far from it. But with her magic blocked and no other weapon, the odds of her getting out alone disappeared by the second.

"You think I don't know it's a long-shot?" I said. "Sciras works. I punched a hole in a stone wall, and it didn't even hurt. I'm not sure I can do that and the invisibility at the same time, but it's better than nothing."

"Yes, but what about the rest of us?" asked Alber. "Also, aren't there like a bunch of those stone freaks? More than one?"

I shrugged. "Yeah, but I want to get Ada away from them first. Once she's back, the Alliance will have to acknowledge there's a threat, and they'll figure something out. We should have the support of several universes on our side if the Stoneskins mount a mass attack."

"*Should,*" said Nell. "I've never trusted you people. You stumble into the middle of things you can't begin to understand—"

"If you can tell me you understand magic, I'm all ears. Don't suppose you've told Ada the truth?"

Nell froze, her face a surprised mask. "You what?"

"Thought so," I said. "You're hiding something from her about Enzar."

Nell's eyes narrowed. "That's my business."

"It's Ada's business, too," I said. "She's in the hands of creatures who would exploit her powers. If she doesn't understand them herself…"

"She *does* understand," Nell snapped. "I taught her what I could. But—she *can't* go back to Enzar."

What? "I wasn't aware she wanted to. They were planning to use her as a weapon, right? To win the war? Or do you know something else?"

Nell lowered her gaze. "I've been… keeping up to date on what's happening in Enzar, through a source."

That's it? "Right," I said. "And if it threatens Earth? Like the hidden Passage, which Cethrax has been using to attack patrols and sneak into Valeria unguarded and god only knows what else? I understand why you kept it a secret, I'm just saying the best intentions don't always lead to the best results. I realise that Earth's Alliance ought to have taken action immediately upon discovering it existed—which, by the way, is something else I don't understand."

"And you're an expert in inter-world security?" Her eyes narrowed. "The hidden Passage didn't contain any doorways, aside from Earth's. That's why we used it. The doorways to the transition points which link with Enzar, as I'm sure you're aware by now, are within *your* territory."

"And could these Stoneskins be using the same routes?"

Considering they'd somehow made a doorway that had never existed before, I doubted it. But I had to be sure.

"No," said Nell. "Your people control every inch of the place now. I've spent the past three months explaining to your superiors that my colleagues and I know more about cross-world security than the Alliance does. Anyone who comes through the escape route has to traverse ten levels of security, including magic scanners. I can assure you that we'd have noticed those… *creatures* that took Ada if they came through our system. Even if they had human appearance."

I considered this. "And bloodrock..." But I wasn't sure even bloodrock solution would work on creatures made out of pure antimagic.

"Is strictly reserved for those of us operating the shelter network," said Nell, eyes flaring. "At least, it was until your people confiscated it."

"All right," I said. "So how do you know what's happening on Enzar? Does the Alliance have access to that information?" It was the first I'd heard, but then again, I hadn't been involved with the Offworld Aid division lately.

"I wouldn't know," said Nell. "They've certainly interrogated my colleagues and me enough times. The transition points keep a close watch on the worlds they deal with—even Enzar."

"Okay," I said. "So, what's the latest?"

"The Royals are missing," said Nell, her voice flat—but not so much I couldn't sense a hint of some unidentifiable emotion beneath it. "And have been for some time."

"Presumed dead?"

"Yes," Nell said. "The magebloods outnumber the nonmages three to one, even if you count the outside worlds they dragged into their war. The Royals are the only nonmages with power, and with them gone, the direction of the war has turned."

"So if Ada goes to Enzar..." Both sides would want her.

"They'll know who she is," said Nell. "Or *what* she is. There's no disguising it on Enzar, not even with bloodrock."

"And you think her... blood parents will be after her?"

"They're dead," said Nell, bluntly. "They were killed when the palace fell, not long after we escaped."

I stared at her, mildly shocked. "She... she doesn't know, does she?"

Nell shook her head. "I found out later, and the less I tell her about what her family did, the better."

"That won't make it better," I said, quietly. Better to have the truth, just for finality's sake. But what did I know?

As Nell's eyes narrowed dangerously, I said, "So you're in contact with the transition point. Is it directly linked to the war zone?"

"The war isn't on Enzar anymore," said Nell. "Most of the fighting is offworld now. There's nothing of Enzar left to defend now the Royals are dead. Our operation only started when it became clear the Royals and magebloods intended to bring all the worlds they could find under their own control. When our last doorway was closed by the Alliance…" Her expression hardened, and a sense of dread stirred inside me —Lawrence Walker had closed those doorways. Cut Enzar out of the Multiverse for good.

I'd never heard what it looked like on the other side.

"When the doorway was closed," Nell went on, "an underground initiative went into motion to help people out of the capital after the magebloods destroyed it. They built secret tunnels for the purpose."

"And who directs them to the Passages?" I asked.

"Why do *you* need to know that?"

"I'm an Ambassador," I said, evenly. "And something is wrong in the Passages. Those Stoneskin creatures shouldn't have been able to get in in the first place. Cethrax, the hidden Passage—it shouldn't be possible for that place to even exist. I talked to someone today who told me the good reasons it's not possible to build a doorway directly between two worlds without using the Passages. But if the Passages are all under Alliance control, how are the Stoneskins getting around without being seen? They must be using the hidden Passage." Which linked with Enzar.

"They can't be from Enzar," said Nell, "because there are only two ways out, and one is buried underground. That's the way Ada and I escaped, but nobody has had reason to go back to the capital since then. It's caved in, as far as I know. And the other Enzar transit point is at the far edge of the continent, underground, and disguised using bloodrock solution. We put it there ourselves."

"And it leads to the second floor of the Passages?" I asked.

"Yes, and it's under Alliance control, as your people like to remind me on a regular basis. There has certainly never been talk of these *Stoneskins.*"

"Right," I said. "So Enzar never used soldiers made of pure adamantine?" It'd be a hell of an advantage in magical warfare if they did.

A pause, in which the last word hung like a weight. I'd had to say it. There was no other way to get the answer.

"No," said Nell. "I've never heard of such a thing. I wouldn't have thought it even possible…"

"I'm hazarding a guess they're artificial. Someone made them." Or they did it to themselves. But I was inclined to believe the former.

The experiments… no. Adamantine was a precious commodity within the allied worlds because it was so hard to get hold of. Worlds with adamantine were worlds of high magic, and most had burned themselves out fighting over it. Including…

I looked sharply at Nell. "Enzar didn't have links with Thairon, did it?"

If Ms Weston and Mr Helm hadn't brought it up, I probably wouldn't have thought of it. But the last world where adamantine had been mined was the world that had blacklisted itself against the Alliance by having an entire team of Ambassadors executed for trying to win freedom for the people enslaved under its government. I didn't know the specifics. I *did* know my mother had died there thirteen years ago. Maybe it was paranoid to think it might be linked at all. But the change in Thairon's government had started the same time as Enzar had been cut off. And both were high-magic.

Nell shook her head. "I have no idea. I've never met anyone from that world."

No. Because whatever the governing class had done, they'd made it impossible for anyone to escape.

I had good reason to hate the place. It didn't mean Thairon had anything to do with the Stoneskins.

"There's a loophole somewhere. Wherever they came from, they must be using Cethrax to transit between worlds." I couldn't track Ada's signal. But if I got into the Alliance's records, surely someone would have noted down which worlds Cethrax had been involved with. And someone had to watch the hidden Passage constantly, to see if they came back.

I checked the time. I had a few hours before Central closed.

Alber came back into the room. "Jeth wants to know if you're going to amplify that signal now."

"Sure," I said. "I can't promise it'll work, but I'll try."

Jeth waited outside the kitchen, eyes red with tiredness, hair standing on end like he'd been running his hands through it. "I can project the signal across five worlds at the moment—the standard reach for a communicator. How do the council contact distant worlds for meetings, anyway? They can't always send people, right?"

"They use videoconferencing," I said. "I've never been in a cross-world meeting, but I think they have to send people to worlds further out than the main Passage because the signals won't reach that far."

"Huh," said Alber. "Thought you knew the council. Did you tell *them* about Ada?"

"My boss said she did, but they aren't prioritising it. They're busy dealing with the repercussions of what happened in Vey-Xanetha, and apparently they need more proof." I drew in a breath, frustration rising again. "What about the computer?"

"It's ready."

I followed him into the darkened hallway. This was a new house, I remembered; Ada had only been living here a couple of weeks. Her bedroom was the attic, and when we'd once spoken on the phone, she'd been lying on the roof...

I shook the memory away.

Ada's older brother's room was more like a cave. Computers on every wall, wires criss-crossing the floor. In the centre, one computer had an odd string of symbols on the screen. The code.

"That's our message," said Jeth. "I can send a signal across the worlds, and if she has her communicator switched on, we'll be able to talk."

"Would it work in reverse?" I asked. "If she was offworld, would she be able to warn the Alliance? I need to find some way to prove to the council the Stoneskins are out there, and they're a legitimate threat. They won't take my word alone. But they know Ada's a powerful magic-wielder, and once they know the truth, they'll prioritise rescuing her."

Either way, I'm going after her.

"Hmm. I suppose, if I linked this device to Central, her message would go through to our computers in the tech department, too. But I'd have to go to Central to set it up. I thought our priority was to get Ada out."

"It is," I said. "But imagine a whole race of invincible monsters that hate the Alliance. If there's anything we can do to warn them—if we prove it, we might be able to get their approval to go after Ada."

"There is that," said Jeth. "They said I didn't have to come in tomorrow... I think they knew something was up." His face tightened. "Okay. What are you planning to do if she does pick up the signal? It won't help you track her, if you need her magic signal or whatever."

"I know," I said. "But if she sends me a description or a picture of where she is, I'll be able to match it with our files. I need a new communicator, though."

Which was problem enough in itself.

"Get one," he said. "You can go to the guard office without getting your boss involved, right?"

"Technically," I said. "Carl knows there's a threat in the hidden Passage now, and I've asked Simon to talk to the senior staff at New York's Alliance, too. But there's something about the Passage I don't like, aside from the obvious." I glanced over my shoulder, but Nell wasn't around. "Look—when you helped the refugees. Did you only use the hidden Passage to get from first level to Earth?"

Jeth blinked. "I only went there a few times. Ada and Nell were always the ones who used that Passage. I was never the best fighter." His fist clenched. "You'd better save her, Kay."

"I'm trying to find out about this Passage. The Stoneskins opened a doorway. They dragged us through Vey-Xanetha and then took Ada through the door again—not to the Passages, I don't think. It doesn't add up. I know they'd linked Cethrax to Vey-Xanetha before, but it doesn't explain how they did that." I hadn't asked Mr Helm either. There were too many goddamned mysteries surrounding the whole scenario *without* getting into who the Stoneskins actually were, and where they'd come from.

"If it helps us find her..." Jeth tapped the keyboard. "Want to try the amplifier? You said it takes skin contact, right?"

"I think so," I said. "You're using your communicator?" It lay on the desk, connected up to the computer via a series of wires.

"Yeah." He held it out to me and I took it, careful not to knock the wires out.

"Wait, what did you do to it?" I said, flipping it over. "Those aren't Earth power cables. Did you turn it into a battery using *Klathican* tech?"

"How'd you know?" Jeth asked.

I shrugged. "I've read theory books. If we had time, I'd ask how you made it compatible with Earth tech without blowing it up. Someone tried to sell me a hover-battery for an Earth motorcycle once and I'm pretty sure that'd end badly."

"Depends how you wire it," said Jeth. "I've worked with this crap for years."

"Is it turned on? I can't trace a signal. Not sure this is something I can amplify."

"Might as well try it." Jeth tapped the keyboard. "Okay. We're set."

My fist clenched around the communicator. The power bar didn't look any brighter. I frowned at it. "Guess not. I can try the tracker, but it only works for magic." I took it from my pocket with my other hand. Traces of a familiar magic lingered in the air, but it was from Ada's younger brother, not Ada herself. Her signal had disappeared even from her own house.

Dammit. "Okay. Clearly, I can't amplify just anything." I checked the communicator screen. "It's at the highest level, though, those extra batteries must be working."

"The message is on a loop," said Jeth. "All I can do is keep sending it out."

He watched the screen in silence for a moment.

I put the communicator down. "What now?"

"I'll keep watching this," he said. "I'll tell the tech department—not about Ada, but I'm sure I can come up with an excuse to try long-distance communicators. They won't need an explanation."

I nodded. Damn it to hell. I didn't have an excuse in line

for where I'd been all day, but Ms Weston had insinuated I wouldn't be welcome at the office anyway. Now it was too late to head back in without running into the evening guard. I resigned myself to another night sneaking in and out of the Passages.

Wait. The ladder to Ada's room was right there in the landing. If anywhere might contain a trace of her magic...

Before I could question whether this was a good idea, I'd climbed the ladder into Ada's room.

The dust hadn't even settled. Though she'd moved in recently, there were no boxes—just shelves stacked with books, martial art trophies, a dusty set of folders. Folded, ironed clothes on the bed. A well-worn copy of a fantasy paperback on the bedside table, beside her old mobile phone, the one I'd given her back after Central had confiscated it. A laptop—also an old model, ten years old or more. Probably second hand.

I stopped dead, the fight punched out of me. I'd never appreciated, until that moment, how thoroughly Ada had messed with my head. I was breaking to pieces because of a girl I barely knew—who I'd helped out of impulse. And who'd implied I was worth something. Not because of my name. Not because of some over-exaggerated story about saving the goddamned Multiverse. She'd seen me as I was, and in the end, she hadn't run away.

So the Multiverse had found another way to take her from me.

I backed down the ladder, and jumped the last few rungs. No point in sticking around here when it hurt to breathe more by the second.

"Kay," said Jeth, as I passed by his room. "For the record, I think you can find her."

I nodded, more in acknowledgement than agreement, and left Ada's family behind.

9

ADA

The thought that Kay was alive, searching for me, kept me walking without complaint for the rest of the day. That night, we camped under a constellation of stars in a deep purple sky. Once we'd left the mud behind, we'd walked through forests of dead, decaying trees, and past the ruins of cities. Nobody knew which world it was, but even the echo of a civilisation once here was enough to give me a brief sense of hope.

We'd stopped by a river to clean the filth of the swamp water from our skin—the Stoneskins were even slower-moving with mud all over their feet. I took a moment to turn my back on the group and quickly change my contact lenses, breathing a sigh of relief when the stinging pain ceased. I could still see as clear as before, but there was no magic here. The world was as stark and bare without lenses. I blinked the sting away, glad no one saw the tell-tale blinding white colour of my real eyes. They showed I was from Enzar, and I was a descendant of the Royals. But I should be in more pain than this, with the amount of filthy water that had gone into my eyes. Must be to do with the magic in my blood.

My clothes were soaked in swamp water, but that was the least of my problems. Even if I'd managed to find spare clothes, my Alliance uniform was far more sturdy and practical than any other material. Plus it was one of few links I had left to the world I'd left behind.

As for this world, it had little to offer except grey, lifeless trees. Like the trees on Vey-Xanetha, when Xanet's power had been drained. At least the smell of decaying leaves was an improvement on the swamp.

Kay had left me a message. Now I had to figure out how to leave him one in return.

The Stoneskins weren't watching me closely anymore, but the looks some of the humans kept shooting me were hostile enough I didn't trust them not to throw me into the next swamp. And that wouldn't end well for any of us. Walking while keeping an eye on everyone was even more exhausting when we had to navigate our way around dead trees and thick undergrowth. The heat made it difficult to think clearly, though at least the branches above gave a little shelter. I'd soon drained the water canteen, and walking all day on Valerian ration bars was starting to take its toll. What'd they do if I collapsed, pick me up and carry me? I might be important to them, supposedly, but why?

I had my communicator, tucked in the inside upper pocket of my coat, where the swamp water couldn't wreck it. People had once lived here, or some kind of intelligent species, anyway. The forest had overgrown the small buildings, then died, the trees becoming skeleton-like shells. Maybe the humans—or whatever lived here—left first, because I didn't see any signs of an attack.

"They protected you," said Aric, and I jumped, not realising he'd moved to walk alongside me. The Stoneskins had stopped to talk amongst themselves and the humans were in a disorganised huddle, crossing the ground with their heads down.

"I have no idea why," I said. Not like I could deny it, seeing as everyone must have seen they'd formed a human— or not human—shield between me and the selver. Which meant they'd probably jumped to the conclusion the Stone-skins and I were on the same side. *Great.*

"Huh," said Aric. "Guess you really are something."

"I don't suppose you know which world we're on?"

He shrugged. "A dead one."

"They're all dead, aren't they? How do the Stoneskins even know where they're going?"

"Ask your buddies," he muttered.

"They are *not* my buddies," I said. "You think I wanted to watch people die? I don't know why they need me, but if it means there's a chance of us getting out of here? Yeah, I'll use them if I have to."

"Us?" Aric snorted.

"All of us," I said, with a gesture around at the other people. No one seemed to be listening, and only a handful looked remotely alive. The others moved like robots, like they'd already given up hope of ever escaping.

It struck me like a blow to the heart. They were like the refugees, stripped of all hope. But no one had come to give them a way out.

I have to do something.

"Give it up," said Aric. "The Stoneskins think they're gods, and they're probably right."

"If you fall on your knees and start worshiping them, I'll leave you behind," I said, checking my jacket for water damage again. Lucky the pockets were tightly zipped, because if I lost my communicator, I'd be screwed.

"Very funny," said Aric. "You and Walker are a match made in Cethrax."

I snorted, though Kay's name bit through me. "Yeah, you'd know about that place, wouldn't you? Your family took holidays with the goblins. Pity you didn't keep any of the source for yourselves, isn't it?"

I realised my mistake as soon as I closed my mouth. *Oh, shit.* Had he even known the potential of bloodrock, not to mention the source his family had found? Though it didn't matter, seeing as they were dead and he and I were stuck out here. I stumbled back as his fists clenched.

"You know all about it," he said. "I don't get why the Alliance let *you* get away with murder. You're no one. Didn't your friend kill people in disguise?"

Skyla. He'd gone there. My own hands curled into fists, and only the huddled, blank-eyed people close by kept me from knocking him out there and then. Like it or not, he was one of the few with the desire to escape.

"She wasn't my friend," I said. "And that's none of your business. Your family almost destroyed a world using a source I'll bet they didn't even understand. Guess they didn't give you a piece of whatever they used to open a doorway?"

Was *that* what the Stoneskins were using? From what I'd seen, the source looked like any other magic-based substance. But although the different sources appeared the same, magic-wielders could tell the difference. I'd thought *I* could. Maybe the Stoneskins' presence stopped me from sensing it.

"What do you know?" he said, arms crossed. But his angry defensiveness hid genuine urgency. He wanted a way out of here as badly as I did.

"Not enough," I said. "Didn't your family tell you anything? Jesus, they really didn't like you, did they?"

I regretted the words the instant I spoke them. Not because I felt sorry for the idiot as much as I knew I'd blown my chance of any tentative alliance. And it reminded me too much of *my* family, who were probably frantic by now. When Central had arrested me, Nell had knocked the crap out of a dozen guards to break me out of jail. In her eyes, everything that happened to me was their responsibility. And Kay's, most of all.

Oh, god.

Aric didn't hit me. His hands dropped to his sides. "Fuck you," he said, and strode off to the far end of the group.

I didn't follow. *Way to go, Ada.*

Hours of walking later brought us to—miracle of miracles—something resembling civilisation. Judging by the over-grown train tracks and tall metal structures, it had once been a thriving town, even if it was deserted now. We were worlds away from Earth, yet I couldn't stop myself noting the simi-larities. The tall buildings, the scrap metal heaps that might have been cars once. All decaying, eaten away by an odd black plant-like substance which covered everything. It crept along the ground and filled gaps in the concrete-like floor, very slowly. But it didn't attack us. Just slowly submerged the town, and the remnants of human civilisation, like black algae covering the buildings and street lamps. Like an aban-doned Earth town, almost. *How long has it been like this? What happened to the people?* Had they emigrated, like the Vey-Xanethans? If there were doorways all through these weird, backways worlds, maybe it was easier to move around. Or it had been in the past.

Even in the Passages, with the vastness of the Multiverse contained behind doors, I'd never truly appreciated how *empty* most of it must be. How many miles of uninhabited ground, of raging oceans, of endless skies with no stars. It was enough to make me feel the size of a pinhead.

A shout from the front brought me back to the present. Some of the Stoneskins had walked off in a separate group, and a line of others barred the way, preventing us humans from following them.

"Why are we stopping?" I whispered.

Gervene, who stood nearest, shook her head. "No clue. They do this in every town or city we find. Even an abandoned old house once. Maybe they're looking for new recruits."

"Hmm. The place is dead, though." That did strike me as odd. Then again, I didn't understand these people, if they could even be called people. Not at all. Maybe there were more of them hiding out in this creepy place. They had to come from somewhere

If only there was some way to get out, to escape. To hijack a car, or sneak into one of the buildings to find some otherworldly equivalent of a working radio or telephone. Whoever lived here had clearly been a technologically advanced people. They might not be dead—by the look of the abandoned cars and doors hanging off their hinges, they'd left in a hurry. They might not even have gone far. Like through a doorway.

I stood on tiptoe, trying to see through the windows of the nearest buildings. All were covered in more of the ink-like plant, and holes had been carved into the walls. No sign of anything living. The guards had been forced to move to the other side of a long split in the middle of the road, like it had been hit by an earthquake. Long swathes of the unfamiliar, black plant covered it like a net.

"They must have left before that thing showed up," said Gervene, who'd surreptitiously moved closer to me. "I don't think that plant is carnivorous."

I opened my mouth then closed it again. I'd been about to say the Stoneskins wouldn't have left us here if it was. But I was the one who was valuable to them. *Not valuable enough to let in on their plans, though.*

And I wanted to know. The choice was either to avoid their attention and make a plan, or use their interest in me to my advantage and get the information I needed to get home. But how to do it without unintentionally dragging everyone else into danger, too?

I inched a few steps to the side, but didn't quite dare get any closer to the tentacles snaking along the side of the nearest building. Some kind of writing was underneath it. Well, more like spray paint. But I couldn't read the script. Not an Earth language. Still, an odd ring of familiarity went through me. As the slow-moving tendrils shifted slightly, another line of script was revealed ... definitely familiar. Symbols, next to an arrowhead, white against the soot-coloured metal.

An arrowhead...

That was the symbol used to open a doorway. But there definitely weren't any signs of magic here. Not of the usual sort, anyway. Whenever I was in the Passages, I detected a kind of resonant hum from being near a door. This time... nothing.

What *was* this world?

The skeleton of what might once have been a telephone post gave me an idea. I unzipped my jacket just enough to reach the inside pocket, and, double-checking no one watched, pulled out my communicator and hit the "on" switch. Even if there was a signal, it'd take a while to connect, but I couldn't help watching the bars in the corner.

Gervene bent to examine the tendrils of inky plant on the ground. "I don't recognise it. It's not a cross-world species, it can't be."

"Bloody fascinating," Aric muttered. "Wish those vehicles worked. I know how to hot-wire a car."

"Even if they did work, they're not like Earth cars," I said. At least, I didn't think so. Worlds could reach the same level technologically even with no contact with one another, but they were unlikely to turn out *exactly* the same. Even worlds that had been in contact for centuries had evolved differently —just look at Earth and Valeria.

Speaking of...

"So whereabouts in Valeria were you from?" I asked Gervene. Native Valerians were distrustful of magic-wielders in general, which had always struck me as odd given their reliance on magic-fuelled batteries to power their hover-tech. But they'd been open to offworlders for centuries, long enough to see the worst magic was capable of. They were one of the worlds to first implement the rule of the Balance, the three laws.

"Neo Greyle, like ninety per cent of the population," she said, rather sharply. "Does it matter now we're out here?"

Whoa. "Just curious. Valeria's more offworld-savvy than Earth, so I thought you might know..."

"I don't know where we are." Her expression darkened. "We aren't anywhere on the Alliance's radar. I think these worlds are either cut off or abandoned. There are hundreds of locked doors in the Passages."

"But Cethrax can reach them," I said. "I don't get it."

"It's Cethrax, does it matter?"

"They've never directly invaded another world, have they?" I said. "Why can they get into these worlds?"

"Because no one's here to close these doorways," said Gervene. "I honestly have no idea. I know someone who used to work with a physicist on Neo Greyle, looking into door-way-theory, but that tends to be classified. I'm not Alliance. But..." Her gaze found the communicator in my hand. "You are."

I'd pulled it out to check, not expecting to see anything. When the icon appeared telling me I had a signal, I nearly dropped it. "What—no way." I opened the settings. No joke. "Holy hell."

"What?" said Gervene, with a glance over her shoulder. The Stoneskins were way off, but if any of them saw...

"There's a signal," I whispered. It wasn't any network I recognised, but there was *something* there. Something that shouldn't exist out here in a desolate world. An incoming message alert flashed across the screen, and I almost dropped it.

"Is that an Alliance communicator?"

I nodded frantically, hiding it inside my jacket again in case the Stoneskins looked in my direction. "I had it turned off, it still has battery. Someone—someone's messaging me. I don't know who it is..."

Kay. Or my family. *Maybe it's the Alliance,* whispered a voice in my head. No—I couldn't afford to get my hopes up.

But I lifted the communicator with shaking hands, switching onto the flash-free camera. I snapped a couple of pictures of our surroundings and attached them to a message draft. "I'm alive, offworld. We came through Cethrax." I typed feverishly, all the while keeping one eye out for movement, expecting a hand to knock the communicator out of my grasp, to hear raised voices. I noted all my suspicions about the Stoneskins' plans, the threat they posed to the Alliance.

I clicked the Alliance's general list and hit "send to all". Every member of the Alliance was logged in, including Jeth and Kay. I put the communicator away as Gervene looked on, curiously.

"What are you doing? There's no signal out here."

"My brother's a genius with tech," I said in an undertone. "If anyone can reach us, he can."

Gervene shook her head. "I'll believe it when I see it."

"What's that?" Aric had sidled over to me, not very subtly.

"You texting someone? There's nothing. My communicator died weeks ago."

Huh. I was surprised he was talking to me after what I'd said.

"I picked up a signal," I muttered. "Don't tell anyone, or say it in front of them."

"Like I would." Aric's expression shifted to his usual glare. "I've had enough lip from you. Those Stoneskin bastards were talking about you. Mentioned a source."

"Saying what? Tell me." A shiver went through me at the word *source*. It never meant good news.

"They said you're important. What's so special about you?"

"No clue," I said. I checked the communicator again. No response. I'd been a fool to expect one, even for a second.

"If they catch you with that, you're dead."

"I know," I said. *But it's the only chance we have.*

A yell made me jump. I spun around, and my mouth fell open. Tendrils of inky plant lifted Long-Toothed Guy above the ground. He screamed, fighting frantically against the thick vines. Everyone turned that way, even the Stoneskins, and those too close to the edge scrambled back onto the roadside away from the plant—a bit tricky seeing as it covered almost every inch of the ground and walls.

"Hell," said Aric. "Thought it was dead."

The plant snaked around Long-Toothed Guy's throat, and squeezed.

"Someone help me!" I said, shoving through the unmoving pack of blank-faced people. "It's killing him."

"Wouldn't be the first," said the dirty-faced teenage boy I recognised from earlier.

"You're despicable," I shot at him, and reached for the magic.

The resistance nearly knocked me off my feet. A *presence* pushed me back, and I staggered into the nearest person.

I'd felt it once before. But it was impossible. Magic was *dead* here.

There was a final *crack,* and Long-Toothed Guy went limp. The plant dragged him down, through the gaps in the road, leaving us staring after him.

"Holy shit," said Aric. "Holy fucking shit. Did that just happen?"

"Apparently," said Gervene, looking faintly nauseated. "*Stars.* What was that? Did he touch it?"

A general murmur confirmed he had.

"He touched the plant... and it did that?" I stared. The creeping black mass was barely moving now. But it had devoured him.

And it was *alive.* Not in a human way but like... like the gods on Vey-Xanetha. The same way that I'd felt the malevolent presence of Veyak working through people... but it was Xanet I was reminded of now. The god whose power could control plants and even heal people. The inky plants lurking in gaps in the road were like a corrupted version of that.

A sick feeling rising in my throat, I looked away. The other humans edged away from the gap in the road, but the Stoneskins blocked every side of the path. No way out. We were trapped like animals marked for slaughter.

"That's it." Aric shoved through the crowd. "I'm through. Killer plants are the last straw."

"Wait!" I said, barring the way before he walked right into the Stoneskin at the nearest street exit. "Are you mad? If you run, they'll kill you for sure."

"Get out of my way, offworlder," he snapped.

I burst out laughing. More hysterical than anything. "You're deluded," I said, trying in vain to hold in the giggles. "Offworlder? Aric, we *are* offworld. A million miles from

Earth. Or more. I'll bet you're the only person from Earth here. So what does that make you?"

"Shut the hell up," he snarled. "At least I'm not a walking bomb."

Now he'd drawn everyone's attention. If they weren't looking already.

"Are you off your head?" I whispered. "I thought we had an understanding neither of us wanted to *die*."

Aric started to say something, then stopped. It had gone deadly quiet, and my skin prickled all over.

The humans parted to either side, making way for three Stoneskins. Heading right for me.

"Adamantine," said the Stoneskin who'd first guarded me, loud enough for everyone to hear. "You are to come with me to the StoneKing."

Crap.

My heart thudded. *He won't kill you. He needs you.* But as Aric had oh-so-kindly reminded everyone, I was a walking bomb. He might be a dick, but I didn't want to *kill* him, nor any of the other humans even if they hadn't tried to defend me. I wasn't a murderer—not a cold-blooded one, anyway. Though the memory of all the crimes I'd committed did absolutely nothing to reassure me.

The main group of Stoneskins had gathered around one building in particular. It was as deserted as the others, steel-framed walls and windows covered in swathes of creeping plant. The Stoneskins didn't seem to mind it.

The group parted, allowing the three Stoneskins to lead me through. I hadn't spoken to any of them before, not that I could tell them apart easily. But the central point of the group was a pair of tall and brutal-looking Stoneskins, at least seven feet high with bulging muscles under their rock-hard skin. As the three guiding me stopped before them, the two of them moved apart—slowly, boulder-like feet dragging on the ground—revealing…

I didn't know what I'd expected to see. A particularly big and ugly monster wearing a crown, maybe. But the Stoneskin at the centre of the group wasn't remarkably different in appearance to the others. Marbled black and grey skin beneath ragged grey clothes. Six feet tall, maybe. His green eyes—the one part of him with any colour other than grey—fixed on me.

I didn't say anything. But I hoped he couldn't read minds, because something had just hit me—something I should have seen from the start. The Stoneskins *did* have a weakness.

"You should know we have been searching for you for some time, Adamantine." He spoke with a faint trace of an accent. Not any from Earth, at least I didn't think so.

"Right." I should be terrified, and yet, after being confronted by that plant… thing, speaking to my captors didn't seem so frightening. "Are you going to tell me why you need me so badly?"

The StoneKing blinked, eyes momentarily disappearing into stone in an unsettlingly creepy way. "You are bold, Adamantine. I did not know what to expect of you, given how you spent your life on a low-magic, sedentary world."

The hairs stood up on my arms. *How does he know?* "Uh, firstly, you don't get to insult my homeworld. Secondly, have you been spying on me?"

"If I were able to spy on you, I'd have taken you with me long ago, Adamantine."

"Oh…kay." I looked him dead in the eyes. No way was I showing weakness in front of this deluded guy who, for all his posturing, was hardly the most intimidating-looking of the Stoneskins. So why was he their leader? "So you know all about me. How?"

"I know almost nothing about you, I confess, Adamantine. That is in part why I wish to speak with you."

Huh? "Any particular reason you picked now? In the middle of a nest of killer plants?"

"The xethec? It will not harm you unless you provoke it."

"Yeah, 'cause that's not creepy." A voice in my head warned me to tread carefully, but the whiplash of finding proof someone was out there trying to contact me coupled with the near-miss in the swamp and watching that plant devour Long-Toothed Guy made me shaky, uncertain. "So why are we here?"

"This is an outlying world," said the StoneKing. "Not a particularly useful one, but it does provide a shortcut through the Janx territory on Cethrax. My assistants are searching the ruins for anything we might use to our advantage. I confess it has been a pointless exercise for the most part, but it keeps them from complaining that we have yet to reach our goal."

"What, you actually *wanted* to go to Cethrax? Are you completely crazy?" Stupid question, really. "Wait, don't answer that. Where even are we, anyway?"

"It was once a high-magic world, not unlike your own."

I had to suppress a shudder at his tone. He knew *way* too much about me. And how?

"Look, StoneKing, or whatever the hell your real name is, as much as I'm curious to know how a high-magic world got itself strangled by plants, I'm more concerned with why you decided to come here."

"Traces," said the StoneKing. "Did you know it was once much easier to pass between worlds than it is now? Before the Alliance popularised the concept of the *Balance*, as a ploy to make every world in the Multiverse play by their rules. Considering the alternative was to be excluded from the Passages and shoved onto the wrong side of Cethrax to rot, I cannot say I'm surprised so many chose to give up their power. But I'm sure you know there were some who used the situation to their advantage."

"I don't have a clue what you're talking about. Except it sounds like you're pissed with the Alliance. Why not take it up with them?"

"I have absolutely no interest in the Alliance, Adamantine," said the StoneKing. "Let them play their games. The real power lies this side of Cethrax, amongst worlds not shackled to a lie."

Holy shit. We were in the non-allied worlds, the ones with no link to the Passages... and my knowledge ended there. I'd heard the phrase *this side of Cethrax* when Alliance staff talked about the allied worlds and the Passages, but I'd never really considered what else might lie on the other side, unclassified.

"Dead plants. Real powerful," I said, affecting indifference. Because something had occurred to me, a suspicion I wouldn't face just yet. "What's your goal? Why drag us through the back end of nowhere if you don't know where you're going?"

"We have a destination," said the StoneKing. "Now we have you."

"You still haven't told me what you need me for," I said. "Nor how you even know—if you didn't know I was on Earth, then how..."

The answer came together in a horrifying rush a split second before he spoke the word—the word I'd dreaded to hear—"Enzar."

10

KAY

T he next morning found me near Central with a plan—kind of. Simon had promised to come up with a plausible alibi for yesterday if I needed one. I sat in the far corner of a local coffee shop with my old laptop, using the shitty Wi-Fi connection to access my Alliance network account and attempt to find anything relevant in the files.

Obviously, the Alliance didn't have anything useful open to the public, but it was worth a shot, and stopped me going insane. When I'd almost run into a patrol twice in the Passages last night, I'd gone back home and attempted to recuperate. I was still riding on panic, adrenaline and caffeine, making it impossible to sleep, focus, or otherwise act like a rational human being.

As soon as Central opened, I'd go to the archives. What Nell had said yesterday reminded me that Cethrax's files occupied a whole section of the upstairs floor, and contained files on every single time a person from Earth had interacted with the swamp world—which was a lot. And that was just the tip of the iceberg. Paranoia had sunk its claws into me, and I had no idea if the patterns and connections I was making were far-fetched or inevitable. Certain worlds were closely linked. If anything might give me a clue as to where she was, I'd take it. I had the earpiece on so Jeth could contact me if he heard anything from Ada. For now, I'd see if I could talk Carl into getting me another communicator.

I also needed that freaking probation lifted, but that wasn't likely given how I'd been AWOL for a full day. *What a mess.* To think of all the times Ms Weston had chosen to believe my version of the truth, however outlandish, she just had to put her foot down now, when Ada's life was at stake.

What would happen if the signal didn't work? Or if her communicator was lost, or broken like mine? If...

Quit it. I rubbed my temples, irritated with myself. A few people at the tables nearby gave me wary looks. Maybe I'd been muttering to myself without realising. I checked the time and returned my laptop to its case, leaving the barista a tip for the food and coffee.

Central's first patrols would be leaving now. Perhaps I'd be able to leave them a message. I wore my guard uniform just in case I got a free moment to sneak into the Passages again.

Like I'll be that lucky.

Through Central's wrought-iron front gates, I saw an unusual number of guards gathering. *Did something else happen?*

I passed through the gates and spotted Carl amongst them, giving orders. Throwing all caution out the window, I approached the group.

"What's going on?"

"There's been something odd in the Passages," said Carl. "An anomaly. It doesn't seem harmful, but we're gathering a team... where in god's name have you been?"

"Simon," I said, remembering the rehearsed story. "He

noticed something odd, too, wanted to talk to me about it. Simon Anders—he works for New York's Alliance," I added. "We both went to the Academy."

"Yes," said Carl. "I was under the impression you were indefinitely suspended from travelling offworld. Including to our own world."

"He called me yesterday," I said, not missing a beat. "Said there were noises coming from down in the hidden Passage, and he followed it. It looked like a doorway somewhere else, actually, but it closed before he could get a closer look."

Carl blinked. As senior guard he'd be well-practised at reading people, and I was far off my game. Not to mention he thought I was unstable.

"You can ask him," I said, silently thanking the universe we'd agreed on a cover story last night. "He's reporting to the senior staff at New York's Alliance branch, as far as I know."

"Later," said Carl. "Right. We need to move. Kay, your boss is looking for you, and she's none too happy. You don't have a working communicator? Again?"

In answer, I took the smashed remains from my pocket. Carl stared. "What happened to that?"

"The creatures that took Ada." I turned towards Central. "Do you need my help?"

"You're on probation, Kay."

Of course I was. And I fully intended on going into the Passages later. But still…

Shouts rang out from the street alongside Central. More guards ran towards the open back gate, shouting. "Carl, we need backup! There's an unregistered doorway, and Cethrax is using it!"

A heartbeat's pause. Then: "All right," said Carl. "Kay, you can come, but you're to stay where I can see you at all times."

I hadn't intended my next trip into the Passages to involve an entire guard patrol, but if it meant I was one step closer to being taken seriously, I'd fight any number of Cethrax's monsters. Our small group crossed the threshold, in formation, and my eyes were instantly drawn to the little-used doorway to Valeria, now ajar and level with the skyline. It opened several hundred feet above the city, near the platform several metres away where I'd used magic to jump from the Passages when Ada had been kidnapped by the Campbells. But that wasn't where the screaming came from.

"That shouldn't be open," I said quietly to Carl, who'd already moved to close it. "Who's using it?"

"Routine checks," he said in a low voice. "After those invisible ravegens." He stopped speaking at the guards' reaction to the words *invisible ravegens*. I bloody hoped *that* wasn't the cause of the trouble again.

We headed past the doorway, armed. At least Carl had trusted me with a stunner, but didn't seem to have noticed I had two daggers I shouldn't have. Probably because the novices were giving him grief again. Two had made excuses to get out of patrol. For once, I was glad of their idiocy, because it had given me the chance to get back in here and do something useful.

At least, until we turned a corner and the screeching cries turned into something familiar. *Really, universe? A wyvern?* These cries were quieter than the usual ear-shattering screams of Cethrax's most vicious predator, but it wasn't like I'd forget in a hurry. Must mean they were further away. *Yeah, I take back what I said about the goblins.*

Wait. Wyverns were drawn to magic. Had I drawn their attention myself, when I'd been using the world-key in here? No, there was enough magic flying around the place already. I readied my stunner as the noise grew louder, and the sounds of shouting and footsteps surrounded us.

Another screech, and a reptilian body pelted towards us and slammed into the group, breaking formation. Daggers swiped, stunners sparked, and a rush of déjà-vu reminded me of an eerily similar scenario a few months back, on my second trip into the Passages. I shook off the thought and aimed my weapon at the small, writhing body in the midst of the group, snapping its teeth at the guards. Not a full-grown wyvern—a smaller one, more human-sized. Adolescent wyverns were ten times as bad-tempered. Another screech told me there was more than one of them. The group had scattered as three guards took down the threat, and somehow, I knew where the screech came from.

The dead-end corridor with the hidden stair to the lower levels. Of course.

Cursing the Multiverse, I made my way in that direction, stunner at the ready. A second reptilian creature shot through the corridor, screeching, leaving a trail of blood— someone had cut off its barbed tail. But it had six-inch-long claws and armour so thick, even adamantine daggers couldn't slice through it.

The wyvern dived, and I swiped my dagger, severing three claws. A noise from behind made me spin around, cursing. Three more of the little bastards were flying at us. I hit at one with the dagger's edge, knocking it into the wall. Spitting, eyes wild, it swiped at me with its tail. I jumped to avoid the poisonous barb and tackled it from behind. As the tail swiped again, I brought the dagger down in a fountain of blood. Then I aimed the stunner at the open wound. The wyvern writhed, screaming as the magic-sparks bit into its skin.

But the hidden stair was open. I slashed at the wyvern's claws, severing them and sending the monster staggering back, and ran for the gap where light gleamed onto the corridor. Not natural light, but reddish-purple. It could be only one thing: magic.

Someone had drawn their attention.

And at the foot of the stairs, I found the answer.

A doorway had opened where there hadn't been a door before, tearing a hole in the wall. Three more wyverns swooped in and out, swiping at the guards who stood guarding the entrance. Some Earth, some not. Swearing, I jumped the last few stairs to join in the attack.

Behind the door, I caught glimpses of swampland. It confirmed my guess—a doorway to Cethrax had opened. Naturally or not, I had no clue. Between us, the guards brought down two of the three wyverns, and when the third dodged and flew away down the Passage, I chased after it.

One knife through the wing brought it down, and I let the other guards finish it off, staring at the open door nearby. It one was one of the doorways I'd marked with my knife. The wyverns hadn't come in this direction... but something made me pause all the same. With a glance at the guards, I went that way.

The code remained carved into the ground. Nothing else worth noting. But I swore something tingled against my skin... I tapped into the tracker, and for a brief moment, I sensed a magic trace.

A familiar magic trace.

It was gone in another instant. I walked past the doorway, one hand on the tracker. *Ada...*

"Kay, what are you doing?"

"Checking there aren't any more of them," I said to Carl. "There are a lot of doorways down here. What opened that one?"

Carl shook his head. "No clue. Kay, you should leave. I appreciate the help, but we've more than enough here already. I don't think you should be getting involved in these situations while you're recovering from—"

"I'm just saying what I see with my own eyes. Is the Alliance planning to take any action against Cethrax?"

"For the wyverns? They'll claim it's not their respon-sibility."

Yeah, but half their leaders are dead. The Stoneskins killed them, somehow. But again, I had no freaking *proof.*

"Can you at least get me a new communicator?" I said.

"I need one, too," added one of the novices. "Bloody wyvern swiped it from my hands. And I think Gerry's passed out over here."

Carl sighed, glancing over his shoulder at the novices. "All right. I'll get the communicators. Kay, you help this lot."

Great. Dealing with a bunch of cowardly novices was obviously getting to him.

Once I'd helped carry the passed-out novice to Central's doors and handed him over to the other guards, I slipped away. Outside, I tapped the earpiece. "Anything from Ada?" I asked in a low voice.

"Not yet," said Jeth.

"Just checking." It was too much to hope she might have left a message in return.

I went back inside Central. Ms Weston would have noticed the missing world-key and Chameleon, for sure, and she wasn't stupid. She knew I'd have good reason to take both of them. I'd pretty much told her I would. Not my brightest idea. Nor was going walkabout yesterday, come to that.

And as luck would have it, the dragon was in the entrance hall, already in conversation with Carl. It was too late to turn back.

Ms Weston glanced up, then carried on speaking to Carl. "That's all there was?"

"It's clearly part of something," said Carl. "Something offworld."

Close to, I saw he held a piece of a familiar metal in hand.

The same material that made up the Passages—and the world-keys. Auros.

"Hey," I said, figuring I couldn't possibly do any more damage than I already had. "I've seen that before."

"I also found this," Carl added. "A Valerian-style bottle cap by the look of things. Maybe one of the guards dropped it."

"I think this is more important," said Ms Weston, taking the metal fragment from Carl. "You think it's defunct?"

"I'll need another magic-wielder to check—maybe ask Iriel, if she's around."

"I can check," I said. "Was that on Cethrax, or in the Passages?"

"Just inside Cethrax's entrance," said Carl, with a glance at Ms Weston. Unsurprisingly, she hadn't given me the piece of Passage. "It's not much use without power, but it'd be able to open and close doorways."

"Maybe someone was trying to close the door to Cethrax?" I was grasping at straws, true, but something told me the Passage fragment was important. Unless I'd imagined that second when I'd thought I sensed Ada's trail.

"Someone?" said Carl. "This substance isn't something the Alliance hands out to anyone. I've never seen it outside of storage, and we don't have any at Central."

"There was a slight anomaly in the stores," said Ms Weston, without so much as a subtle look at me. Great.

"The stuff's worthless on Earth," said Carl. "On its own, anyway. Did you find the world-key?"

My heart beat faster. *Focus, Kay. Don't give her a reason to accuse you until she has proof.*

"No," said Ms Weston, "thanks to that centaur's obsessive-compulsive desire to rearrange my entire office."

"You can't blame him for that," said Carl, "seeing as you're the one who brought half the archives down."

"I'll thank you to stop the gossiping," said Ms Weston. "It's with very good reason. And some of them are missing."

"Missing files?" I said, with my best attempt at nonchalance.

Ms Weston narrowed her eyes. "I want a word with you, Kay. I told you to stay out of patrols."

"Carl asked me to help," I said. "I'd have spoken to you first, but I forgot I don't have a working communicator. It was broken..." I reached into my pocket and held up the remains of the metal contraption in demonstration. "Not the first time it's happened." Given my habit of breaking the things, that was unfortunately true.

"So I see," said Ms Weston, in cold tones. But it was a million times better than her accusing me of what I'd really done—robbed Central and gone offworld illegally. For once in my life, I was actually grateful for the damned magic that made it possible for me to break the law and get away with it. If that wasn't a sign I'd lost the freaking plot, I might as well declare allegiance to Cethrax's undergods.

"I'll get you a communicator," said Carl. "Did you say you knew about this?" He indicated the metal piece. The auros.

I didn't have to feign confusion. "I honestly have no idea where it came from," I said. Or what it was doing near the doorways to Cethrax. I hesitated before saying, "I found something similar by the place the Stoneskins opened the doorway they took Ada through. On Vey-Xanetha."

"Is that so?"

My heart missed a beat. She didn't know. But using the auros to find a doorway hadn't worked anyway. No—I'd need a trace to follow. But it was pretty clear the Stoneskins *had* been opening doorways. Right there in the Passages.

"Was there anyone guarding the Passage at the time?" I asked. "Because it seems to me it ought to be a priority, given what's happened."

Ms Weston's eyes flashed. "Thank you for your concern, Kay, but I've told you before that I'm quite capable of doing my job."

"He has a point," said Carl. "I did say we should keep the whole corridor under guard, not just the stairs. Especially with those reports coming in from New York's Alliance."

"This again?" said Ms Weston. "They can station their own guards there if they're worried. We have too few staff to spare for a twenty-four hour guard."

"There are more corridors than I realised," said Carl, with a look at me. "Kay was right when he said they go on for miles. Parts of them are hidden, too—I think only magic-wielders can see the hidden stairs on the eastern side."

If it was true, I was willing to bet Central hadn't tracked all of them. Carl had been running patrols and the other magic-wielders were exempt from missions after the Vey-Xanethan fiasco. Which meant I'd probably seen more of the place than anyone else... apart from Ada.

"I see," said Ms Weston. "In that case, Carl, you will focus your attention on making sure patrols cover the area along-side the hidden Passage. See to it. And Kay, I'd like a word now. In my office."

11

ADA

I stared. "You're from my homeworld."

The StoneKing shook his head. "No. We are not. But it is our destination."

"You're taking me back there? Why?" I clamped my mouth shut before I said, *there are easier ways of getting there than the back end of nowhere.* What if the Stoneskins were unaware of the paths used by the refugees? It would be a stupid idea to clue them into the hidden tunnels Nell and I had used. But how did they know where they were going?

"You are Adamantine," said the StoneKing. "You are the only surviving Royal outside of the Empire, and you are going to help us have our revenge on the ones whose orders condemned us."

My frantic heartbeat pounded in my ears. *No. No.*

"Who?" The question came out as a whisper.

"The magebloods."

My pounding heart missed a beat. "Huh?"

"The mageblood scum were the ones who sent out the order to the allies of the Empire. They needed soldiers to overcome people who made themselves invincible. The Royals, with their magic sources, *were* invincible, or so I am told. Anyone who got close to them on the battlefield was obliterated. The magebloods lost millions, and the magic channelled through the Royals was enough to knock off the Balance across ten universes. They had to be stopped. Therefore, the magebloods' surviving leaders, safe in their adamantine bunker, came up with a plan: us."

I stared, mouth hanging open. *An experiment. Just like...* And it gave me a weird, guilty sense of relief that the *Alliance* hadn't done that to them. No, someone else had.

"Damn," I whispered. "You weren't created on Enzar, were you?"

"We were created in a laboratory on a world capable of holding us captive--created to be the magebloods' shields. They created thousands of us—starting with volunteers, then resorting to kidnapping and coercion across a dozen worlds. Nobody stopped them. Our group escaped by pure chance." His gaze drifted over the other Stoneskins. "They thought we forgot where we came from, but all that's left for us is revenge. We needed a weapon of our own to take down the people who turned us into monsters. We needed you."

What the hell? My thoughts were scrambled. Sure, I'd guessed they might be an experiment, but *Enzar?* It made sense, horribly so, but that didn't make it any less unbelievable. Enzar had been cut off from the allied worlds for twenty years. There was no way in aside from the transit points, and if there was one thing I was sure of, those places had nothing to do with the fighting. No way could anyone we worked with have known the Stoneskins existed.

Created on another world capable of holding us captive...

"You haven't said how you even knew I existed," I said. "There were a lot of Royals... right?"

"There were," said the StoneKing. "Until the magebloods killed them."

A shiver ran down my spine. He'd seemed... coherent, when he'd been speaking to me. But now real madness burned in those green eyes, and his face was more stonelike than ever. Menacing. Unhinged. The magebloods had damaged him, made him into a monster, and I had to look away from his eyes, squashing down the part of me that whispered we were more alike than not, on the inside.

"Okay," I said, as if we were chatting at the bus stop. "So you found out I..."

"Escaped? I heard tell of a servant who fooled the whole palace, and who killed a dozen guards smuggling a baby out of the capital while the Royals were fighting. Most dismissed the rumours, but who could have carried out such a plan? The Royals were dangerous, their abilities capable of wiping out whole cities, and even the magebloods didn't dare fight them directly. The idea of a mere servant nonmage with no magic stealing one of their children—would you not find it intriguing?"

Nell. I stopped breathing as a sharp pain struck me right in the heart. Where was she now? She'd never give up on me. I could picture her right here, coming to take the StoneKing down.

Nobody was invincible. Even the Royals, with their unlimited magic.

"How'd the magebloods kill the Royals?" I asked. *My real parents.* Of course I'd known they were most likely dead, but still...

"Magic, of course. The Royals might have been more powerful, but the magebloods outnumbered them."

"Wait. You said you want to use me for revenge on the magebloods. But you implied you were working together, with them."

"We are on neither side," said the StoneKing. "We have methods of tracking magic-wielders, and either will be fair game for us when we reach Enzar. Your war has ravaged half the Multiverse. I imagine there are many who want to see an end to the fighting."

He's actually insane. "So you hate all the Enzarians... but you want to work with *me?*"

"You aren't one of them," said the StoneKing. "And I would hazard a guess you only know half of what you can do. You are listed as dead in the Empire. Nobody alive knows you exist, save for us. You will be our silent assassin. You will win me the Empire, Adamantine."

"You," I said, "are insane. You're crazy if you think I'd ever do that, for you or anyone else."

"I never said you had a choice, Adamantine." The Stone-King shook his head, almost sadly. "We will break you if necessary."

"Listen to yourself," I said. "What are you planning to do with the other humans you picked up? Aside from let them get eaten by killer plants and Cethraxian monsters?"

The StoneKing's mouth twisted into a smile. "What use is an army of only one magic source?"

"You don't know anything about me, do you?" My heart beat too fast, but he was pissing me off, and if I gave the illusion of confidence, maybe it would buy me the chance to get in a question of my own. "What did you do, run around kidnapping people who looked like me until you found me?"

But there were no other Enzarians amongst the group.

"Of course not," said the StoneKing. "We merely made use of a certain area of Cethrax with links to the Passages and to other worlds. We were stuck there for some time, though it gave me the chance to bring the Vox to an understanding to allow us free access to their territory."

"You trapped the Vox?" I said. "How? It's magicproof, like you."

"And astonishingly easy to trap in chains. It is amazing how willing most races are to comply when you threaten those they care about. We are stronger than any creature even on the desolate world of Cethrax. Everyone bowed before us, and as an added bonus, we were able to enslave a magic-creature for a brief time, too."

"So you were using Vey-Xanetha as your source—for what?" I asked. "I'm lost here. I don't see what that has to do with me."

"We were told you are a source in yourself, Adamantine. I never expected to find a lone girl so easily, which is why it came as such a shock when I returned to find the doorway closed, the Vox free from chains, and Veyak once again reduced to a puppet to serve humans. A pity. But we had what we wanted. You left a trace that was easy to follow, Adamantine."

"A trace," I said, grasping his meaning. "You have an Alliance tracker?"

"*I* am the tracker, Adamantine. It was built into my skin long before the magebloods tampered with me."

A moment passed. *He's serious.* Built into his skin... like a magic boost. An injection. A *tracker?*

"You can find *any* magic-wielder?" I stared at him, unable to help myself. "On any universe?"

"Including Enzar," said the StoneKing. "Even though the Alliance has closed all direct Passages, we finally found a signal."

An icy sensation shot down my spine. If the StoneKing *was* the tracker, it meant I couldn't steal it and use it to find my way back to Earth. I'd have to find another way out.

I didn't let any of my thoughts show on my face. "You

have a world-key. Why not just open a door straight to Enzar?"

"I can track magic-wielders, individually, not worlds," said the StoneKing.

"But you found Vey-Xanetha."

"Through tracking an individual. Veyak—magic given consciousness—was a perfect fit for our purposes."

"For *what?*" I said. "What did that have to do with me?"

"Nothing whatsoever," said the StoneKing. "But it helped us recharge our transporters. There are few places outside the Alliance with the required energy stores to do that."

I shook my head. "You're saying you cut open a doorway between Vey-Xanetha and Cethrax, enslaved a Vox *and* a living magic source, all because you couldn't charge the batteries on your... transporters? You mean world-keys, right?" I shook my head. His plan seemed more like a joke by the second.

The StoneKing blinked at me. "The doorway itself opened naturally, as part of the cycling seasons on that world. We merely prolonged it from our temporary base on Cethrax."

The doorway on Vey-Xanetha opened naturally... they'd mentioned a chasm. And if this guy was a walking tracker, he'd have been drawn to Veyak as soon as the doorway opened. Holy shit. How had whoever created him let the StoneKing and the others escape?

"You know how many people died because of that doorway?" I said. "The summoners sacrificed their own lives trying to close it."

"It is no concern of ours," said the StoneKing. "We did not use that world to its full extent, but it proved useful to have a union with the Vox. It certainly helped us to find *you.*"

He really was batshit crazy. "You chased me based on a rumour, thinking I'd be your assassin? I won't kill people, for you or for anyone on my homeworld."

"That remains to be seen," said the StoneKing. "I think I can give you an incentive. You don't want revenge on the people who murdered your family?"

My heart dropped, fists clenching. Did he think I was so naive? I'd never met my birth parents, but from what Nell had told me, I'd had a lucky escape.

"No," I said. "My family were as bad as the rest of them, from what I heard. They're *not* my family. My real family is…"

"On Earth," said the StoneKing, with a chilling smile.

Oh. God.

The StoneKing's smile widened. "I think if we need an incentive, then it will be a simple matter to track them down. I'm sure they're worried about you… worried enough even to illegally enter the Passages, am I right?"

God. No. "You bastard." I dug my nails into my palms, simmering with anger.

"Now we have an understanding." The StoneKing shook his head. "I'd rather avoid coercion, but if you give me no choice in the matter, I'd be happy to restrain you until we reach our destination. I have allowed you freedom, haven't I? I've allowed you to speak to your human friends. But we are more than human. Where would you go, even if you could run?"

My fury boiled over the edge. "I'd go to hell before I'd be your assassin." The words tore loose from my throat as I jumped at him.

The two giants moved faster than I'd expected considering their size. My fingers grazed the StoneKing's face before they dragged me back. I clenched my teeth as their rock-like hands crushed my arms—they could break both of them in a second. I cursed inwardly, not stupid enough to struggle.

"Enough," said the StoneKing. "We will reach Enzar in a

few days, and I would not have her incapacitated. We need our assassin to be whole."

"I am *not* an assassin," I spat.

"You have killed. That makes you a warrior."

No. A sour taste rose in my mouth.

"It doesn't make me *yours*," I said.

"Your only option is to stay with us, Adamantine. There's nowhere for you to run. This world has no source. A dying plant is all that remains of a once-prosperous world." He looked around. "It's a shame what your parents' war did to the Empire."

My heart dropped, and it took every ounce of willpower not to tear myself free and leap at him again. But the Stone-skin giants would rip my arms clean off before they let that happen. *No. He's trying to provoke you.*

"Shut up," I said.

"You don't want to hear of your family's achievements?" His eyes gleamed with menace. "You can call *me* a murdering bastard, but I've no desire to destroy what's left of these sorry worlds. *Your* people, however... I believe they've sacked ten worlds, maybe more—not counting the ones drained of resources to fuel the Empire before they went to war. In assassinating the major players in the conflict, you will be assisting in bringing this regrettable war to an end. Don't you want your homeworld to stop destroying itself? Your people to stop killing each other? A person like you, Ada, can make all the difference."

Waves of fury crashed over me. "You don't see me as a person at all," I said. "You see me as a weapon. And you're forgetting what caused the conflict in the first place."

People like me. Weapons created by the Royals. And deep down, maybe I'd always known I'd wind up going back.

I'd rather die than be responsible for any more deaths. On a high-magic world like Enzar, I wouldn't dare use magic at

EMMA L. ADAMS

all even if there wasn't a war going on. Every human in a hundred-mile radius would be collateral damage. But it was no use saying any of this to the StoneKing. He and his soldiers were made out of antimagic. They had no reason to fear me. Why would they care about whoever got in their way?

"Yes, but the magebloods have never had an effective defence against the devastating power of the Royals, Adamantine. We were created to be shields. Thanks to you, we'll take their power and become gods." An inhuman grin stretched his marbled face.

He's going to kill us all. The proof of it was enough to stop me in my tracks. Was there any hope of escape at all? If I ran, they'd catch me, and if I hid, I'd either starve to death in the wilderness or get eaten by killer plants. And the other humans would die, too. I'd stuck with them for the sake of self-preservation, but there was no denying it: on a high-magic world, I was a walking bomb. I could use magic under my own power, but trapped between the magebloods, who had extraordinary levels of power of their own, and the invincible Stoneskins...

"I will give you time to consider, Adamantine. Your fellow humans will have plenty to say to you, I am sure."

Shit. They would. Not only did everyone know my name now, they knew I was his target. It would be quicker for them to kill me, not to mention a slap in the face to the StoneKing.

Stop it, Ada. You're not going to die. Until the last hope faded, I'd fight for my life, and for the others, too. Just because the options seemed nonexistent didn't mean there was no way out. I'd escaped Central before, a building made out of the same material as these creatures. There were always chinks in the armour if you knew where to look, and evil or not, the StoneKing's so-called master plan was full of gaping holes. Like doorways. They used keys to open doors, so they were dependent on them. Maybe that was kind of a weakness. *Come on, Ada. You've thought your way out of tough spots before.*

"As it happens, I do have a special plan for your companions," said the StoneKing, with a jerk of the head in the direction of the group gathered on the roadside. "But they're expendable, magic-wielders or not. It would be a crying shame to build up their hopes now, Ada, whatever you're scheming. If you were as ruthless as your parents were, you'd already have worked out how to use them to your advantage. Think on it." He addressed the giants holding my arms in place. "Let her return to her own kind."

I stumbled back, heart in my throat. *He's planning to make me do* what? I could absorb other magical abilities through skin contact—but what had he implied? I could take power from other people?

The large Stoneskins barred the way as I attempted to approach the StoneKing again. "Wait," I said. "What are you planning to do with—?"

"Later, Adamantine," he said, green eyes glittering. "I will tell you the details of my plan when we reach our new world. I believe I have located a new magic signal to follow, and so we will leave this sorry wasteland behind."

Hell. I had to check to see if my message had got out. If I hadn't imagined that signal. Maybe my communicator was glitching. Maybe the Multiverse was playing an elaborate prank on me, to build up my hopes. But that was hardly more ridiculous than the StoneKing's insane plan.

The humans all stared as I made my way back through the crowd. Several edged away from me, muttering. I caught the word *adamantine*. And *like them*. Maybe they thought the Stoneskins and I were close relations.

The StoneKing was worse even than I'd feared. My head

hurt, and my eyes were starting to sting again. Maybe I *had* picked up an infection from the swamp water. Maybe I'd go blind before we reached Enzar. No—I was pretty sure Nell had said Enzarians' eyes were particularly resilient. Something to do with magic in our blood.

I'd always been aware I was different—it seemed a superficial term. I'd lived on Earth most of my life and if it wasn't for the ties I felt to the Passages, to the shelters, to offworld, I *could* have had a normal life on Earth. And perhaps that would have made me happy. I didn't feel pure Enzarian. I didn't speak the language, and what little remained of the culture had been burned away by the war twenty years ago. Most people didn't know how the war had begun. Not that my parents had probably started it.

The last Royal's child. Nell took you from the palace. Those facts had followed me throughout my life, but I'd thought nobody else knew. We kept a pretty low profile even amongst other Enzarians, and none of them knew the truth about my magic. Nell had never even been back to the transition points. She'd only been in the Passages a handful of times, to show *me* the way. Seeing as she'd had three kids and a bunch of refugees to take care of, I'd never questioned it too much.

Jesus. No wonder she kicked up a fuss when Delta and I went wandering off around the Passages. But she couldn't have known she had a reputation so far offworld, otherwise she'd never have let me go out at all.

I wished the other humans would stop staring. I wanted to run somewhere quiet, just to think. To process. The StoneKing's words replayed, interspersed with things Nell had told me. Things she'd let slip. How magebloods and nonmages alike had used magic for generations to wipe out diseases, and that was why I'd never had so much as a common cold. And most Enzarians looked like they might be related, at first glance, because of selective genetics. On both sides of the war. Only eye colour separated them. Nell had said...

God. I wish I'd listened better. I wish I'd questioned her. She hadn't shared most details of her life before she came to Earth. She hated talking about it. I didn't know the full story of her escape. But if I was going back there, to a war zone on a high-magic world—if I couldn't get away, then what?

Hands shaking, I checked my communicator. No response. I closed my eyes, my body trembling. *Keep it together.* If I fractured now, if I gave in, more than my own life would be forfeit.

"Ada?" Gervene's concerned eyes looked at me. With difficulty, I forced my thoughts back to the present. To the pitiful, half-formed escape plan I'd been contemplating.

"Yeah?" I said. "Sorry. Just found out they're planning to take us to our deaths. Enzar." My voice was too loud, and I didn't care. "A high-magic world, an empire, at war. I'm their freaking *assassin.*" I clamped down on the hysterical laughter before it broke out of control. "They think I can win a war and stop the Empire that enslaved ten universes. The only thing I'm good for is blowing shit up." I didn't even care who could hear anymore.

"Ada." Gervene's hand on my shoulder steadied me. "There's something I didn't tell you, too. I... when I was on Valeria, I used to be an assistant researcher at a research station run by a man called Dr Campbell."

Her words distracted me. I snapped my head up. "You— you worked for the Campbells?"

Gervene studied the floor. "I didn't know them person-ally. That's no excuse, but it's the truth. I was support staff. I didn't know what they were planning to *do* with those pieces of old tech from Klathica they bought from the KimaroTech labs. But when we got caught, they arrested the whole department. I was going to be jailed for life, like the others."

"Yeah, they all deserved it," I said, panic and hysteria giving way to anger. "You know what the Campbells tried to do to me? They tried to use me to ignite a bomb in the middle of London. It would have wiped out the entire Earth's council, maybe even the world, and the Balance across the Multiverse would have been knocked out of sync. That's what you were working for. Just like what those lunatics over there are planning to do to me."

Gervene shook her head, her face chalk white. "It's not like they *told* us," she said. "Those machine parts are common trade. The Campbells' sister company uses them in hover-tech. That's not illegal. The KimaroTech labs supplying the tech from Klathica work for the Alliance. How was I to know the Campbells were working against it? They were respected across the Multiverse."

"I've had enough of dodgy people from Valeria trying to ruin my life," I said. "First the Campbells, then the Conners—don't suppose you know about them?"

"Conner... Gavin Conner? I think I met him once."

"Mr Conner and some of his friends decided to raid the Campbells' place after they'd been arrested, looking for whatever they'd left behind. They stole magic sources and nearly caused a cross-world war. And they killed even more people."

Aric, who'd moved closer, shot me a sharp look. He'd probably heard his family's name.

"Stop that," Gervene snapped. "You think anyone could possibly have known? You can't know the consequences of all your actions. If you weren't here, that selver might not have killed people because the Stoneskins were protecting you."

That was a cheap shot. "All right, all right," I said. "I get it. You were an innocent bystander, who—"

I cut myself off. I was going to say, *used an illegal Passage.* But I'd done the same. Knowing it was connected to Cethrax and the likely source of all the Alliance's problems.

"That's my story, anyway. I think you owe me yours."

I glanced ahead. "They're packing up soon. We won't have the chance to attack them later. I sort of have an idea. But I'll need help."

"What?" said Aric, who'd been listening in. "I wanna get out of here, but I'm not risking my neck. Unless you prove you're not gonna get us all killed."

"I'm not," I said, in a low voice, "if you don't do anything stupid. The Stoneskins have a weakness."

"They do?" Aric's interest sharpened, as did Gervene's.

"Yes," I said. "Their eyes are the only part of them that isn't protected."

"So?" said Aric. "You think I didn't notice? We're outnumbered by a mile. We can't blind all of them."

"Can't..." I hadn't even thought of blinding them. "What if we used magic?" But most people couldn't use magic in a world where the levels were non-existent.

"No way," said Aric. "There are a hundred of them. We'd never be fast enough. They'd crush us."

True—literally true. I suppressed a shudder.

"Yes, but it's a start," I said. "I can't blind all of them permanently. But what if all of us used magic at once? That's enough to dazzle a normal person, right? What happened when you used magic in the Passages?"

Aric blinked. "Guess that's true. But they'd all have to be looking the same way. *And* you'd have to get everyone to do it at once."

"I know," I said. "It's not ideal. This place is without magic, anyway. But... it's *something.* Better than being chewed up by a plant, or sacrificed—or whatever they're planning to do with us." I hesitated. "I sent a message out. I don't know if anyone will get it, but they're about to move us all offworld, and we'll be back to square one even if someone does pick it up. The only thing I can think of right now is stalling them."

"Huh," said Aric. "So what's your plan?"

I looked around at the other humans, all of whom were blatantly listening in. "Anyone want to really piss off that plant?"

12

ADA

Unsurprisingly, Aric said, "No way."

"No one's going to go for that, Ada," said Gervene. "It's too risky."

"They're moving us," I said, in a low voice. "When they tell us to walk on, head over there." I pointed at one particular section of road that was, miraculously, free of creeping plants. Provided no one strayed too close to the edge, we might be able to avoid a horrible death.

If I provoked the creeping plant, hopefully it would turn on the Stoneskins. It was a terrible idea, in all honesty, but if I distracted them, I could get the others out of harm's way. And after... no idea.

Would the other Stoneskins sacrifice their lives for their king? The StoneKing seemed to have been picked as the leader because his built-in tracker would lead them to their destination, and because of his batshit-crazy plan. Surely they couldn't all be hellbent on revenge. Either way, if they lost their leader, the other Stoneskins would have no way to Enzar because they'd lose their tracker. But the StoneKing was protected by his giant servants. It'd take a major disruption to get him on his own. And I had no time to think of a better option. But then, I wasn't exactly inexperienced in causing a ruckus.

I checked my communicator, and the odd signal was still there, but no response. No indication anyone had received my message. I couldn't rely on blind faith.

"Right," I said to Gervene. "We need to get everyone over there. As far from the plants as possible."

I'd controlled one god-like magic-creature before, and I had no idea if this one worked the same way. But I knew what would draw its attention.

Gervene moved through the crowd, telling people our plan in a low whisper. Most of our fellow prisoners wore blank expressions. Resigned. Hopeless. My fists clenched. I wouldn't sacrifice other people's lives for a last-ditch plan, but impatience prickled under my skin all the same. They had to at least *want* to get away, even if they'd long given it up as an impossible dream.

"Come on," I said, beckoning to everyone close by. "If you don't want to die, get over there."

"That's it," Aric muttered, and started bodily lifting people over onto the raised section of road. "Get over here if you don't wanna die, you bloody idiots."

"That's one way to do it." I edged through the crowd to the place where the road cracked, where the tendrils of killer plant waited within. Three Stoneskins had spotted me and headed my way, anger evident on their rocklike features.

I pulled on magic—the little magic I could get at—and the presence of the living plant pushed against me. The tendrils began to move.

Come on! I was a living source, apparently, for god's sake. Ignoring the presence of the magic-creature, I concentrated on magic itself, the magic inside me. I hadn't used it in so long, but it didn't just disappear. Sparks flew, and I pushed the charge higher. Every hair on my body stood on end. More power built, too much to be coming from me. I was pulling it from somewhere else.

From the other humans. They were magic-wielders, every single one of them. Some of them shifted, blankness clearing from their faces as they picked up on the magic. They must have internal sources. But none of them tried to stop me taking their magic. *Sorry. I'll have to borrow your power for a bit.*

Most of the humans had moved over to the safe place now, or been lifted there by Aric, giving me a clear view of the Stoneskins' camp—and beyond it, the doorway opening. A piece of the world was peeling away... but even as I watched, magic flowing through my veins, the door began to close, the edges shifting.

Holy shit. I wasn't just dragging power out of the magic-wielders, I was draining every source within reach. Including the world-key, or whatever the Stoneskins were using to open the door.

I pulled on it, hard, and magic sparked brighter than ever, a vivid red glow settling over the abandoned buildings, and around me. A rush of inspiration struck. I had to release the energy before the Stoneskins got too close otherwise they'd block it altogether, but none of them seemed to want to get near the creeping plant.

A vine snagged my ankle. I yelped, and the magic escaped in a thunderous crash, shaking the ground under my feet. The sky lit up, red, then white. I'd almost hit third level without even realising it. Several people screamed.

"Let me go!" I snarled at the plant, blinking the glare from my vision. "I'm a magic source, like you." Lights burst behind my eyes, and my skin tingled. Just as Veyak did, it was attempting to use me as a vessel. Anger buzzed at me, like when I faced a kimaros. The plant was a living source, and it must have been conscious once, before someone had overloaded it with magical energy. Same as Veyak and the others. *Stop. I'm not the enemy.*

"That won't work," I said, kicking at the tendril around my leg. "I'm adamantine. I'm not your enemy. Attack *them!*"

The vine tugged my leg, without warning, and my elbows scraped against the concrete floor. I struggled, glimpsing several Stoneskins caught in a similar trap, vines wrapped around them like ropes. To my relief, the humans were out of reach, on the other side of the road, and most of them had the sense to move away from the plant. For now.

I kicked out again, letting magic flow through my limbs. I concentrated all my effort on the place where the vine curled around my leg, and released the charge.

The vine let go, and I stumbled back. The doorway had closed, and the Stoneskins headed towards the other humans, and what had been a safe place had turned into a trap with no way out. *No.*

Seeing the plant had let go of me, two of them marched towards me. It was a weak magic source, and couldn't do any damage, least of all to magicproof creatures like them. Helplessness sank its claws into me again.

The communicator buzzed in my pocket.

"Get over here, Adamantine, or I will order my soldiers to kill them. *All* of them."

The StoneKing himself marched towards me, knocking his fellow soldiers aside. They stared after him, mouths hanging open.

I went still, my heart thudding. *Crap.*

"Adamantine, if you use magic again, your friends will die. You've left me no choice in the matter."

The two large Stoneskins climbed over to the humans and had Aric and Gervene trapped within seconds. *Dammit.*

"You bastard," I whispered.

"Did you really think a decrepit source like the xervec would serve you?" He tilted his head on one side, pityingly. "You will be my personal prisoner, Adamantine. I think that's a wise decision, don't you?"

Fuck you. Before I could say the words, the Stoneskins lifted Aric and Gervene off the ground. Gervene gasped for breath.

I just nodded, the fight knocked out of me.

This isn't over. I glared at StoneKing as he took me by the arm and steered me through the group.

The Stoneskins herded the other humans back over the road, and towards the place where they'd been opening the doorway. The StoneKing dragged me along with him, several other Stoneskins on either side, barring all chance of escape. With the StoneKing touching my arm even lightly, I couldn't so much as access a hint of magic.

Two more Stoneskins stood either side of the road. Between them, the air shimmered above a carved symbol on the ground. They were opening a doorway again. I hadn't drained all the magic from their source.

Not Enzar. Please. No.

But the blue gleam through the gap in the world was familiar. The Passages. A shiver of dread washed over me. If he didn't have such a tight grip on my arm, I could use magic again, and stop that door.

Too late. The two Stoneskins stepped into the Passages and the StoneKing dragged me after him. The icy air and the smooth metal under my feet were so familiar... I twisted to look to either side, but the view blurred, distorted, and where the corridor should have been was what appeared to be a solid wall. The Stoneskins had done something to isolate this part of the Passages. So no one would be able to find us. Bastards thought of everything.

"Lead the way," said one of the two, and the StoneKing

stepped forward, holding something in his free hand—a gleaming piece of metal, black with a bluish sheen.

The world-key. It had to be.

A wild desperation clawed at me, and before I could contemplate how stupid it was, I lunged and kicked the StoneKing's hand with everything I had. The StoneKing hadn't expected the attack and his grip was loose, as was the other Stoneskin's as my foot connected. The piece of metal fell, bouncing on the floor, and for a moment, the shimmering barrier fragmented, images flashing across it one after the other—the view of a night sky, then a desert, then the tops of towering skyscrapers with cars parked in mid-air. Valeria. I struggled desperately, but the StoneKing's grip went so tight, my hand numbed, then broke out in pain like white fire.

"Pick that up!" he shouted, and one of the other Stoneskins grabbed wildly at the fragment—it skittered out of sight, bouncing off the Passage wall, and the vista of Neo Greyle grew even larger, filling the Passage from floor to ceiling. High in the air, on a level with the rooftops—several kids with hover boots shot past, and we were so close to a parked car I could almost touch it. Close enough to be heard.

"Hey!" I shouted. "Over here!"

A rough hand cut off my words, smacking my face, and blood filled my mouth where I'd bitten the inside of my cheek. Two Stoneskins grabbed at the Passage fragment, but the doorway moved, and they fell into empty air.

"*No!*" The StoneKing shoved me back. I slammed into one of the giants, whose huge concrete arms closed around me. The StoneKing seized the Passage fragment, but it was too late—the two Stoneskins had already fallen through the doorway. Which closed, leaving only blue walls behind. Valeria was gone, and two of the bastard's servants along with it.

I didn't know whether to yell in frustration or laugh, so instead, I spat a mouthful of blood onto the Passage floor. The StoneKing turned back, the metal fragment in hand, and moved to the door once again, grabbing my arm roughly.

"You'll pay for that," he said in a low, dangerous voice. "You do realise we could all have been pulled through that doorway?"

The StoneKing shook me. Not hard, but my teeth rattled in my head all the same. *Holy shit. He's going to kill me. Or the others. Dammit.* Why had I been such an idiot? I didn't know the first thing about world-keys, and I'd kicked a dangerous object around the Passages when for all I knew, it might have blown the place up.

Still. He didn't need to know I hadn't known what I was doing. I met his gaze, stared into those green eyes, and wished I had a free hand to scratch them out.

"Adamantine," he said, "I was under the impression Earth did not allow most people to access information on inter-world travel. I thought lowly Alliance guards such as yourself wouldn't know how to manipulate your way around the worlds."

He thought I knew something? Kay knew more than I did about world-keys, but then again, he was an amplifier and could open a door to anywhere if he had a signal to follow. Like on Vey-Xanetha. If he had a tracker, maybe he could find me.

That's too big a leap. I said nothing, watching the StoneK-ing. He frowned at me, looking me up and down.

"Do you known how to reach your homeworld?"

I shook my head. "No."

"Yet you knew how to reach... Valeria? You chose that world?"

I did? I hadn't a clue why the doorway had opened there. Yeah, if he'd let go of me, I might have had a shot at escape, but I could just as easily have fallen to my death. The mental image of those two Stoneskins falling out of the sky was so outlandish, I couldn't help a smile.

"You think it's funny?"

"Your face is," I said, grinning at him. *Go on. Hit me.* I'd lost him two of his minions—*and,* if anyone came through this part of the Passages, they'd see the blood on the floor. At this point, I'd take every small victory. I was cracking up.

The StoneKing sighed, turning the piece of metal over in his hand. Then he pressed it to the wall, gripping my arm tight. Dread rose within me again. *Not Enzar.*

But instead, the world that appeared in the doorway was none other than a familiar swamp.

"Again?" I said, disbelieving.

"You dislike the swampland?" asked the StoneKing. "I admit, I do find it distasteful."

"What was the point in dragging us through that city if you're planning to go back here?" I said.

The StoneKing pulled me alongside him. "I am following the nearest magic trace. The closest leads back to this world. Unless you *do* know something, Adamantine?"

We stepped onto boggy ground again. This part of Cethrax looked no different to the world we'd left behind— just mud, rotting, sharp-branched trees, and a cloudy dark purple sky.

"Tell me," said the StoneKing, and the two minions closed in. "I need you, but I will not hesitate to kill your unfortunate human companions. Two of them in particular. What is it you know about world-travel?"

"No," I said. "I've no idea. It's true."

And there went my brief advantage. Not that I could have kept up the pretence for long. If I *had* known how world-keys worked, I might have been able to do more. Get some people out of harm's way. Just one person. I couldn't condemn everyone along with me.

The other Stoneskins passed through the doorway in formation, then the humans, guarded either side. Guilt rose within me. Stoneskins held onto both Aric and Gervene, the former of whom seemed pretty subdued. At least they hadn't hurt either of them.

But that put my ideas to dust. My heart sank when the last of the Stoneskins at the back of the group came through, and the StoneKing dragged me over to where the gleaming piece of metal lay. I expected him to pick it up, but instead, he brought his stone foot down with a thud that jarred through me. The stone was broken—as was our way back. His adamantine skin must have killed what was left of the magic inside it.

"Nothing to say, Adamantine?"

"What, you want me to congratulate you? Why are we back here?"

"I told you: it's where the trace is leading me."

"So you're leading us around in circles?" I said, incredulity rising by the second. I couldn't believe the other Stoneskins put their faith in a lunatic who freely admitted he didn't even know where he was going.

"If you have a better way, I'd be glad to hear it, Adamantine."

"Stop calling me that." I swore as I sank up to my ankles in mud again.

"It's your name, isn't it?"

"Only one person gets to call me my real name, and it isn't you." I yelped as he lifted me out of the thick mud. "What's *your* real name?"

"None of your concern," said the StoneKing, sharply. "Come. We have ground to cover, and I would assume you have no desire to spend the night in the swampland. Nobody will defend your friends, should Cethrax's perils strike."

Cursing him, I had no choice but to let the Stoneking lead me through the swamp.

"You're following a magic trace," I said. "But none of the creatures here can use magic. If anything, they repel it."

"Someone used magic… near here. Fairly recently."

I blinked. Looked around. I couldn't sense anything, but the StoneKing held my arm.

A horrible possibility hit my heart. He was blocking my magic—was he blocking my signal, too? Would anyone be able to find me now?

My blood chilled as my eyes rested on a human-sized, reptilian body, half-sunk into the swamp, wings splayed out.

A wyvern.

Hell. The scaled monster was definitely dead, and there was more than one of them. Dead lizard-like monsters slumped across the swampland. *Someone killed them?* Someone from here… no. Sparks sizzled from the wounds on their scaled bodies. They'd been zapped with Alliance stunners.

I turned back to the doorway, but it had gone.

13

KAY

"So," said Ms Weston, resting her hands on her desk. "What exactly were you researching in the archives? Markos tells me you were there all yesterday."

Oh, hell. Markos had actually covered for me. Who would have thought he'd go that far? Only the centaur knew the archives backwards. And he'd apparently rearranged the whole office, too, and stolen Ms Weston's files. I'd have found it amusing, but for the circumstances.

I played at nonchalance, my gaze drifting over the rearranged filing cabinets on both sides of her office. Someone—and I could hazard a guess who—had swapped the contents of each shelf with the one below, and by the look of her desk, rearranged it so everything faced backwards. I'd never underestimate the centaur again.

"Doorways," I said, without missing a beat. "Seeing as those Stoneskins did something I've never seen before. More than once. It takes a certain type of source to keep a doorway open, right?"

Maybe I was pushing my luck, but I figured the closer to

the truth I stayed, the more likely she was to believe me. Besides, maybe she had more information.

"Yes, but I cannot say I've ever had a particular interest in magic-based sources, Kay." Again, that penetrating look. She'd guessed *something*, and it was a matter of time before she landed on the truth. It was bad enough she'd compared my attempts to rescue Ada to my mother's last fight to liberate Thairon. God only knew I was grasping at straws.

Maybe even part of me knew that odds were, it was too late already. But the Stoneskins posed a threat to the Alliance whether they had Ada or not. It was my job to stop them.

"I just wondered, seeing as that's what the Conners did. It's in the report. It looked similar on Vey-Xanetha, too, when the Stoneskins—whoever—opened the door to Cethrax and imprisoned the Vox." That, too, was a mystery. If Vey-Xanetha was usually cut off aside from the single Passage doorway, how had those Stoneskins even found them? I didn't think they'd come from there. The ones who'd taken Ada had spoken English, which suggested at least some of them were from the allied worlds. They weren't from Cethrax, either.

But Mr Helm had said sources from certain matching worlds *could* open direct doorways. And the two worlds had previously been linked. But that left the question of who the Stoneskins actually were, and what they'd needed the magic they'd been amassing from Veyak for. Unlimited energy meant unlimited possibilities, for anyone with an imagination. You could use it to blow things up, like on Enzar, or make invisible cars, like Mr Helm had. Or make implants for humans to give them superpowers, like on Klathica... or a more extreme version, like the Alliance's experiments. Like the Stoneskins themselves, maybe.

Ms Weston sighed. "Your fellow Ambassadors couldn't

confirm your story. The council won't take the word of one person alone."

"Because Ada and I were the only ones to go through the doorway," I said. "Vey-Xanetha's stable now it's closed, right?"

"Yes, it is. I recently spoke to Kevar. He had a report from a young follower of Xanet, who told him someone saw an Alliance guard in the city. Might that be you?"

"Yes, like I told you," I said. *Goddammit, we're past that now!* "The girl saved my life after the Stoneskins almost beat me to death. But they'd already taken Ada. I can't pick up her signal."

"Pick up her signal?"

"You gave me a tracker," I said, throwing caution to the winds. "I can normally trace a signal. But it's like it's vanished off the face of the Multiverse. Is that not enough proof?"

"Proof she's beyond our reach," said Ms Weston. "You are right about the hidden Passage, Kay, but you should concentrate on what concerns you—your duty to the Alliance. Not *magic source theory.*"

I met her eyes evenly. "I told you the truth."

"You told me you intended to violate Alliance code," said Ms Weston. "I asked every department what they could contribute to the investigation, and the tech team seem to think it's possible to project a radio signal offworld. Further than the close allied worlds, like our communicators can reach. This sounds awfully like one of your theories, Kay."

Damn. Jeth must have told the rest of the department.

"I've no idea," I said. "Really. I don't even have a working communicator—why would I be interested in contacting anyone offworld?"

"Ada has her communicator, does she not?"

"Yes," I said, "but you said yourself her tracker's disappeared."

"Yes, I did," said Ms Weston. "I'm glad you remember that detail, at least, Kay. But I meant what I said—some things aren't worth risking your life for. It seems you were the one I should have warned, from the beginning. When I promoted you to Ambassador, I was under the impression I was putting responsibility in the hands of someone who could keep a level head in a crisis, and who would put the Alliance above his personal concerns."

"You can't expect me to ignore something that has the potential to pose a threat to the entire Alliance." I wouldn't give up on Ada. I couldn't. But the threat to the Alliance—it was my job to deal with it. And right now, the two were aligned.

"If we had *proof*, Kay, there is a threat to the Alliance, we would act immediately. We know well of the dangers of Cethrax, and were it not for your revoked Ambassadorial status, we would consider sending a team to negotiate with the Vox leaders over these doorways in the hidden Passage..."

"When?" I asked, barely managing to keep my voice steady. If there was a chance Ada might have been near the place—I had to know. "The Vox leader will confirm he was under the control of the Stoneskins, chained under a doorway to Vey-Xanetha."

"Kay, what you're telling me is *impossible*. Creating a doorway between two separate worlds without the Passages as an intermediary would damage the Balance on such a level, the repercussions would be felt across the Multiverse. World-keys themselves are highly unstable when misused, as I suspect *you* did—even if your report is true, you broke several of the Alliance's rules."

"I gave my reasons. Have you spoken to Raj and Iriel? They can confirm the Vox's account of events. The two worlds of Cethrax and Vey-Xanetha were linked in the past, when the population first migrated across the worlds a thousand years ago. They have legends about a chasm, a kind of crossroads between the worlds. Raj and Iriel both heard the story, too. They can verify it."

Not that I wished a trip into Cethrax on either of them.

"As it happens, Cethrax have agreed to a meeting with Earth's collective Alliance, based on reports sent in from New York. You know Simon Anders, I assume?"

"Yeah, he called me." Again, I figured an approximation of the truth was my best option here. "Seeing as I was the one who found the Passage."

"Yes, there is that," said Ms Weston. "Why, Kay, is it always you? Half the team sent to investigate the place got lost in the lower levels."

"Because I'm a magic-wielder," I said. "I think some parts of the Passage are hidden from non-magic-wielders. That's why I wanted to be involved with it."

"Carl has been trying to pinpoint all these doorways to Cethrax. They seem to change of their own accord... unless someone else is meddling in there."

Hell. "I have no idea," I said. "Do you mean recently?"

"Several times. I've asked all novices to send an alert straight to me if they find anything out of place."

"Good," I said. "Is there nothing I can do to help? I can see through magic-based illusions." I'd explored every inch of the place already, but if anywhere was close to Ada, it was Cethrax's hidden Passage. I *had* picked up a hint of her trace, I was sure of it.

"Kay, you'll go into the Passages again *only* when I give my permission. I'm glad you remember your place here. But that doesn't mean I won't be keeping a close watch on you."

Glad to hear it. "Right," I said. "Does that mean I can return to Ambassadorial duties?" I was far from in the mood for offworld politics, but if it gave me legal access to the Passages again, I'd take it.

"Not yet," said Ms Weston. "As a matter of fact, Markos could use some help cleaning up the abominable mess he made of our records. I'm sure it will keep you busy."

Figures.

"That's more important than searching the Passages?"

Ms Weston sighed. "Kay, I'm still covering for your actions on the Vey-Xanetha mission, while trying to keep on top of fifty offworld mission reports, including some urgent messages coming from the upper-floors on cross-world negotiations. If the information you gave me becomes relevant, I will take note."

"Urgent messages? Which world?"

"That's none of your concern," said Ms Weston. "Now, go and help Markos. And if you should happen to see a world-key or Chameleon lying around, you will return it to my office."

"Sure," I said.

That was a close call. And I couldn't read Ms Weston at all, so god knew if she'd worked out who'd taken them. She was certainly sharp, but maybe she was giving me a chance to make amends. To work with the Alliance again.

But to do that, I'd have to give up on Ada.

"Oh, and one last thing," she said. "As of now, the main entrance to the Passages is locked down until we've solved the issue with the hidden tunnel. I considered lifting your probationary ban, but I think it would be wise to wait until it safe."

Dammit. Even if I walked in there invisible, the guards would notice the Passage door open. So much for sneaking around.

Later. I left the office and heard raised voices on the stairs. With a glance over my shoulder, I slipped out into the corridor to find Carl in conversation with several other senior staff.

"This is ridiculous," he was saying. "We don't have enough people to spare. Simple as. Sixty percent of the guards are barely-trained novices, and we won't be able to hire any new Academy graduates until next August. Overseas applications are down since the attack on Central, and so are offworld ones—as expected." He spotted me. "Kay, you don't happen to know about this ridiculous plan to send an envoy to *Cethrax*, do you?"

"Something has to be done," I said. "Didn't the council send representatives there after the Campbell family made a deal with them?"

"Certainly not," said Carl. "We dealt with the matter in a neutral zone. Danica's talking about sending people into the swampland. That place is a death trap for anyone, Earth or otherwise."

"It's also halfway into the Passages by now," I pointed out. "If you need me for anything, let me know."

"Yes, your new communicator is set up," said Carl, handing it to me. "Maybe there's something to the wyvern-hide cover idea…"

That, or sciras. Speaking of which, I hadn't asked Jeth how it was coming along.

I'd have gone back to the Passages, were it not for it being under close scrutiny right now. I paused on the stairs, making sure no one was around, and tapped the earpiece.

"Anything?"

"No. Whereabouts are you?" asked Jeth.

"Central. They're combing the Passages. A bunch of adolescent wyverns got loose from Cethrax. But they didn't find anything of Ada's. No magic trace, either."

"Worth a try," said Jeth.

"Have you managed to do anything with that sciras yet?"

"Kind of. I've added a layer to one of the Chameleons. Like bloodrock solution. Took a few goes, but Alber used it and put his hand through the living room wall. He *said* it didn't hurt, but I can't say it would stand up to those... Stoneskin, whatevers."

"Let me try it," I said.

"I'm fine-tuning it. Should've known you'd volunteer to run yourself into a wall."

"I got beaten up by a wall twice in the same day. Anyway, my boss keeps hounding me. I'd go offworld, but the Passage entrance is probably sealed by now, and there might be a team going to Cethrax to negotiate with the Vox. I tried to persuade her to send me there, because it's the last place I know Ada was, apart from Vey-Xanetha. It might be the Vox saw her in their territory. A group of monsters made of rock —no way could they get through Cethrax unnoticed, even in the middle of nowhere."

"Or you might get eaten," said Jeth. "Even sciras wouldn't protect you from a wyvern's poison barb, or drowning in the swamp."

"It's a start," I said. "I need to check in with my department. Let me know if anything happens."

"All right," said Jeth. "I'll see if I can get the other Chameleon upgraded. Then you can test-drive this one if you like. Al's destroyed enough furniture already."

"Yeah," I said. *Damn.* Nothing from Ada, *and* the Passages out of bounds. I'd have more luck trekking through Cethrax's swamps.

"There you are, human," said Markos, withdrawing his head from a filing cabinet. "Come to help?"

"Unfortunately," I muttered, glancing out the window. London sat under gloomy fog. Inside the office was an entire forest's worth of paper, by the looks of things. "Did you move the contents of *every* cabinet?"

"And her desk," said Markos. "Some of the other senior staff, too. The novices are all in training, so every anomaly on this floor is being blamed on me. I did tell them it was Evan, but they all saw a centaur. Pity I don't have a fancy invisibility trick like you do."

"You don't want one," I said. "Where is Evan, anyway?" I'd forgotten the idiot novice was even here.

"Around. I think he thought the falling cabinets were the work of the ghost."

"Good," I said, absently, picking up a sheaf of paper. "Pity we can't send him to Cethrax."

Ada might not have got the message yet. But I checked my communicator every other minute all the same. Better than speculating on whether Ada was still alive after two days with those monstrosities.

And thanks to bloody Cethrax, the Passages were off limits. I scanned through the Alliance's files on my communicator—again—checking for any information that might help. Cethax's file was more focused on the varieties of monsters than on how it violated all the natural laws of the Passages and doorways. That figured. But I bookmarked a section on how to diplomatically argue with a Vox leader, just in case. Come to think of it, one of those bastards owed me a favour.

I moved files without really paying attention to where I put them. An idea began to take shape. If the only way to find the Stoneskins was to go through Cethrax, I *did* have a little piece of information which might save my life. Not that it would help against wyverns or other wild beasts, but most sentient Cethraxians answered to the Vox. Unfortunately, Cethraxians didn't understand the concept of owing someone a favour. If anything, the Vox probably thought sparing my life was enough compensation. Typical.

Maybe I should just go to Cethrax, with or without

EMMA L. ADAMS

Alliance permission. Except it was a hundred times more dangerous even than going into the Passages alone. And dragging Ada's family into it? It wasn't an idea I was keen on. They weren't magic-wielders, aside from Alber, and even that wasn't an advantage in the swamplands. Not that there was a method for long-distance travel through the place anyway. The Stoneskins must be travelling on foot. But Cethrax was riddled with doorways. I couldn't count on anything.

My communicator buzzed. *It's not her,* I told myself.

It wasn't Ada. A message had gone out from Valeria's Alliance reporting dangerous magical activity in the capital, and requesting immediate assistance from any available magic-wielders. Marked as *urgent.*

Hellfire. The very last thing I needed. I wasn't sure whether probation extended to situations like this. I'd say not, but the same reasoning had got me blacklisted in the first place.

A magic-wielder was loose in Valeria? For a world with pretty consistent second level magic, natural-born magic-wielders were surprisingly rare. Which meant something had gone wrong, or they were offworlders. On the other hand, volunteering to help would get me instant, legal access to the Passages.

"I just got a call," I said to Jeth on the way downstairs. "There's something happening on Valeria. If I sign up, I've an excuse to get into the Passages."

"Valeria?" said Jeth. "What does that have to do with anything?"

"Unusual magic-wielders, they said. Would I be able to pick up one of those adjusted Chameleons?"

"Oh, for—fine, I'll come. But don't get yourself killed. Nell will be pissed off if you die before finding Ada. Wouldn't surprise me if she tries to follow you."

"She can talk to the Alliance, then," I said.

At the foot of the stairs, Carl waited again, looking incredibly riled. "Back *again*," he said. "I have twenty novices in the Passages wanting to get a free ticket into Valeria, but none of whom are qualified to go one-to-one with a magic-wielder. And I'm told these are particularly brutal."

"Great," I said. "Cethrax or dangerous magic-wielders. Maybe I should flip a coin."

Carl's eyes narrowed. "Kay, this is no joke."

"I know," I said. "Listen—Ada's brother's coming, and he has something that might help us fight the Stoneskins, or whatever's attacking people. Can you let him into the Passages? I should probably check what's happening."

Carl sighed. "No. Kay, you're treading the line between anti-authoritarian and unhinged already, and to be perfectly honest, neither of those things qualify you to enter the Passages." His communicator buzzed, and he looked at it, alarmed. "Damn. Fine, Kay—you go. The attackers aren't magic-wielders. They're using antimagic."

It's them. It had to be. "I'll go," I said, already breaking into a run.

Ada.

14

ADA

Walking through the swamp was even more excruciating accompanied by the StoneKing. He switched between taunting and enraged every other minute. Worse was the threat the other Stoneskins would hurt the human prisoners, twisted with the guilt that I'd almost got them killed already, and the screaming sense of urgency. I had to get away before the Stoneskins succeeded where the Royals had failed.

Monster. The Multiverse seemed to want to make me into one. I'd die before I hurt anyone else, but what had happened with the living magic force, not to mention that piece of Passage, drove home the idea that it was too easy to hit people by accident. If it came down to it, and if I couldn't escape my own fate, maybe I could set the others free. The StoneKing was expecting me to make a bid for freedom. But the next time they used the doorway key, I had an idea.

First, I had to distract the bastard holding my arm.

We followed a meandering path through marshy ground. The swarms of flies in the air had no interest in the Stoneskins but really went for me. I swatted at them, pretending to be more annoyed than I actually was, searching for any opening. I tensed at a screeching cry, and a group of hideous three-headed birds descended—but they swooped over our heads in the direction we'd come from. Maybe towards the dead wyverns. The birds looked pretty similar to another monster I'd faced in Vey-Xanetha.

"How do you expect me to fight off those things with no weapon?" I said, as another monstrosity swooped low enough that I ducked to avoid its claws.

"They won't attack you." But the StoneKing called his soldiers into a closer formation. He didn't bother with the other humans. Of course not.

I pretended to drag my feet more than I needed to in order to get a close look at which Stoneskins he most trusted. Either side was one of those giants, but they didn't seem to understand English, nor to do anything but snarl at anyone who got too close. The two Stoneskins walking directly behind them, though, appeared to be the ones he trusted. One carried a battered rucksack-type bag, not Earth-style. Valerian? Most of their supplies seemed to be from there, anyway. And it was either supplies they carried, or something more valuable. Like pieces of the substance the Passages were made of. World-keys. I'd glimpsed a gleam of blue, before the Stoneskin had zipped it. Definitely a source, but not one I'd used before.

So they must be one-use only, and judging by what had happened, they couldn't be tuned into just one world. For some reason, the one I'd activated in the Passages had led to Neo Greyle, Valeria. Might that happen again? Could I get the others into an Alliance world? If not for the Stoneskins, my magic signal might have been left on Valeria. But if it had, the Alliance never sent people directly into the swamp. Even if their employees got kidnapped, apparently.

I dragged my feet even more. We were in the middle of

the group, but it was more of a loose formation based on who moved the fastest through the swamp. The Stoneskins were more focused on not sinking in the mud than keeping an eye on me, and as we slowed further, one row of guards remained between me and the humans. I pretended to be overly interested in the scenery, which consisted of a handful of ragged trees. The wood was bone-white and the edges of the broken branches looked sharp. They'd actually make good weapons, against a human, anyway.

The StoneKing gave me a shrewd look. "You find the swamp difficult to navigate? Given what I've heard of Earth, I'm a little surprised."

"Enough with the planet-bashing," I said, more to divert his attention than anything. "On Earth, where I live, we take public transport or drive. Trekking through swamps is something only hikers do."

"Interesting." The StoneKing said something to the Stone-skin on his right, and I took the opportunity to twist around, looking at the line of humans. Aric and Gervene were near the front, and as Aric's eyes met mine, I mouthed, *get everyone to use magic. Hit that tree.*

I had no idea if it would work, but combining the powers of several magic-wielders at once might be enough to knock over a large tree. Enough to cause a diversion.

My feet skidded, and I fell to my knees in the swamp. Filthy water washed over my feet, and the StoneKing made an exasperated noise. "I know you're not helpless, Adamantine."

"Clumsy," I corrected him, "because you're dragging me into the bloody swamp. Now my feet are swimming in it. Thanks."

The StoneKing let go, enough for me to stand, and I pretended to make a fuss over shaking the water out of my shoes.

"If I'm supposed to trust you," I said, "then who are you? Which world are you from?"

The StoneKing stared at me, those dark-green eyes filled with more curiosity than suspicion now.

"Does it matter?" he said.

"Just curious, seeing as you're such an intrepid traveller."

The StoneKing's eyes narrowed, a pretty impressive feat considering his face was made out of rock. "You have not yet earned the right to hear my story, Adamantine."

"You haven't earned the right to call me that," I said. "And you never will if you expect me to kill people for you. I'm not your slave, and I'm not gonna use my magic for you or anyone else in the whole godforsaken Multiverse."

The StoneKing's mouth twisted. "You may change your mind, and stalling will not help you or your fellow human allies."

He turned his back on me, and reached for my arm.

"Now," I said, raising a hand and sending magic in an arc of lightning. At the same time, a half-dozen other magic shots filled the air. The StoneKing cursed loudly in Klathican. I let go of the magic and lunged out of the swamp, grabbing for the rucksack that contained our ticket out of Cethrax. A dull pain shot up my arm as I accidentally hit the Stoneskin holding it, but he was too late to grab me, and too late to stop me throwing the bag into the air. It soared over the swamp, and I followed at a sprint.

Swamp or not, the Stoneskins were far slower, and I ran for it, feet skidding on the marshy ground. The other Stoneskins had turned back towards the humans firing bolts of bright-red magic left, right and centre, trying to decide who to stop first, but it was too late. As the sparks of magic clashed like fireworks, the tree trunk split with a *crack,* and it fell in a tangle of branches, crashing right across the Stoneskins' path. Branches splintered, swamp water sprayed over our heads, and I grabbed the rucksack and tipped the contents into the mud. A dozen blue-gleaming fragments fell onto the marshy ground—and the world fractured.

I was hovering at the edge of a void, like a cliff's edge, with nothing to see but fog. I swayed, momentarily transfixed by the swirling mist—then another *crack,* and the scene changed to a beach, waves heaving against the shore… except these were much higher than any I'd seen before, tall enough to swallow buildings, and there were no people around.

The scene changed to a city from above—a familiar city, complete with cars parked in mid-air around skyscrapers, while a train snaked through the gleaming maze of streets.

I staggered back in the mud as my foot knocked the metal fragments. The Stoneskins ran towards me—or tried to, thanks to the swamp—but they were closer to the humans. Aric and Gervene were nowhere in sight, hidden behind the fallen tree.

Crack. Another tree fell in a waterfall of sparks. I bent and grabbed for the metal fragments, but they were sinking fast into the mud.

The StoneKing was metres away. Once he touched me, that was it.

As my hand locked around the metal piece, the world broke apart again. This time, the scene showed a desert under a blazing red sun. Heat crashed over me, as did magic. I yelped as my skin burned, teeth chattering with static charge like I'd run headfirst into an electric fence. The world turned pure white, and a gleeful scream rang through my head.

"*Yes*—that's it! That's Enzar! Keep still, girl!"

I was knee-deep in mud, the metal fragment burning my hand, the StoneKing screaming in triumph as his servants surrounded the human prisoners.

Magic brushed against me, welcoming. Like a half-remembered song from childhood. The burning red sky lit up, piercing brightness dazzling my eyes—the scene shifted and suddenly I was closer, at a cliff's edge, and below, on the sand, there were... people. They crouched behind a raised section of land, lined up in a row. Each held a shield above their head, the gleaming metal reflecting the huge red sun. No, those were no metal shields but jet-black, all-too-familiar. Antimagic, adamantine.

Lightning stabbed down from the sky, raining over their heads. The line broke as several people fell, killed by the third level magic. Whoever the enemy was, they must be hidden behind the opposite cliff.

Another fork of lightning split the world in two. My ears rang, dust filled the air, and the line of shields was broken. I was burning in a firestorm of magic, every cell in my body alive, alive.

I was adamantine, and I was home.

No!

I wrenched my hand away, buzzing with magic, in time to see the StoneKing close in from the swamp. The metal fragment toppled onto the ground, the image of the desert floating above it like a hologram. Magic burned under my skin, demanding to be released. Desperate, I pulled the magic from the metal fragments.

The world exploded, and I fell head over heels—a ringing sounded in my ears—the two halves of the world slammed together and Enzar disappeared, leaving the swamp. The ringing noise cleared, and I became aware I lay on my back, muddy water swirling around my elbows. As I pulled myself upright, the StoneKing bent over the place where I'd released the magic—no longer swampland, but a circular patch of burned ground. The humans remained behind the web of fallen branches—still alive, though surrounded by Stoneskin warriors.

The StoneKing turned back to me, and my heart froze at the fury etched into his rocklike face.

Shit. I backed away, the truth slowly sinking into me as surely as my feet sank into the swamp. In draining the magic from those Passage fragments, I'd cut off our only chance of escape. We were trapped on Cethrax now.

~

KAY

I'd never seen the main Passage so deserted. A handful of guards stood in front of the few open doors, but most were sealed shut. A large group of Alliance members had gathered outside the door to Valeria at the far end, including Raj and Iriel, neither of whom looked thrilled to be there.

"What is it?" I asked Iriel.

"Trouble," she said, grimly. "Three people are dead in Neo Greyle. At least."

"Wha—how?" The crowd completely blocked the way, and I wanted to find out what was going on before I ran into the unknown.

"It's no normal magic-wielder," said Raj, who leaned against the wall, shaking. "It's—something else. Not human. And there are two of them. They're on the rampage in the city, they're trouncing everything they come across, and they've hijacked a hover car."

"I'll go," I said immediately. "You need magic-wielders, right?"

"Magic does nothing," said Iriel, shaking her head. "They even lifted the no-magic-shot rule—it doesn't work, it just bounces off them."

My heartbeat kicked up, adrenaline racing through my veins. "I think I know what they are," I said. But what the hell were the Stoneskins doing on Valeria? "They didn't have a human with them, did they? I think they're the creatures that took Ada."

"You think *what?*" Raj stared at me. So he hadn't heard the story. Of course not—everyone I'd told thought I was unhinged.

"I don't have time," I said, trying to see past the guards. "These monsters, made of pure adamantine, they attacked us in the Passages. They nearly killed me, but took Ada with them because they needed her for something. God knows what."

"Because she's a magic-wielder?" asked Raj.

"It's more than that, isn't it?" said Iriel. "I saw what she did on Vey-Xanetha—did you say creatures made from *adamantine?*"

The word spread through the crowd like a flame, and heads turned in my direction.

"Let me through," I said. "Those creatures—Stoneskins— are working against the Alliance."

"How do you know?" asked Raj. The others were too busy arguing amongst themselves to notice me.

"Because they were using the illegal Passage. They were the ones who messed with Vey-Xanetha, they took the Vox hostage and were trying to charge power for something. I know what it sounds like." I raised my voice to interrupt the questions. "Those creatures aren't human, nor are they like anything I've ever seen before, or even in the Alliance's records. Whatever they are, they're vicious killing machines and near indestructible—I know. I've fought one."

Except I didn't have a way to defend myself now. I tapped the earpiece, taking a few steps back from the crowd. "Can you get to the Passages?" I asked Jeth. "Two Stoneskins are loose on Valeria—it's definitely them, and they're killing people. They might have Ada."

"Shit. I'm on my way."

Raj and Iriel both stared at me, along with a half-dozen other people who'd overheard. "Listen," I said, "can you spread the word to the other Alliance members here? Tell them the Alliance is under threat from these Stoneskins, and they have a source. One powerful enough to knock the whole Balance out of sync."

"They *what?*" someone asked. Finally, people were starting to pay attention. I had no idea why the word *source* had slipped out, seeing as I was talking about Ada. But that was what lived in her skin.

Rage quickened my pulse. Like hell was I letting anyone else get away with trying to turn her into a weapon.

"Those creatures call themselves the Stoneskins. They nearly killed me once already, but I know how to beat them." I tapped the earpiece. "If the guards let you in, I'm in the main Passage. I told Carl you were coming."

"Who are you talking to?" asked Iriel.

"Someone in Central's tech team's working on a device that'll replicate the protection the Stoneskins have. It won't stop magic, though—did they use magic at all?" I asked the now-staring crowd.

"No," said Iriel. "But if they're made of *antimagic—*"

"Then they can't use it," I said. "Doesn't matter either way. The point is they're indestructible. But I have a device—"

"Aren't you an Ambassador?" a guard asked.

"Aren't you Walker's son?"

"Have you heard—?"

"Enough!" shouted a voice. Carl. "Kay, I believe you just invited Ada's brother into the Passages?"

I broke away from the crowd, ignoring all the questions,

and found Jeth at the junction to Central's Passage entrance, surrounded by other guards.

"Yes," I said. "Do you have it?"

"I don't know if it'll work," said Jeth, handing me—a Chameleon. "Only way I could get it to work was to adapt a Chameleon. Second switch activates the protection, but like I said, it's probably limited. It might run out of power. If you find Ada—"

"What is this?" Carl demanded. "Kay, you're forbidden from going offworld."

"And Valeria's under attack from those Stoneskins," I said. If I was going to make a scene, might as well go all-out. I raised my voice so everyone could hear. "The Alliance is under threat from a group of creatures made out of unbreakable adamantine, with a source powerful enough to knock out the Balance across the Multiverse. They already almost destroyed one world through creating an illegal doorway, and whatever they're scheming, they're using the hidden Passages in some way, *and* Cethrax. The Vox leader in the Janx territory will confirm what I've said, but I *have* to go after them. This device is our last chance."

"What device?"

"Why did no one say a word about this?"

As voices rose, Jeth attempting to explain the sciras to Carl and Raj and Iriel taking over the explanation of what happened on Vey-Xanetha, I clipped the Chameleon to the inside of my sleeve and hit the switch, letting magic flood through me. There was only one way to find out if it worked.

I pushed through the crowd, and several people backed away with exclamations of pain as I knocked into them. Sciras effectively worked as a shield, so in theory, if something hit me, I wouldn't take any damage. In theory.

"What are you on?" someone demanded. "Is that a magic-boost?" He must be from Klathica, where you could get implants for so-called invincibility.

"Ask him." I pointed at Jeth. He'd just have to deal with the questions.

And I had to find those Stoneskins. Once through the crowd, I took one look at the number of guards on the other side of the doorway and turned invisible.

More exclamations followed me, but I ran, unseen. I sprinted through the entry point, past crowds of guards and Enforcement officers, until I reached a road packed with hover cars, and a pile-up midway.

No time to pause. I ran for the car park, where the hover cars and bikes were parked several feet off the ground, and jumped for the nearest bike. Pulling myself up, I hit the accelerator and switched off the invisibility. Heads turned as the hover bike nearly shot out from under my feet. I dug my hands into the handlebars and slowed down enough to steer around a corner, pausing beside a pair of senior-looking guards.

"Whereabouts are they?" I asked, interrupting their questions. "I'm an Ambassador, I have permission to chase after those monsters. Where are they? Is there a girl with them?"

"You can't have permission—who in the stars are you?"

"Kay Walker," I said, flashing my ID, "and those Stoneskin monstrosities are carrying a source powerful enough to destroy the Multiverse. I don't have time to explain, but there are some people in the Passages who do."

"That way." One of the officers stepped forward, pointing. "But they took a car, and they might be on the other side of the district by now. They've seriously injured twenty-five officers. Enforcement are sending every squad that way. Didn't see a girl."

"Hell," I said. "Right—thanks."

I hit the acceleration, the hum of the engine in line with the roaring in my ears. *Get to them.*

Gleaming skyscrapers wheeled past as the bike gathered speed. Once I reached the main road, the trail of destruction the Stoneskins had left became evident. Hover cars were abandoned in mid-air, glass littered the pavement where windows had shattered, and the entire front of one building was smashed in. Other hover cars were upended on the high pavements, and the gleaming buildings and roads reflected the devastation back in fragments.

The wind whipped against me, cold air cutting through my jacket. I spun the bike around a corner, past another row of shattered windows. All the smashed windows told me they'd moved fast, with no clue how to control the car. *Where were they going?*

I passed by a police station, where shell-suit-clad officers gathered outside. One shouted after me, but I was already wheeling around a corner, towards the sound of screaming.

"Shit." I decelerated, just in time. I'd been about to steer right over the locomotive hover-track, except someone had already done that. The mile-long train had ground to a standstill, half off the rails, and people climbed out the open windows, running from the smoke pouring from the end. Even more ran screaming from a building on my right.

The sign outside reading "KimaroTech" had been smashed through, the foot-high letters scattered on the pavement. The metal gates were bent and twisted out of shape and half-open. Behind, the front of the building had been smashed in, too,

Two invincible monsters and a laboratory full of dangerous magic-based sources was a recipe for disaster if I ever knew one. I swore again when I spotted the limp bodies of guards outside the entrance. The bastards had killed everyone on-site.

I hit the acceleration again and steered the bike through the gap in the gate. The lab now had a car-shaped hole in the glass doors, and the car itself lay upside-down in the entrance hall in shattered fragments of glass tinted red with blood.

The Stoneskins would pay. I'd make sure of it.

The sciras didn't make me invincible to getting cut by glass, so I stayed on the bike until I'd passed by the shattered doors. The entrance hall was eerily quiet, where it had been bustling a few hours ago. Swearing under my breath, I reached the corridor where the walls were dented like a mallet had slammed into them. I switched on the invisibility, and followed the sound of voices.

"Are you happy you let your people die?" said a voice, with an accent I couldn't place. "You can't stay holed up in your lab forever, humans."

"Technically, we can," said Mr Helm's voice. "The doors are reinforced even against whatever in the Multiverse you people are."

Damn. The survivors must have barricaded themselves in. I hadn't tested the sciras enough to be confident I could take on two of them.

Turning the corner. I stopped short. One of the creatures stood to the side, hands in his pockets in a disconcertingly human manner. His face was like the side of a cliff—literally. Grey and white marble covered his skin under the tattered remains of a shirt and trousers. The other Stoneskin, dressed similarly, leaned forward against the metal door as though trying to force it open. The metal coating had chipped, revealing black beneath—just as I suspected. The door was made of adamantine, same as these creatures.

Stop thinking of them as invincible. Think of them as human. No weapon would kill them, true, so I couldn't apply the same logic I did to creatures like chalder voxes—but I didn't know for sure they were immune to other damage. I had my own two hands. That was enough.

If my plan didn't work, I was good as dead. And there was no healing god around to save me.

You won't kill me this time.

"If you don't let us in," hissed the Stoneskin, "I'll kill every human in the city. We were made to kill, thanks to you people."

Despite everything, I paused.

"I don't have a clue what you're talking about!" said Mr Helm. "What the devil *are* you?"

"We are Stoneskin," he said. "We were made to be shields, but instead, we shall be gods."

"Gods?" said Mr Helm. "You're lab experiments, aren't you?"

The Stoneskin pounded on the door with enough force to shake the whole building. "Your people made us what we are, and we *will* have our revenge. It seems it wasn't chance that dropped us into your world."

"No, it was an illegal doorway," said Mr Helm. "How did you do that, anyway?"

"Priorities!" shouted a female voice. "Don't *talk* to it!"

"But Lynn, imagine if we trapped it? I've never seen anything like it before."

Thud. The Stoneskin hammered on the door again. The floor shook.

I crept up behind his partner, and switched off the invisibility, pulling on the sciras instead. In the split-second before one of them spotted me, I got my arm around his throat.

For a heartbeat, I thought that was it—he'd grab my arm and crush it like before. But I found the pressure point, and the monster choked.

Hell. Yes. I'd taken him by surprise, and as the other Stoneskin turned with total shock etched on its face, I kicked his legs out from underneath him and pinned him down.

"If you don't step away from that door," I said, "I'll kill him."

"What—in all the stars." The Stoneskin took a step back, eyes wide.

Revealing another weakness.

"You're a pair of murdering psychopaths," I said, "and I don't think anyone will care if there's one fewer of you in the world."

As the monster I held down struggled against my grip, I freed one hand and jabbed my fingers into his eyes.

The Stoneskin screamed, high-pitched and—again—almost human. Too bad I had no mercy for killers like him. I returned my hand to his throat, and pressed. The Stoneskin's legs spasmed, kicking at me, but it hurt no more than it would if he were an ordinary person. Human.

"You're not one of us!" snarled the second Stoneskin, advancing on me. I kicked him in the kneecap, and he yelled in pain. "We are invincible!"

"You're deluded," I said. The Stoneskin was starting to go limp. His bloodshot eyes closed. He'd passed out. Good timing, because the second was ready to attack. From the hesitant way he moved, he didn't have a clue how to fight—if you could literally crush people with your bare hands, you didn't need to have any kind of skill or training.

I tackled him, the momentum sending us both crashing into the wall. He was cowering after two blows to the jaw. I grinned at him. "How does it feel to be outclassed?"

"Bastard," snarled the Stoneskin. "Human scum."

"You were human once, weren't you?" I goaded him. "Lab experiments, right? On a little revenge plan? Which world?"

"That is *none* of your—argh!" He cowered away, but I had him pinned against the wall.

"I'd say it is, seeing as you broke a hundred laws and murdered a bunch of people," I said quietly. "If you tell me what you're doing here, I *might* kill you fast."

The Stoneskin cried, real terror breaking through, "We were following our leader, but that girl pushed us through a doorway!"

My heart missed a beat, my hand clenching. *Ada.* "Who?" I demanded.

"This redheaded girl the StoneKing thought was so important."

"Ada," I said. *She's alive.* Relief momentarily stunned me, and the Stoneskin shoved his way free and ran.

Too bad he was slow. I tackled him again, sending both of us crashing to the floor—and the door to the labs burst open. Mr Helm ran out, accompanied by three other scientists, and stared at the limp Stoneskin.

"He's not dead?"

"I wouldn't touch him," I warned. "He'll wake up soon."

"Good job we have a cage just perfect for him."

As the Stoneskin struggled again, I knocked him out. Standing, I watched as three scientists dragged the other Stoneskin into the lab. I grabbed the second by the scruff of his neck and pulled him after me.

The lab looked no different to last time, aside from the metal cabinets lying where they'd clearly been pushed against the door. A dark-haired girl held a remote and when she hit a button, the doors to the cage in the room's corner opened.

As one of the other assistants closed the door on the second Stoneskin, Mr Helm turned to his assistant, Lynn, who looked more put-upon by the minute.

"Good job," he said. "I'll be interested to question these two later."

"And report it to the Alliance," said Lynn. "That should be our first priority."

"Well, yes," said Mr Helm, "but think what this will do for our research?"

"They *killed* people," Lynn said.

"And there are more of them out there," I added, with a glance at the sealed cage.

"How in the stars did you fight them?" asked Mr Helm, looking at me as if seeing me for the first time.

"You're Alliance, aren't you?" asked Lynn, eyes wide.

Unsurprisingly, everyone else stared, too.

"Yeah the Alliance sent me," I said, figuring it'd save time just to go with it. "From Earth. I followed the trail here. I fought it with this." I unclipped the Chameleon and showed him. "It's enhanced with sciras."

Five stupefied faces stared at it. Mr Helm's hand reached out, but I shifted the Chameleon out of reach. "I need it," I said. "Ask the tech team at Central—someone called Jethro Fletcher. I reckon the Alliance can make good use of these."

"I will," said Mr Helm, shaking his head in wonderment. "Sciras—shield-enhancement on a *person?* How in the stars…" His gaze drifted over to the half-visible car floating in the opposite corner. "Not bloodrock?"

I nodded. "It has a camouflage switch, too."

"And a good job, if there are more of those things out there," he said darkly. "I didn't understand a word. Why did they attack us? Where did they come from?"

"That's what I'd like to know," I said. "I can't use a tracker on them—they don't have magic, they repel it. But they said they were created… by KimaroTech?"

Mr Helm blanched. "We would never have done such a thing. But there are others who have used the same name— our sister lab on Klathica, which has since moved into researching magic-based enhancements…"

"That sounds familiar," I said. Klathica. Maybe that was why I couldn't place the Stoneskins' accents. Klathica, like Valeria, had had offworld links for long enough that its native language and culture, whatever it was, had been superseded by a mishmash of offworld traditions and mannerisms. What set their world apart was their fixation on human enhancement via magic…

"You don't think they might have been involved? Those Stoneskins—he said something about being made as a shield."

And that meant—no. I wouldn't go there. Not now, not here.

"I have no idea," said Mr Helm, shaking his head. "Stars… you're right, Lynn, we must inform the Alliance. I would contact the Klathican branch, but the Alliance wouldn't want word spreading…"

"I reckon it has already," I said, moving in the direction of the door. "There were guards from a dozen worlds out in the Passages. I'll tell them we caught the Stoneskins."

I really wasn't in the mood to deal with a questioning from half the offworld Alliance—the other Stoneskins were still somewhere out there.

And Ada is alive.

"At least we know our security's sound," said Lynn, indicating the doors. "That was a close call. I thought they were going to bring down the doors." She glanced back at the semi-transparent cages.

"We did have a backup system," said Mr Helm. "Our research is valuable enough to the Alliance that we have permission to set up a temporary doorway port—" He pointed at the cube-shaped machine in the corner closest to the doors.

"Doorway port?" I echoed. "Is that like a world-key?"

"Of a sort. Every Alliance building has one built in for

emergencies only, in case a global catastrophe strikes. Valeria's Alliance's main Alliance branch has one, as do several other branches across the allied worlds."

"Does *Earth* have one?" I asked.

"It might," said Mr Helm, "but it's low-magic, so it's unlikely it'll work to the same extent. Every world *does* have at least one emergency evacuation point put into place by the original Alliance."

"I've no idea..." I hesitated. *The hidden Passage.* But the Alliance didn't know. Still, it was a reminder I needed to check it again. "How many of those doorway ports does Valeria have? And how many worlds are they connected to?"

"All of the allied worlds, as far as I know. It works as a shortcut between Alliance branches, but only in cases of dire need. The amount of energy needed to power it is immense, and it's not equipped to transport more than a few people at a time. Valeria is the only world where you can cross from one part of the city to another, because the level of magic is stable enough to allow it."

"So not worlds like Cethrax?"

"Stars, no. Do you think the Alliance would have been fool enough to set up a direct link between the council and the world that hates the Alliance?"

"Fair point," I said. "I have my suspicions the Stoneskins might be operating in Cethrax. If there was a shortcut there which didn't involve walking through the swamp, it would help."

"Good luck to you," said Mr Helm, with a slight shudder. "That one looks like it's waking up."

He was right; one of the Stoneskins had begun to stir. I crossed the room quickly and crouched. "Can it hear me out here?"

"The cage isn't soundproofed," said Mr Helm. "It *is* unbreakable, however."

"Good." I rapped on the front of the cage. "Who are you?"

The Stoneskin coughed. *Human. It was once human.* I shook the thought away. "Where were you going? Where are the others?"

"Gone." The Stoneskin coughed again. "Far away… our leader is the tracker. Not me."

"Tracker… as in, a source?"

"The StoneKing alone knows our destination. He, and the girl, were to avenge our kind against those who ordered our creation."

"Who?" I asked. "Was it Klathica?"

The Stoneskin laughed. "They wouldn't have the audacity."

"Then *who?*"

The Stoneskin's face split into a grin. "The Empire."

My heart dropped as cold fear washed over me.

They were taking Ada back to her homeworld.

15

ADA

"**Y**ou little bitch." The StoneKing twisted my arm so tight, I screamed. "Do you realise what you've done?"

Crack. Stars burst behind my eyes as he backhanded me. Blood filled my mouth where I'd bitten the inside of my cheek again, and I spat it at him.

"I've stopped your suicidal plan in its tracks. You can't use me to blow up Enzar. Not anymore."

"You've doomed yourself," said the StoneKing, breathing heavily. "And you've doomed your fellow prisoners, too. There's no way out of Cethrax now. There's no escape."

My heart sunk, but I said, "At least you bastards can't destroy the Balance."

"You would have been a queen, you stupid girl."

"I'd have been a weapon, and *dead.*" I glared defiantly at him. "And even you'd be wiped out with the rest of the Multiverse. You're deluded. I was never going to be your assassin."

"No, you weren't," snarled the StoneKing. "You would have been much more, Adamantine, but you chose to doom yourself instead." He pulled me after him, causing another spike of pain in my bruised arm.

"What do you even mean by that?" I asked.

"Thairon didn't know what we know. Even the mage-bloods don't, and as for the Royals…" He gave a mocking laugh. "They know *nothing* of sources, nothing of the true potential of magic. Even less than the Alliance do."

"What the hell are you blathering about now?" I winced as his grip tightened again.

"Thairon created us," snarled the StoneKing, "as a defence, to protect the mageblood soldiers. But their real quest was to gain control of Enzar's ultimate source. The source that almost caused a cross-world war. The source that lives inside our skin, Adamantine. It's ours by right, and we want it back."

"What does that have to do with me?" I asked. "You mean —magic sources? Adamantine—the deposit is on Enzar?"

"They think it is," said the StoneKing, face twisting, "but I intended to prove them wrong. As long as the search for the source continues, the war will never end. I intend to end it and claim all their sources for our own. They took away our humanity. Magic is all we have left."

"Back up a step," I said. "So Enzar are looking for a deposit and you're saying you want it, too? What makes it any different from any other source? They *have* adamantine."

Or, they had, because they'd injected it into *me*.

"There's a theory amongst Klathican researchers," said the StoneKing, "who say every world where magic is above the second level has a major source of its power known as a nexus. When that source burns out, the magic in that world dies. In high-magic worlds, it is common for wars to erupt over control of the source. Like Enzar. In order to turn the tide of the battle, the magebloods believe they need this nexus. Power in such a quantity would wipe out the Multi-verse even with the doors to the Passages cut off."

I stared, open-mouthed. "I thought you wanted me to *assassinate* the magebloods. I thought this was about revenge. Now you're telling me you want to save the Multiverse? Or am I seriously misunderstanding you?"

"You're a living source like us, Adamantine. You must understand. You're pulled back to your homeworld. You were meant to bring an end to it all. If the magebloods die, the war ends. The Multiverse survives. And you will be its queen... alongside me."

I choked on a laugh. "So you want to be king of the world. Right. There I was thinking you might be making sense for once." About the nexuses, anyway. Every magic-high world had a source? It didn't sound implausible with what I knew about magic.

Stop. He's trying to trick you with half-lies. "How do you know?" I asked. "How would you know every high-magic world has a... nexus?" It sounded like the kind of information limited to the higher-ups in the Alliance. Hell. "Did the *Alliance* experiment on you?"

A pause. We'd reached the other side of the marsh by now, and the Stoneskins had surrounded the humans, forcibly dragging some of them around the remains of the trees we'd knocked down.

"The Alliance are blind to what's in front of them," said the StoneKing. "Thairon created us on Enzar's orders, but Thairon wanted the source for themselves. We were nothing to them."

"Enzar... and Thairon?" I glanced at the other Stoneskins. "They created all of you. So you escaped?"

"They didn't know," said the StoneKing. "They didn't know back on Klathica, I had already volunteered to be implanted with a tracker. Even the adamantine coat has not affected it, because it lives under my skin. I broke out, gathered my comrades, and set out to find the one person who can end the war—the one surviving Royal with a heart of adamantine. You."

"Holy shit," I said. "No offence, but you could have done better. You're saying you were used as experiments, but instead of revenging yourself on the people who imprisoned you, you decided to go searching for a random girl who'd never even been in the war? You expected to find me, or find the nexus. Or destroy it?"

"You don't understand at all, Adamantine," said the Stone-King. He looked into my eyes, long enough to set my heart pounding and my skin prickling. "You *are* the nexus."

My mouth hung open. I couldn't move, even to shake my head in denial. *Impossible.*

The StoneKing continued to stare at me, a blazing intensity rising in his green eyes. "You're our secret weapon. If we tell Enzar we have you, the fighting will cease. If we threaten your life, both sides will immediately call for a ceasefire. All fighting will end, and you and I will have a willing Empire to rule over."

I finally found words. "What... the hell? You think *I'm* the nexus? You think I'm the source of all Enzar's power?" A wild, irrational laugh escaped me. "You're... I have no words. That's the stupidest thing I ever heard, and seeing as I've been listening to your idiotic wittering for the past ten minutes, that's saying a lot. If I'm supposed to be the source of Enzar's power, they sure have done a good job fighting with magic without me the past twenty years."

The StoneKing watched me, expression unfathomable. "It would seem unlikely, if they *knew* you'd been on Earth for twenty years," he said. "But they don't. For all they know, you've been in hiding on their own world or one of the others in their old Empire. They're desperate for an end to the conflict. Desperate enough to believe anything. Adamantine as the heart of Enzar… it seems plausible, doesn't it?"

I laughed again. "You get points for originality, I'll give you that." I had to taunt him, to crush the creeping sensation under my skin. There was no way—absolutely no way I could have a *source* living inside me. Magic, yes, but not the heart of all magic on Enzar. That wasn't possible.

It couldn't be possible.

"Well, congratulations," I said. "Only one flaw in your plan—we're stuck here."

"Precisely," said the StoneKing. "We are stranded in a world which is severely hostile to your kind. My fellow Stoneskins will not leap to defend your fellow humans from attack."

"You don't scare me," I snarled through gritted teeth. "I'll make you sorry. You wait."

"You mean your Alliance friends you sent a message to?" he said, and this time, real horror coursed through me. "You are sadly predictable, Adamantine, but I rather fear your efforts will cost many lives. You told your friends to follow you to the ruins of Xervec, did you not? Pity… I almost decided against leaving the bomb there."

I stopped dead, the panic rising to a fever pitch. "You— what? You're lying. You don't have a bomb!"

"You were the one who provoked their plant," said the StoneKing. "Two of my own nearly died stirring it up, but the energy gathered would kill anyone who set foot near the place. If the Alliance has picked up your signal, I'm sure they'll take the initiative and send representatives there to find you—as you're so valuable, they'll send their best. But they'll never find you. Xethet will devour them, if they don't step on the bomb first." His face stretched into another inhuman smile. "None of them would be fool enough to step into Cethrax, even if they did know you were here. And they don't. Adamantine blocks magic signals, even yours. As long as you are with us, no one can track you. No one can find you."

As his words hit me one after another, like rocks, the last lights of hope burned out. If he hadn't been holding my arm, I swore my knees would have given out.

A bomb. He'd rigged that city with a bomb. And I'd given an exact description. If the Alliance sent anyone there, they'd be blown to pieces or obliterated by high level magic.

I'd seen, not fifteen minutes ago, what that level of power could do.

"Nothing to say, Adamantine?" said the StoneKing.

I wasn't sure I *could* speak. I reeled, images of Kay and the others being caught in the explosion warring with stark images of my homeworld, lightning raining down from the sky, magic sources, death and destruction, and Kay.

My breaths came shorter and shorter. *Kay.* If only I had a way to warn him. To save one life. *You can't save everyone,* Nell had said to me. Repeatedly.

I couldn't save anyone. Not even the surviving humans following our group.

Did they knew their days—hours—were numbered?

The world shrank to marsh, mud and the red sky, and the StoneKing's grip on my arm, all but dragging me along. *No. I can't let them die.* But neither could I escape, and there was no way back to the Passages now. Not for me, not for any of us.

Maybe it would be the humans who killed me, once they found out what I'd done.

What felt like an eternity of walking later, but was probably less than an hour, we reached a stone building with the odd appearance of a medieval castle. Two towers reached to the sky and a third had crumbled into ruins over the parapets.

"Perfect," said the StoneKing, flashing me another smile.

"I believe the castle was once used as a prison… for human trespassers."

"Lovely," I shot at him, but my heart sank deeper into the mud. *We can't win. There's no way… if he just left me alone…*

"Right." Hauling me by one arm, he led the way into a dark entrance hall. It was icy-cold inside, and pitch-black—for a minute. Then an eerie glow suffused the air, and I drew away from the StoneKing's grinning face as it loomed out of the darkness. The glow was coming from their *skin*.

"You don't know all my secrets yet, Adamantine, do you?"

I said nothing. It was too dim to make anything out, and I stumbled as he pulled me up a narrow stair. The stairs kept going—he was taking me into one of the towers.

"There are dungeons, too, but I thought it would be nice to give you a view of what happens to your friends." He shoved open a door, revealing a circular room containing a wooden bed and nothing else. It stank, like the swamp, but worse. The hairs rose on my arms.

People had died in here. I was sure of it.

Oh, God.

"There." The StoneKing shoved me, sending me sprawling onto the mattress, which instantly emitted a cloud of dust and insects. Scrambling back, I spun around in time to see the door slam, and hear the click of a key turning.

"Convenient of them to leave a key in the lock, isn't it?"

"Fuck you," I snarled, and threw myself against the door. Pain shot up my shoulder, but the door didn't budge.

Shit. Shit. Shit.

"You have two options," said the StoneKing from outside the door. "There is a window, is there not?"

Yes… a small one. No glass. I might be able to wriggle through, but it was a hundred feet off the ground. And below, the other humans gathered. No Stoneskins were out there at all.

"There's no one left," said the StoneKing. "I wonder what will come to kill them first? I've heard the area is a common wyvern nesting ground. Lucky we're all protected inside this stronghold, isn't it?"

The humans on the ground below looked to be panicking, arguing in groups, even hiding. Several had run, but there was nowhere to escape to. The horizon was unbroken. Just swamp, and mud, and decaying trees. I picked out Gervene and Aric amongst the others. They'd been confined to one area, and someone shouted out, but even magic wouldn't get them out of there. The monsters could smell it.

The StoneKing's voice spoke from the other side of the closed door. "Your options are as follows: watch your friends die before I kill you tomorrow at dawn, or climb out the window and die before you hit the ground."

Sure enough, more Stoneskins gathered on a balcony of sorts, directly underneath the window. If I climbed out and jumped, risking death, they'd catch me before I reached the others.

"Fine," I said.

He'd forgotten one thing—one *major* thing. I had magic, and he wasn't holding me anymore.

Quick as a flash, I took out my communicator. *Please let there be a signal.* Nothing.

Why did there have to be a signal on that distant world, but not here?

Wait...

I tapped the message screen—and it lit up, buzzing loudly.

Crash. The door slammed open again, and the StoneKing stood there, his expression livid.

Someone had sent a reply all right, but I had five seconds before he reached me. Backing to the window, I fired a jolt of magic directly at the floor, where he was about to tread.

A crack spread across the stone, but not deep enough to break it. There wasn't enough magic. I had to go with Plan B. If I couldn't use the communicator, someone else could.

"Don't you *dare!*" snarled the StoneKing.

"Aric!" I yelled out the window. "Catch this!"

I took aim, and threw the communicator out the window, propelling it with the smallest jolt of magic. The StoneKing stared for a moment, as though totally confused as to what I was doing. I didn't blame him, seeing as I'd thought of the plan on the spur of the moment. But at least I'd aimed right. From the window, I watched Aric jump up and catch the communicator. He might be an idiot, but he was also a trained Academy graduate with insane reflexes. I hoped either he or Gervene came up with a reply before the Stone-skins got to them.

I fired magic directly downwards at the ledge. The Stone-skins on the balcony stumbled as the stone broke under their feet—pity it wasn't enough to knock them down.

"Get them!" the StoneKing shouted, and this time, I couldn't run. He grabbed my arm so hard I yelped in pain. "You *dare...*"

"Yeah, I fucking dare, you psycho," I spat. The world swam before my eyes.

Hopefully, death would be quick.

Wingbeats, and a hideous screeching noise. I looked up sharply, dread coursing through me. No way. That couldn't be...

"Perfect," said the StoneKing, his smiling face too close to mine. "I think I'll let you die alongside your friends, Adamantine."

He dragged me to the window, and threw me out into the empty air.

KAY

We couldn't get another word out of either of the Stoneskins. The first lapsed into speaking nonsense in a language none of us understood while the other remained unconscious until the first Alliance guards started to arrive. Valeria's Alliance. I didn't want to stick around, but the Stoneskins had left no clues as to where the others might be—when I questioned the guards, they said the common rumour was the two Stoneskins had fallen out of the sky. Given how most of Valeria's doorways were at a high level, that was surprisingly unhelpful.

The story I'd told the guards in the Passages had spread by now, as had the notion that I was using some top secret Alliance tech. I had to tell them I'd been told not to let anyone touch the Chameleon. Luckily, the Stoneskin had interrupted by rattling the cage, trying to get out, and I slipped away. Mr Helm followed me from the lab into the corridor. The Stoneskins had left hand-size dents in the walls.

The colour drained from Mr Helm's face as he saw the damage. "If there's anything I can do to repay you…"

"I want to buy that car. The one with bloodrock enhancement."

Mr Helm gaped at me. "You what? It's not for sale. It's priceless."

"I think I have a use for it," I said. "There are more of those Stoneskins out there, and they kidnapped a friend of mine. I've been tracking them, but they're most likely offworld, in a hostile place. An invisible car would be pretty handy. And so would that doorway port."

"It's not authorised," said Mr Helm. "It requires an

Alliance member to activate it. As for the *car,* it's untested in the field."

"It doesn't matter," I said. "This wasn't tested in the field, either." I tapped the Chameleon. "Look, if I have a car, I can follow them through whatever doorway they came in by. There are too many of them for me to fight alone, but the source they have—trust me, you don't want it unleashed on the Multiverse."

Not if they really were taking Ada to Enzar. A high level magic world already steeped in conflict. Pieces were starting to slot together in my head, and not in a way I particularly cared for. The Stoneskins had to be linked to Enzar, too. They'd been created on the *Empire's* orders? But what did they want with Ada? Before she'd joined the Alliance, she'd lived as far under the radar as possible, even from her home-world. Only when she'd joined the Alliance had the rumours started spreading. Sure, it might have reached that far... but how had two of those bastards ended up here on Valeria?

The guards were talking on their communicators, and I caught the words *lethal source* and *war.* Mr Helm, deathly pale, shook his head. "All right, Kay. I can trust you not to damage it?"

Given my record with Valerian transport, probably not. "Sure," I said. "But I'm taking it offworld."

"Let me know how it goes," he said. "It's one of my most inspired ideas, but I would be *very* interested to have a talk with the designer of that remarkable device of yours."

"I'll let him know," I said. Speaking of which, I needed to update Ada's brother. But first, the car. Luckily, it seemed the same as a regular Valerian hover car once Mr Helm freed it from the metal circles holding it in place and switched it on. I climbed into the driver's seat.

"Thanks," I said, again, as he got out the way. I hit the accelerator.

I hadn't mentioned I was no expert in this particular type of steering—not to mention driving through a building wasn't what the car had been designed for. But compared to getting those Stoneskins into the cages, it was child's play to navigate my way out, past the bodies of those the Stoneskins had killed and the wreckage they'd made of the front doors. My hands clenched over the dashboard. They were crazed killers, the lot of them. But whether there were ten or a thousand, I'd get Ada back or die trying.

I hit the button marked 'camouflage' and vanished along with the car as it soared out of the building, and into the sky.

Several frustrating minutes combing the skies later, I gave up and steered through the first open doorway to the Passages I found, coming out into a deserted corridor. The hover car remained in the air even in the Passages, though sparks danced off the surface as the residual magic came into contact with the chameleon-coating.

Frustration buzzed under my skin as I drove down more corridors. At least the car made traversing the Passages a hundred times faster. But I had no clue if it would work offworld or if the hover batteries would give out when faced with another world's atmosphere. As I reached the corner that led to the main Passage, I paused the engine. I didn't want to draw attention to the fact that I'd just broken a dozen laws. The car was invisible, so I killed the engine at the corner and hoped no one walked into it.

All things considered, it hadn't been my best plan.

Jeth's voice sounded in my ear: "I got a reply from Ada."

I hit the earpiece with the palm of my hand, convinced I was hearing things. "You what?"

"I got a message from Ada. I'm forwarding it to the Alliance."

I was already jumping out the car. "I'm on my way." *Ada. She's really...*

I hadn't counted on half the Alliance being gathered in the corridor. I shouldered my way through a pack of guards, ignoring the heads that turned in my direction, ignoring the questions. *Ada. Get to Ada.*

First—her brother. I found him arguing with Carl.

"It's not illegal," he said. "And her message—look, it says quite clearly, they're a direct threat to the Alliance." A buzzing sounded and he pressed his communicator to his ear. "Nell, don't—for god's sake. She's coming here."

"She's unauthorised," said Carl.

"I doubt you'd be able to stop her." Jeth's eyes fell on me. "What happened?"

"I caught the Stoneskins, they're imprisoned in a room they can't break out of. Ada messaged you?"

"Must have picked up a signal. Check your communicator."

Sure enough, the message screen had lit up. A long message, clearly typed in a hurry, but readable, and accompanied by a picture.

"Is she still on that world?" I was already inputting the description into the Alliance's file search window. "When did this come through?"

"Just now, but it might have been delayed. There's no way to tell."

And she'd pushed those Stoneskins through the Passage doorway—before or after? Again, no way to tell. But if we went to that world, we could find the trail. Maybe even pick up her trace.

The description matched a dozen possible worlds. I showed it to Carl, who was fielding yet more questions from the guards. It looked like someone from Earth's Alliance had forwarded Ada's message to the other Alliance branches, too.

One word stood out above all others: *war.* There were a hundred Stoneskins, she said, but they were nigh on invincible. I was one person with a Chameleon adapted with sciras. We sure as hell didn't have an army. If *they* had one, God only knew what we'd do.

I shifted impatiently, trying to find a way through the crowd.

"Where are you going?" asked Jeth.

"After her."

"You can't," he said. "The whole Alliance is involved now. Damn. I need to make more of those sciras things—no way can one person take out a hundred of those monsters."

"Yes, but getting Ada away from them ought to be the priority," I said.

"It ought to," said Jeth, tapping buttons on-screen, "but —*Dammit.* Nell's going to the hidden Passage."

"She's *what?*" said Carl, looking aghast. "We cannot authorise this—Jethro, you aren't even supposed to be in here yourself."

"Yeah, that reminds me," I said to Jeth. "Valeria's tech labs are interested in your Chameleon devices, *and* the sciras. They might be in touch."

"Damn," said Jeth. "Any other time—" His communicator buzzed and he held it to his ear. "No, Nell, I told you I haven't tested it. She's got the other Chameleon," he added to me.

"Right," I said. "I'll go and find her. Don't argue with me," I said to Carl. "You can't deny Ada's message confirms my story."

"No," he said, "I can't. But I don't have a world-key authorised for use."

"Well," I said, "I'm going to find Nell before something attacks her."

I ignored the questions that followed me, and ran back around the corner to the place I'd parked the car. I climbed back into the vehicle, switched on the acceleration and steered it a roundabout route to the nearest stair to the lower Passages.

Now for the tricky bit. The stairs were too narrow for the hover car. I had to leave it parked at the top of the steps and hope nothing was lurking below. Jumping the last few steps, I ran through now-familiar corridors, pausing near each doorway, searching for anything, any trace.

My feet skidded in the mud and metal fragments on the floor. Their dull blue colour left no doubt—they were pieces of auros. Defunct, by the look of it. No trace.

And there was blood on the floor.

Ice chilled my spine, and I stiffened as my communicator buzzed again. Jeth sent me a file for the world that matched Ada's description. A world abandoned, lifeless, choked by magic-fuelled plants. The native population had emigrated, and the Alliance had listed it as dangerous, cutting off its former doorways. I had no idea what the Stoneskins wanted with a place like that, but I didn't trust them at all. They wanted to take Ada to Enzar, but it didn't sound like they were close yet.

Footsteps. I tensed, turning on the spot, but it was Ada's guardian. Nell glared at me. "I should have known I'd run into you down here."

"I found where Ada is." I held up my communicator. "I'm going to try to open a door. I have on-the-ground transport ready."

"Really?" Nell raised an eyebrow.

"Really," I said, checking my communicator. Another message joined the first—an image of a symbol made of two interconnecting circles. And—"Carl's opening a doorway upstairs. We should probably join him."

"Why should we?" she demanded.

"He knows more than I do." But I was pretty sure he suspected I'd swiped Ms Weston's world-key already. I couldn't help looking at the broken fragment of auros. I didn't sense a signal coming from it at all, but there was *something*.

The blood. I crouched down beside it, and tapped into the tracker.

A signal washed over me, sharp and sudden. I jumped back, heart thudding. "Ada."

"What?" said Nell.

"Her signal. I found her signal. Tell the others not to bother making a doorway."

I pulled the key from my pocket and used it to sketch the symbols on a blank stretch of wall, willing my hand to stay steady, willing the signal not to disappear again. The last symbol… I let the signal guide my hand, like I was following directions I only half-understood. My hand moved as if of its own accord, but magic was doing it somehow—I doubted even Valeria's scientists could fully explain it. The symbol resembled a clawed footprint.

The door opened… to Cethrax.

I stared for a moment. "Cethrax? No way." It made sense, with it being riddled with doorways, but…

A screech tore through the air.

Damn. Ada was in trouble—I was certain of it. On the other side was swampland, no wyverns visible. Before my eyes, the scene changed to—nothing.

"What the hell?" I said, staring. The scene looked awfully familiar, like the edge of a cliff, nothing to see but thick mist. And on the other side there might have been a shape, the outline of something, but it was impossible to tell. The void.

The world-key vibrated in my hand, snapping me out of the trance. Without realising it, I'd drawn another symbol, and the scene changed yet again.

"What are you doing?" Nell demanded.

"I don't know," I said, attempting to pull the world-key back. "It's like it's stuck—I was trying to follow Ada's signal. Maybe it got jumbled."

"You said it might be blocked," said Nell. "Adamantine blocks all magic. If any of those *things* was touching her—"

"Shit," I said. "You're right. Her signal won't go in a straight line—it'll be scattered. And she might not be there *now*." I hoped she wasn't in Cethrax. That scream... there were more wyverns out there. Blasted wyverns.

The scene changed to a desert. Nothing to see. But it was already changing again—cycling back to the swamp, then to a rocky outcrop—then, again, the abyss with no end.

I pulled my hand back as the scene changed to the ruin of a city. Several Alliance guards turned to stare at me from a few metres away on the other side of the open doorway. Hell —this must be the place Carl had opened the doorway to upstairs.

Sure enough, Carl himself stepped up to the new doorway I'd opened, staring at Nell. "What are you doing? Non-Alliance members aren't allowed in here. Kay, you're *not* authorised to—"

"I think Ada's on Cethrax," I said, scanning the city behind Carl. "I have a tracker, and I can follow her signal."

"Trackers only work on low-magic worlds," said Carl. "What do you mean, follow her signal?"

"What if I told you I was an amplifier?"

A pause. Carl's expression shifted to incredulity before I'd finished speaking. Exactly what I'd expected, and exactly why I'd never told anyone. But I couldn't think of a cover story, and finding Ada was paramount.

"I can amplify a tracker," I said. "Normally, I can zone in on one person's trace, if they're a magic-wielder—that's how I found Ada's brother when the Conner family had him held captive on Valeria. That's when I realised I could do it. But it doesn't work on Ada's signal right now, because it disappeared. I don't know if it's because they took her too far offworld, or if they're somehow blocking it."

"I can vouch for him," said Nell, to my total astonishment. "I witnessed it myself."

Carl blinked, then looked over his shoulder at the ruined town. "This place was in the message she sent."

"Yeah... you don't have any weapons, do you?"

"You didn't steal any along with the world-key?" he said.

Touché. "Look, I wouldn't have done it if I'd had any other choice. You can't deny Ada's message matches what I said."

"No, I can't." He sighed. "But neither do I feel Earth is ready for a cross-world war."

Shit. "That's likely to happen?"

"It depends on how things go with Cethrax."

And if Enzar are really involved... damn.

"Look," I said, "I can follow Ada's signal here." I stepped over the door's threshold, and the signal surged up without warning, as well as something else I couldn't place. Another magic signal—a powerful one. My skin buzzed all over.

The other guards had begun to head towards the ruins of the city. "Wait," I said, hurrying after them. "There's something not right."

The static feeling climbed higher. Like Ada's message had said, the abandoned town in this world was in ruins, most of the buildings covered in a thick, inky-black plant with creeping vines. Not unlike a certain god...

"It's alive," I said. "Don't go near that plant!"

Ada's signal felt oddly muted now, but it was still there,

just about. One road into the town wasn't choked by the plant, so I pointed that way.

"How do you know?" asked one of the other guards. I vaguely recognised him as from the Valerian Alliance.

"I'm using an amplified tracker," I said. "Following Ada's signal—she's their prisoner."

"All right," said Carl. "It looks like Kay's account was entirely true. Lead the way."

"If I lose the signal, we'll have to turn back," I said. "I was picking up on at least five worlds. They've been using the Passages in some way. *Her blood was there.* A chill went through me.

Something's not right here...

But was it just the sense of a world left to ruin? It must have been high-magic once. Maybe that plant-thing was a source.

I led the others past wrecked, crumbling buildings, through streets lined with the skeletons of metal vehicles not unlike Earth cars. How long had this world been abandoned? It was impossible to tell.

A blue gleam caught my eyes. A fragment of auros lay in the middle of the road, surrounded by more of the plant. They'd opened a doorway here...

The plant was *moving.*

"Guys, get back," I said, as tentacles inched along the ground. "I think this is a dead end."

The static rose to a fever pitch as magic surged up without warning.

"Hell," I said. "There's a source—run!"

The road trembled under our feet, and the world exploded.

16

ADA

A scream jammed my throat as I fell from the window. My hands scrabbled at the walls, and I dug them into a crevice and hung on, heart thudding in my ears. Below, the humans had scattered—some ran, others had huddled together for protection. Aric yelled something, but I couldn't make out the words. My fingers dug into a gap between the stones, already hurting. I couldn't hold on for long.

"Give up, girl," the StoneKing shouted from above. "It'll be over quicker."

Screech.

"Hell," I whispered. The sky was marked with bird-shaped outlines, descending fast. Not birds.

I frantically felt for another gap between stones, dropping a foot down. From the balcony below, a Stoneskin reached out and grabbed my ankle. I screamed and kicked, and screamed louder when my foot connected with stone. Darkness crept at the corners of my vision. Maybe I'd get lucky and pass out before I died.

The blood rushed to my head. I hung upside-down over the side of the balcony. The red sky… those shapes…

"Come and get her!"

Laughter. The Stoneskins were laughing at me. The one holding my ankle dangled me over the edge, and a dark shape descended on me, claws outstretched.

A wyvern.

I kicked again, desperately—I'd rather fall to my death than be a snack for a wyvern—but the Stoneskin's grip was like iron.

Screech.

The hand let go, and I fell.

Claws snatched me out of the air. I yelped as one cut through the sleeve of my jacket. The world rushed upright. I hung over the edge of the wyvern's giant curved claws, my head pressed against rough, rock-hard scales.

Holy. Shit.

I twisted in mid-air, the ground spinning below. People ran in all directions. Aric shouted something, and lightning speared the sky. *No. It won't do any good.* Wyvern scales were magicproof, unless you found a weak spot. And to do that, you needed a weapon.

Teeth grazed the top of my head, and I wriggled out the way. "Let me go, you bastard," I snarled, twisting again. I dug my hands into the scales, magic sparking from my own hands.

"Let me go…"

Magic rushed through me in a wave, and everything turned to blinding white.

KAY

Thunder roared in my ears. It took several minutes to become aware someone called my name. The ground under me felt like broken rock. The sky was dark red, like blood. I lay on my back, on concrete, or that was what it felt like. My skin buzzed all over, but the overwhelming sense of magic had faded.

I'm alive...

Disconnected words swam around my brain. *They tried to kill us.* Stoneskins had played all of us. And the others were...

I forced myself to look away from the sky.

The town was gone, the buildings reduced to heaps of crumbling ruin, blocking my view of the street. I shook my head to clear the ringing. Someone had shouted my name.

"Get back here! Now!"

Nell. She was behind the still-open door. But there was no one else. No one...

I lurched to my feet, unsteadily. The Chameleon remained in my hand, miraculously untouched—*the sciras. Of course.*

Voices shouted. I spun around to see several feet away was another doorway, the path was blocked by guards.

"What happened?" yelled a voice.

"An explosion?"

I ran to the ruins. The way was blocked, but there must be bodies buried under there.

God. No.

How many had died?

"Kay, get *back* here," said Nell. "There's another message from Ada."

Ada. She was alive. Somehow that notion slotted through the chaotic jumble—the truth I hadn't quite yet grasped—I'd survived.

The sciras. It had likely saved my life.

But Carl had been with the other guards. I moved to the other doorway. "There was a bomb," I said. "But there might be survivors. If you want to send people through, make sure they have some kind of protection. Jeth…" I tapped the earpiece. "You don't have any more of that sciras, do you?"

"Nell has the other one," he said. "What happened?"

"It saved my life," I said. Numbly. A bomb. A fucking bomb. "The Stoneskins set a trap. But there might be survivors. I can't reach them."

Someone shouted from the other side of the ruins, "The street's caved in! We need help over here!"

The guards in the Passage parted to let two people through, both wearing the shell-like suits of Valeria's enforcement officers. "We'll search," said one of them. "Our armour has protection built into it. If we'd known—"

"This breaks protocol," someone said. "Sending people into a hostile world."

"Screw protocol," yelled another guard. "Our people are out there."

No. It was my fault. I led them there. I moved aside to let the guards pass, only now aware just how hard I was shaking.

"Hey!" a male voice called from the ruins. Carl.

Relief flooded me. At least one person was alive.

"We need help over here!"

"Is it safe?" The two shell-suited men approached the blockade warily.

"I think the blast—whatever it was—was in one of the buildings," I said. "It felt like it came from that way."

"The plant absorbed most of the blast!" Carl said. "Lucky this was an open space—we had room to run."

Lucky. *That was too close.* And the others should have had the same protection as me. I should have thought first, not gave orders I didn't have the authority to give.

Enough.

"There's a message!" Nell shouted at me from behind the other doorway. "Says it's from someone called Aric."

I spun around and stared at her. "What?"

Now I knew I wasn't hallucinating. A hallucination would make more sense.

"Ada—she's on Cethrax. There are wyverns."

Guilt at leaving the others warred with fierce urgency. *The Stoneskins are with Ada. You have to get her.* With a last quick glance at the rescue operation happening behind me, I pulled out the world-key, tracker at the ready, and moved to the doorway. To Nell. I couldn't wait. I'd have to check on the others later. Ada needed me.

"Do you have a weapon?" I asked, crossing into the Passage again.

"Do you think I'm stupid?" Nell stood beside a blank stretch of wall, glaring at anyone who came near.

My hands shook from the adrenaline and it took several attempts to redraw the symbols on a free patch of wall with the world-key. This time, Ada's signal was clear, pointing one way. The door opened with barely a sound. Swampy water washed against the floor of the Passages, and the red-tinged horizon was marked with several bird-like shadows. Below, the ruin of an old stone building was outlined against the sky. I gripped the dagger Carl had given me.

"Stay back," I said to Nell out of the corner of my mouth. "I know this place..."

Screech!

One of the shadows dived, and I ran through the doorway, turning invisible. Get to Ada first, kill those bastards later.

The shadow dove at me, forcing me to run out of the way. The doorway snapped closed, and I heard Nell's angry shout from behind, but two more shadows passed over my head. Wyverns. Fully-grown ones this time. They'd seen me.

I swore as the thick mud slowed me down. A gigantic fallen tree blocked the path, and throwing patience out the window entirely, I sent a blast of magic at it.

The recoil was stronger than I expected, sending me staggering back into the mud, but it also sent the wyverns soaring out of sight with loud screeches. I had no clue where Ada was, but the fortress was the one landmark, and the wyverns approaching it told me they'd fixated on something there.

The sky lit up, white, as magic seared the air. Someone over there had used magic. In fact— sparks were flying, arcs of lightning piercing the sky. But magic wouldn't harm the wyverns.

I ran. Two wyverns circled the fortress-like building and as someone fired magic at them again, the recoil rebounded, lighting up the sky. A nearby tree fell, split in two. And there were people, at least a dozen, running in all directions, some hiding behind trees, others cowering on the ground.

Screw it all. "Ada!" I shouted.

My heart stopped. A wyvern flew overhead, Ada clutched in its claws, as magic struck in a haze of white. I blinked to clear my eyes.

No. "Ada!"

The world cleared. Ada clung to the wyvern's claws. I couldn't fire magic at the creature in case I hit Ada instead. Unless…

I let magic spark from my hands, aiming it at the ground. The boost sent me flying ten feet in the air. Breathlessly, I yelled, "Come and get me, you clawed bastard!"

The wyvern flew at me, screeching. The momentum was already driving me back towards the ground, but as its claws swiped, Ada wriggled free and jumped. We both hit the ground, rolling over in the mud, and I came upright to find her staring at me, dazed.

"Kay," she said, swaying on the spot. "You're not dead..."

"No, but we need to move." That goddamned wyvern wasn't going to quit. And like hell was I going to let it at Ada again.

"Agreed." She staggered forward, but she didn't seem hurt, only shaken by the fall. "The others." She turned back to the other people, who the second wyvern was dive-bombing. The first fixed its eyes on me, and soared downwards.

Cursing, I drew my dagger and handed her the stunner, which she took in a shaking hand just in time to aim at the wyvern. Sparks shot from the end, striking the wyvern in its less-protected wings, and it screeched, wheeling higher, out of reach.

A human body fell from the sky, dropped by the other lizard—those people must not be armed. No wonder they were fighting with magic. It wouldn't do much good against the wyverns' thick armour. And these wyverns were clever bastards, not flying close enough to the ground to make them vulnerable.

Hit the weak spots... the joints in its armour and wings. I took aim and shot magic from my fingertips again as the second wyvern flew at the cowering humans. Ada shot magic at it, but it had already grabbed a human—they didn't even struggle.

I let sparks fan out from my palms, challenging the nearest lizard to dive-bomb me. The wyvern levelled its flight path, claws swiping at Ada. Sparks filled the air, and something whizzed past my head. Not magic. Amongst the humans, a woman straightened up and caught whatever it was in her hand. A sharpened tree branch?

I twisted in time to see Aric, of all people, sprinting across the marsh, arms full of more branches.

"You wanna live?" he yelled at the cowering people on the ground. "Fight, you bloody morons!"

I had to give him credit, those branches were decently sharp to make improvised weapons. But only Aric would be idiot enough to draw attention to himself with two angry wyverns above. The second dropped the human it held and flew at him. The first circled above Ada and me. I sent a jolt of power at the joint on its right wing, burning a sizzling hole through it. The wyvern screamed, knocked off balance in the air, and circled lower. I stabbed at its swiping claws with the dagger, severing at least one of them—and Ada was ready with her stunner.

Its barbed tail thrashed, and I jumped, swiping the dagger through the air. Blood poured from its tail, but I hadn't severed it. Ada shot magic right into the wound and the wyvern bucked and screamed, droplets of blood spattering the ground. The other wyvern screeched at it, wings flapping frantically as Aric and three others stabbed at it with branches sharpened to wicked points.

"Get away from here!" Ada shouted, magic flaring from the stunner in her hand. The wyvern took the hint and flew lopsidedly sideways, colliding with its partner. They fell in a pile of thrashing limbs and blood.

Aric ran at them, stabbing with a branch. They took off again, tangled together, blood spattering the marshy ground.

"We need to get out of here." Ada turned to me, wide-eyed. "You're really here. Holy hell…"

"Yeah," I said, keeping one eye on the wyverns, which flew higher, out of reach. I dug my free hand into my pocket and got out the world-key. Better to open a door here than run all the way back, but I couldn't let the wyverns into the Passages.

"Kay, *hurry!* Aric, Gervene, get the others over here, quick!"

I couldn't figure out why she was freaking out so much—she'd seemed composed fighting the wyvern. I activated the world-key, and crouched to carve the symbols into the ground. It wasn't ideal, but most of those people hadn't been fighting—they were either hurt or in shock, and we had to get them to safety.

Damn it all to hell. I drew the last symbol, the one I'd seen on Vey-Xanetha—for the Passages.

Something rock-hard collided with the back of my head. Stars burst behind my eyes, and the world-key was snatched from my grasp.

A Stoneskin held the world-key up to the sky, mouth stretched in an insane smile.

"Thank you, human!" he said. "You have given us a way out! I can feel Enzar calling."

Shit. "No way," I said, amplifying the sciras. But the world was hazy, and the back of my head throbbed. I missed with my first strike, and he hit me on the jaw. Not hard enough to break it—the sciras had taken care of that—but it made my vision swim again. And he was getting away. With the world-key.

"No!" Ada shouted, and then yelled in pain as the Stoneskin knocked her into the marsh. Cursing my blurred vision, I pushed to my feet, sprinting to place myself between her and the Stoneskin monster. But he wasn't alone. There were others—at least a dozen human-shaped monsters with marble skin. And further out, another group were rounding up the humans—one woman struggled and a particularly large Stoneskin hit her with enough force to send her flying ten feet across the swamp.

"You bastards!" Ada yelled.

We were outnumbered by far. I had the one sciras-chameleon, and even if I transferred the effects to Ada, there were too many of them to fight off between the pair of us.

And the other humans—at least ten lay unmoving in the mud already. The ones huddled together wore dazed, deadened expressions. No sign of Aric. Maybe he'd run.

"Ada." I walked over to her, unsteadily, and took her hand. She looked at me, and her eyes reflected everything I couldn't put into words.

"How touching," said the Stoneskin who seemed to be the leader. "I'm impressed with you, human, impressed enough not to kill you right away. In fact, I want to drag our game out a bit longer. Lock them both in the tower until I find Enzar. I don't trust them."

Enzar. He was looking for Ada's homeworld. And I'd brought him the means to do it.

I squeezed Ada's hand, hoping she'd get I was transferring power to her. She could absorb the effects of the Chameleon, so I hoped the same applied to the sciras. But I couldn't use both at once, and in any case, we couldn't just turn invisible and run for it when that lunatic held the means for destroying the Multiverse in his hands. No—I had to get a warning to the Alliance.

But two massive Stoneskins had turned in our direction. Whatever they were, they'd never been human. Their grey-marbled skin covered bulging muscles and curved claws, like some relation of Cethrax's voxes. No way could I go up against one of those even with the sciras.

Shit.

17

ADA

My arm throbbed, my head ached, and the StoneKing had the world-key. But hope stirred in my heart every time I looked at Kay, even as the two gigantic Stoneskins marched us back into the fortress, up the stairs to the tower. He was alive. They hadn't killed him, and he'd been trying to find me all along.

And he'd *hit* one of them. He had some way of fighting them I'd not seen yet. *I never doubted you.* I wished, stupidly, they'd leave us alone to talk. Even though every minute brought us closer to our doom.

Into the tower room. The guard locked the door behind us.

"Shit," said Kay, pacing to the window. One look outside told me it wouldn't do any good to try to climb out. The platform below had collapsed when the wyvern had crashed into it, and there was no escaping a hundred-foot drop, right in the middle of the Stoneskins. They'd take us to pieces.

"God." He hammered on the wall. "I can't break it."

"I think I'd be worried if you could break down a wall," I said shakily.

"The sciras," he said, "it should have worked." He braced his shoulder against the door, but it didn't shift an inch. He cursed, drew back and threw himself against it, making me jump in alarm.

"Jesus, Kay, calm down!"

"Calm—" He looked at me, eyes wide. If anything, Kay looked like *he* was the one who'd been kidnapped by monsters. Bruises marked his face and neck, and there was a half-healed cut on his forehead. His skin was so pale, the bruises and the shadows under his eyes were even more vivid. "We're fucking locked in."

No shit, I was tempted to say, along with *you could at least act like you're pleased to see me for half a second.* I gave myself a mental shake. We were both utterly screwed. And Kay hadn't looked so terrified in all the time I'd known him.

"Do you have your communicator?"

He uncurled one tightly clenched fist to dig in his jacket pocket. "Shit. *Shit.*"

"It's broken?"

"Water must have got into it." He threw it at the wall, where it smashed into pieces, swearing in languages I didn't know.

"Kay…" I'd never seen him on the edge of losing control, not like this. He paced around the room, hammering at gaps in the wall, shoving at the door again. It didn't budge.

"Ada." He turned to me, breathing heavily. "Sorry." He took a couple of steps towards me.

"I'm not overly happy about being locked in either, you know." A lump rose in my throat. "They killed Gervene. They probably killed the others, too."

"Aric," he said. "How did he end up here?"

"They caught him in the Passages when they were looking for me." I shuddered all over. "They want me to dominate Enzar. They have a crazy scheme."

"Yeah?" He ran a hand through his hair, which, like mine, was soaked in swamp water. His hands were dark with blood, the knuckles shredded from pounding on the door. "Always with the crazy schemes." He closed his eyes, then focused on me. "I'm sorry. I should have known this would happen."

"My second imprisonment in a day," I said, in an attempt to lighten the mood. "Can't say I care for the décor in here."

"You were in here before?"

"Until a wyvern took me for a ride." I half perched on the edge of the bed. "They threw me out the window, can you believe it? I really pissed off the StoneKing."

"StoneKing?" He arched an eyebrow. "Because that doesn't have 'ego' written all over it."

I half-smiled despite myself, my chest aching. I'd missed him.

"He's raving mad," I said. "Yeah. He's been dragging us across the Multiverse for days searching for a signal that probably doesn't even exist. I wrecked his plans when I destroyed their—whatever it was they opened doorways with."

"Auros," he said. "Two of the bastards escaped onto Valeria. Said you pushed them through a door."

I gaped at him. "They—it was when I tried to escape in the Passages, I didn't know what I was doing. They—they hurt people, didn't they? God…"

"It's not your fault," he said, and I remembered him saying the exact same thing when I'd killed with magic the first time. I whimpered as guilt rose, choking me. *I couldn't save the others.*

"Ada," he said, softly. "You're all right."

Tears pricked my eyes. His arms wrapped around me as I sobbed for Gervene, for the other people who'd lost everything and died out here in this hostile world. For the people I'd unintentionally put in danger.

For everyone whose lives the Stoneskins had destroyed.

"We have to get out of here," he said. "Your brother adapted the Chameleons with new tech. A source called sciras. Now there are a couple of Chameleons that can make you a shield as well as invisible, but not at the same time."

"Jeth did that?" I wiped my eyes. "I've never even heard of sciras."

"Neither had I, until I looked up all the sources. I was trying to find a way to get you away from those bastards, and I stole it from Central—and adamantine, too. And bloodrock."

"You... *you* stole from Central?"

"Your brother's the one who set up that signal," he said. "But the message must have been delayed."

"Shit," I said. "The bastards. The StoneKing told me he set up a bomb. He said it would kill all of you before you found me. You didn't..."

He was as unreadable as ever, though his fists were clenched, his body tense.

"No," he said. "I got lucky. I think some of the others survived..."

The world tilted. More lives taken by the Stoneskins. I leaned back and my head struck the wall.

"Ada. You okay?"

"Yeah..." I rubbed the back of my head, confused. "That should have hurt more than it did. Wait, did you transfer sciras over to me?"

"I hoped I could," he said, glancing down at where his hand lay over mine, "but it still won't help us kill all of them. I can't fight more than one of them, and I can't bring down the door."

"Maybe both of us could," I said, standing. "We have to do

something. That world-key must be more powerful than those Passage pieces they were using, if they think they can get directly to Enzar."

"Auros," he said. "Must be true. How were they navigating?"

"The StoneKing has a built-in tracker," I said. "I think he got it before they did whatever they did to him."

"Damn."

"Auros? Is that the metal in the world-keys?"

He nodded. "Yeah—same stuff in the Passages. I tried to amplify it. I talked to a scientist on Valeria who knew about doorways and he said only magic-wielders can make world-keys, because you need to pick up on the signal of an individual world. Or a magic-wielder, I guess. They're drawn to other sources, too, that's why I kept opening doorways right next to the door they opened on Vey-Xanetha. But you can't usually do it within the same world because the signal gets muddled, and you can only jump between two worlds of the same level without the Passages."

"Like Conner did," I said, nodding. "The Stoneskins wouldn't know. It's why they're using their own tracker, but it keeps bringing them back here, for some reason. That reminds me."

I told him what the StoneKing had said about imprisoning the Vox, and Kay's incredulous expression matched mine when I'd found out.

"They were charging the auros, at the expense of an entire world?" He shook his head.

"I know," I said. "Hell, maybe they were the ones who created the chasm in the first place. The one that destroyed Vey-Xanetha's old world."

"Maybe," he said. "The chasm... I forgot to ask. It's like a between-world, but it leads nowhere. I tapped into it when I amplified the world-key the first time around..." He trailed off, running a hand through his hair. "Theories won't help us here, but the StoneKing isn't an amplifier, right? He doesn't control where the world-key, or auros, leads him. Even if he sensed a magic signal."

"He follows the signals," I said. "No one's mentioned an amplifier. But the world-key is drawn to the nearest magic source. Like when we came here, it was where someone had just used magic. Those dead wyvern."

"Dead?"

"Killed with Alliance stunners," I said.

"That... actually just happened." He shook his head. "We must have missed each other by hours at most."

"Damn," I said, shaking my head, too. "And I found your message in Cethrax as well. I'm starting to think the Multi-verse is messing with us."

The faintest hint of a smile touched his mouth. "Yeah, I get that feeling a lot," he said. "Wish I'd been able to leave a default setting on the world-key that'd knock them into the middle of the abyss."

"Wanna try? I'd rather die fighting than in here."

His expression darkened. "You've no idea. Sorry I freaked out on you. You don't need that right now."

"No," I said, sucking in a breath, trying to focus on him, not the rest, just for a second. I'd feared, the whole time I'd been imprisoned, that I'd never see him again. "I need *you*."

The tiniest flicker of a smile stirred at the corner of his mouth.

"But first," I said, "we're going to take those bastards down."

"Or die trying." He smiled faintly at me, eyes burning with a fierce light. "Okay. Want to try breaking the door down?"

Crash. I jumped, and Kay turned to the window. "That came from outside."

So it had. It sounded like rocks sliding against one another. Or like someone was—

Crash.

The ground shook, the walls trembled. I joined Kay at the window, trying to see. Human-sized shapes moved below... what had happened to the other prisoners? I shifted, trying to see, and the walls quaked again, as did the floor. The whole building felt like it was about to fall off a cliff.

A flash of light lit up the darkening sky. Blue light, not magic.

"Hell," said Kay. "Bastard must have figured out how to use the world-key." He shoved at the wall again.

More crashes sounded below, and then the noise of someone running upstairs. Kay ran to the door as it burst open.

"Some rescuer you are!" Nell shoved him aside and had wrapped me in her arms before I could blink.

"How did you get here?"

"Another doorway," she said, hugging me tightly. "Thank you for leaving the other device behind... the Alliance were *quite* understanding of my need to borrow it, after a fashion. Some idiotic policy on not allowing Earth civilians to access the Passages."

"Nell," I gasped. "I can't breathe."

"Sorry." She drew back, checking me all over. Another bright blue flash. "Whatever they're doing out there, it distracted them. I had no trouble breaking in."

"They're opening a doorway," said Kay, heading for the door. "We're outnumbered, but we can't let them go offworld, especially to Enzar."

"Enzar?" Nell's eyes narrowed. "They're not. Tell me they weren't taking you back there."

"They were," I said, pulling back. "I have to stop them.

They were going to use me to win them the Empire. The StoneKing's convinced."

Kay was already out the door, and I hurried after him, Nell at my heels. We descended the spiralling stairs as fast as we could.

"Of course they're batshit," said Kay. "They've really been wandering around the universes at random, with no plan?"

"Apparently so," I said breathlessly. "They had a plan, just not a well-thought-out one."

"Figures," said Kay. "They were going to kill you because you broke their auros?"

"The StoneKing was. They all do as he says."

"Of course they do," he muttered.

No one was in the entrance hall. It was eerily quiet, unguarded, and dark. The hairs rose on my arms.

"Everyone must be at the doorway," I said, picking up the pace. "Damn—if he's opening doors at random…" *Like Valeria.* Like I'd done.

Nell had knocked right through the front doors. They weren't made of stone, but bone-coloured wood. And she'd used the sciras booster-thing to literally break down the doors.

"In case we die, I should probably say you're awesome," I said to her, as she kicked the remains of the door out the way to make a path.

"We are *not* going to die," she said, "and you are not going to Enzar. I'm taking you back to the Passages. The other doorway's not too far from here."

"We can't leave them out there!" I said. "The other prisoners were snatched up, same as me, from the Passages."

"Aric," said Kay. "Figures I'd run into that bastard again. But Ada—we can't fight them alone. We should get backup from the Alliance."

I turned to him. If we waited, more people might die. Another blue flash lit up the sky, and someone screamed.

Ignoring the others' shouts, I sprinted in that direction. It was just around the corner... and blood spattered the marshy ground.

"Shit," I whispered.

They were dead. The humans had been lined up, bodies marked with terrible wounds—crushed limbs and skulls—stark red in the blazing light coming from their left. The Stoneskins were gathered in a wide circle around what at first glance looked like a glass panel. A doorway. The Stone-King stood beside it, making swiping motions.

"The hell is he doing?" Kay's voice was a whisper. "That's not how you use the world-key..."

The scene changed, and half the circle of Stoneskins was obscured by fog.

All heads turned in our direction.

Oh, crap.

"Get behind me," Nell snapped.

"You can't fight them by yourself," I said. "Nor you—Kay!"

Magic sparked from his hands, right at the StoneKing, but the other Stoneskins moved to form a wall before he knocked the world-key loose.

The two giants broke away from the group and advanced on us. One grabbed for Nell, the other for Kay.

"No!" I screamed, torn in two.

The world shook, and tilted sideways. For a heartbeat, I thought I'd been knocked down, but it couldn't be right because my feet were on the ground. The view through the doorway was dark swampland, but not the same scene surrounding us. Another, tilted at an angle.

He'd opened a doorway *within* Cethrax.

"Perfect," said the StoneKing. "I have had quite enough of

you interfering Alliance people. I will tear reality itself apart if I must, but I *will* take Adamantine to her homeworld."

"No," said Nell, struggling, "you won't. I'll kill you first."

"Sadly for you, I don't think that will be the case." The StoneKing stepped forward, and the doorway *moved,* along with him. He held the world-key in his hand. "Come, Adamantine, and I might spare your friends."

"Like hell," said Kay, struggling, but even with the sciras, he couldn't break the giant's grip.

The StoneKing stood a metre away, the world-key glowing, illuminating the wide smile on his face. And he reached for my arm.

If I ran, I might get away. But I'd lose Nell and Kay.

Damn him.

He grabbed my arm.

"No!" Nell screamed, fighting hard. But she was outmatched.

"I'll kill him," I said, dragging up the last shreds of conviction I had. "I'll kill him, I promise I will."

"You won't be able to find us," said the StoneKing, to Nell and Kay. "Cethrax is bigger than Earth. We leave no trace because we have antimagic in our skin. Good luck with your little trackers, Alliance scum."

I opened my mouth to say something else—what, I didn't know—but he'd already dragged me through the doorway, into empty swampland.

18

KAY

I'd lost her again. And I had only myself to blame. From the dagger-looks Nell was giving me, she felt the same.

I should have had a better plan from the start. I should have tried to fight my way through the Stoneskins no matter how many there were, because anything in the Multiverse was better than losing her again.

But the doorway was closed, and that bastard was on the other side. Wherever they were, I couldn't track Ada as long as the StoneKing had his filthy hands on her.

And a giant Stoneskin had his hands on *me*. The sciras was useless with his rocklike arms crushing me. Nell had the other sciras-chameleon, but the effects wouldn't last forever, and unless Ada got that world-key away from the StoneKing, there was no way back.

But no one was around to give these guys orders. They'd hold onto us unless we struggled, then they'd crush us. I thought hard, scrambling to think of something. I had nothing but the Chameleon and tracker, and I could only use one thing at a time.

Which meant this was really going to hurt.

The doorway was closed. The other Stoneskins' blank expressions proved they were at a loss without anyone to give them orders. And they weren't particularly bright.

Bracing myself, I switched off the sciras, and went invisible.

Pain shot up both arms where the Stoneskin gripped me —for a moment. Then his arms went slack, and his eyes widened, seeing his prey had disappeared. I slipped free and, in a second, switched back to the sciras and knocked him out with one blow. I spun around, turning invisible again, but the other Stoneskin had already shifted, jaw hanging open, and Nell broke free and hit him so hard in the mouth he actually staggered back.

I switched off the camouflage. Neither of us spoke, but ran as fast as possible in the direction of the doorway she'd left open. None of the other humans we passed were alive. The bastards had killed them. Kicking up speed, I kept my eyes on the Passages ahead, a square cut into the world, and pelted through the doorway.

I spun around. Nell had opened the door just down from the main corridor, where guards were gathered, but now there were at least twice as many of them. Some were by Valeria's door, others were crouched down, carving symbols into the walls. World-keys. They must be searching the Multiverse for those monsters. But they had no signal to follow, and now, neither did I.

"Nell!" said Jeth, breaking away from talking to some of the guards. "You made it—where's Ada?"

"They took her again," I said. "Bastard StoneKing—their leader—took the world-key and jumped to somewhere else in Cethrax."

"We need another world-key," Nell said, loudly. "They're taking my daughter back to Enzar. That's against your policies!"

"We can't use it indiscriminately!" shouted an official. "There's a procedure, and Enzar is a war-zone. Is it worth provoking war on the Alliance?"

I didn't have a fucking clue. My mind was clouded, because Ada was gone, and so was any chance of going behind the Alliance's back.

And I couldn't think about it. No matter how painful it was, getting the Alliance to take out these bastards was paramount. It had been their standpoint not to interfere in suicidal magical warfare. I'd even agreed with it. They wouldn't drop the rules for one person. No matter how powerful a magic-wielder she was.

Even if Nell killed them, which was becoming more likely by the second.

"If you don't give me that damned world-key, I'll rip out your eyes!" she yelled. "My daughter is out there, and if they find out what she can do, there won't *be* an Alliance. We'll *all* die!"

"Even the whole Alliance can't take on magebloods, let alone the weapons the Royals were using," shouted the official.

Maybe not. Maybe it was worth dying for a shot at rescuing her, because anything was better than doing nothing at all. If war was coming no matter what, if the Stoneskins insisted on stirring up conflict across the Multiverse...

"Wait," I said, another possibility striking me. "The Stoneskins are using a magic-tracker to find the nearest world where magic's been used. That's how they're navigating. They don't even know which world they're going to end up in when they open a doorway. If we created a mass-use of magic in a certain place, we can draw their attention."

"Out of the question," said one of the men from Klathica's council. "That would cause a disruption to the Balance no matter which world we picked—not to mention the potential casualties."

"Zanthar," said Iriel suddenly—I hadn't even realised she was close by. "The world's mostly evacuated, and it's high magic so it won't take much to cause a disruption. *And* it's mostly sunk under the ocean. I'll bet those Stoneskins don't float."

I looked to the council. "That sounds reasonable," I said. "It won't harm anyone, and isn't it the better alternative than the Stoneskins getting to Enzar?"

A pause. The council members lapsed into discussions while Nell shouted impatiently.

I'd almost forgotten the door to Cethrax was open, but everyone went silent when a roar erupted from behind it.

"Damn," I said.

Before anyone could so much as move, a group of drevy-erns scrambled out into the Passages, goblin-like faces twisted in terror. "The Vox!" they shouted. "You humans invaded our territory!"

It looked like Cethrax had finally picked up on the tres-passers. Which meant…

A shadow curled out of the doorway, and there was the collective noise of weapons being drawn as it extended, floor to ceiling, and partly solidified to show the cliff-face of the Vox. Horns curled down either side of its face, its tusks were taller than the goblins, and its eyes were like fathomless pits.

"You have got to be shitting me," I muttered, dagger in hand already. He was the same Vox I'd freed from chains. I stepped forward before anyone attacked, placing myself between the Alliance and Cethrax's king.

"You," said the Vox. "I should have guessed you were responsible for using magic in my territory."

"Because of the Stoneskins," I said. "You owe me a favour, and they're still out there, on your world. I can stop them."

"Nobody can stop them," said the Vox. "They are invincible. They slaughtered hundreds of Cethraxians, and would crush the Alliance in their palms."

It was deadly quiet in the Passages. I didn't blame the higher-up Alliance members for their expressions of sheer terror. I doubted a Vox had ever set foot in here—relatively speaking, anyway, seeing as it was half-shadowed. They never needed to leave their territory, nor did they want to— and any attempts to reason with them about letting their underlings wander into the Passages and kill anyone they came across were generally met with indifference.

But Ada and I *had* freed this Vox from captivity.

"I have something that can beat them," I said, with as much conviction as I could muster while facing a beast whose head alone was bigger than me, and could crush me even with the sciras activated.

"He isn't the only one," said Jeth, to my surprise. I'd expected him to be cowering like most of the other guards. Only the senior guards and council members hadn't edged as far away as possible. At least someone was setting an example.

"No," spoke up a council member from Valeria. "We have devices that will enable us to fight those monstrosities. They've trespassed into our territory, too."

Whispers broke out, along the lines of suspicions about what he meant. Did he mean implants, like Klathica? They were illegal on Valeria, the last I'd heard. And Jeth wouldn't have had time to make any more of those updated Chameleons.

The Vox blinked his plate-sized eyes. "You humans have always thought you can outwit those far superior to you. You've committed too many crimes against my people for me to allow you free passage into my territory. It is irrelevant, besides. You cannot win this fight. My people have migrated to another territory, where we will remain."

"You're giving up?" said another, familiar voice. What was Aric doing here? He must have fled when the Stoneskins started killing the others.

"What would you do, if it was your world, human?" asked the Vox. "Wait to die? Evacuate? We have nowhere to run, and thousands have died at the hands of the Stoneskins."

"I told you," I said. "We can fight them. Nobody is invincible," I added, with a sideways glance at Nell. "We can track them down and kill them—but we don't have much time left before they unleash their weapon. They have a source powerful enough to wipe out the Multiverse, not just your world." Not that it was worth the effort to explain to any Cethraxian why other worlds than their own mattered. "If you let us do this, we'll be happy to negotiate over anything else. Even the doorways into the Passages."

There were a few discontented mutters from behind, swiftly silenced by the higher-up Alliance members with the sense to see telling the Vox what he wanted to hear was the only way to win the argument. We didn't have the luxury of negotiation.

"They're in your territory because they intend to open a doorway, into a war zone," I said. "I don't need to tell you what that would do to the Balance in your world. But there's time to stop them, if you give us access to the doorway."

The Vox glared down at me. "One hour, human. If you die, I get to feed you to my kin."

Nice.

"Seems fair," I said. "Right—I need a world-key. I can go after them if they've already opened a door. They're travelling at random, following magic-signals."

"They interrupted several of my kind, who barely escaped with their lives," said the Vox. "They tell me their location is… two miles west of the doorway. You will never make it, human. Your doorways are not exact, are they?"

"Yes," I said, "but I have on-the-ground transport."

"He does," said a voice, and Mr Helm of all people pushed through the crowd. "I've given him permission to test a certain prototype of mine."

Well, damn. "Exactly," I said. "I'll catch them. Someone else will have to lead the way to Zanthar." I glanced over my shoulder at Iriel, who hadn't fled like some of the others. "That sound fair?"

"If it's all we have…"

"There's no time for debates," I said. "I'll get a doorway open. That much, I can do." Even if I couldn't fight them all head-on, I could slow them down. If I caught up to them on Cethrax, invisible… it was leaving a lot to chance, but as long as they didn't see me, they wouldn't be able to stop me using magic.

No time to consider the odds. If we didn't get to them *fast,* there'd be no Multiverse to defend. Ada could fight them, yes, but even the Alliance was far outnumbered.

Good job I'd had enough practise facing odds highly stacked against me. "Someone have a world-key?"

"The one to Cethrax is that door already open," said Valeria's council member. "It'd take too long to recharge it."

Should have seen that coming. "Right," I said. "How about auros? Any going spare?"

"We can't go around handing them out."

"Here," said Mr Helm, interrupting and handing me a piece of the metal. "I took it out of the machine in the lab—I think you need it more than I do. But try not to lose it—*or* break any of my equipment."

"I can't promise," I said. "But I'll go after them."

"And we'll go to Zanthar," said Iriel. "Come on," she added to the crowd, at least half of whom were too terrified by the appearance of the Vox to really get what was happening.

"Listen," I said to the Vox. "You're not to harm anyone. That's part of the deal. You let us use your territory to rid the Multiverse of the Stoneskins, and let every human out unharmed. Understand?"

I sensed the incredulous stares behind me, from people who couldn't believe I'd have the nerve to barter with a Vox. But they hadn't seen what I had. Anger had obliterated every trace of fear. I was going in, and I was going to save Ada no matter what it took. I would *not* lose her again.

"Deal," said the Vox, in its gravelly voice, and its gigantic head shrank, becoming shadow again. I hurried down the corridor, finding the camouflaged hover car where I'd left it. Luckily, it cast enough of a shadow I didn't run into it. Climbing into the seat, I nearly ran down Nell as she pelted through the corridor.

"You're not leaving me back there," she said breathlessly. "I'm going after my daughter."

"Fine. Hop in." I'd figured as much. *Probably shouldn't tell her I'm not sure this thing works offworld.*

But driving over the threshold to Cethrax gave no reaction—the car stayed off the ground, the engine kept humming, and I steered it west, like the Vox had said. Cethrax had magic, and apparently that was enough to keep the engines running.

Very good job we were invisible. Wyverns flew overhead, screeching, probably drawn by all the magic used. Dreyverns and ravegens scrambled on ground level, jabbering in Cethraxian. Even the insects had sharp teeth and claws. And yet all that paled in comparison to what was waiting at the end of the road.

I upped the acceleration, and drove on. Towards Ada.

19

ADA

Captured again. I couldn't fight. Not unless I somehow got hold of the world-key, and that wasn't happening any time soon.

Think. God, I was exhausted. The StoneKing had dragged me a good half-mile across the swamp—literally, whenever I slowed down. There were no other people left. Except a bunch of Stoneskins who'd crossed over with us, to make sure there was no chance of escape.

No one but me could kill him. When I had my chance, I would. Yet the Stoneskins were winning through sheer force of numbers. Aric had my communicator, my one chance of contacting anyone. I had nothing. Just a worn-out stunner tucked into my pocket, which I couldn't use as long as he had his hands on me. And he knew, too. I'd never be free.

I hadn't seen Aric amongst the dead, but there had been at least a dozen. Gervene was dead, too. Dead, because of my attempts to break free. Other people had probably died because I'd pushed those other Stoneskins through the doorway.

Stop thinking about that.

The StoneKing finally stopped in a deserted area of mostly dry ground, far away from any semblance of civilisation—or doorways. I'd seen a few wyverns, flying in the direction of the fortress. They must have been drawn to the magic. Guess the Stoneskins weren't interesting enough to them, and a single human went unnoticed.

I'm the only human. They can't threaten to kill the others. But they *could* threaten to wipe out the Multiverse—and the world-key could take them literally anywhere to do it.

Speaking of which… the StoneKing held the device in his hand, crouching to carve symbols into the ground.

"You learned that at the Alliance, didn't you?" I asked, clutching at straws. "You worked for them."

"You can't stop me, Ada," said the StoneKing, etching a second symbol by the first, at the point of the arrowhead.

"Wasn't trying to," I said. "Is it really worth it? Wouldn't you rather target the individuals who ordered whatever they did to you? Isn't that more satisfying than provoking the attention of an entire world at war?"

Silence. *He won't listen.* I twisted around to look at the other Stoneskins.

"Come on," I said. "He's mad—you must see it. You…" I turned to the Stoneskin I recognised as one I'd spoken to on the first day in the swamp.

"Please," I whispered. "You have to help me. Your boss is crazy. He thinks I can talk down the warring tyrants on my homeworld."

"I think you can fulfil your potential," said the StoneKing. "*Our* potential. We were both made to be gods."

"Oh, sure," I said. "It's not like you just tried to feed me to a wyvern or anything. We can be BFFs now."

I'd meant to take him off-guard, and it worked for about

half a second before his eyes narrowed. "Enough, Adamantine. You cannot possibly win, so why not embrace your role?"

"Because you're a psycho," I said. "And I was never interested in becoming a queen of anything. Or an assassin."

The other Stoneskins formed a circle around us. No way out. His grip on my arm ensured that, if nothing else. He carved a final symbol into the ground, and it hit me in a rush, so sudden I almost laughed. He wasn't following a signal. And Kay had already been using the world-key.

"Open your eyes to the truth, Adamantine. This is what you were made for."

And the doorway opened... onto another stretch of swampland.

I grinned. "That was stupid," I said. "You didn't think the world-key would work the same as auros, did you? It's tuned into Cethrax."

"Do not mock me, Adamantine," said the StoneKing. "Did you think that wouldn't occur to me?"

Honestly, yes. You're not the brightest bulb, are you? But the words stopped before they left my mouth.

The scene in the rapidly-expanding doorway changed even as we spoke, from swampland to a beach, from plains to a city of spired towers. Crap. The world-key couldn't just be linked to Cethrax, after all. This guy was a walking tracker, and could find *any* magic source. For a brief instant, the scenes overlapped—the skyscrapers of Valeria, another murky-skied city with old-fashioned cars—world after world blurred before my eyes, but I watched the StoneKing, readying myself to grab for the world-key.

He pulled me forward. The ground disappeared from under my feet, and suddenly Cethrax was the other side of the door, and I was...

Nowhere. No ground, no sky, no—anything. The breath stopped in my lungs. I couldn't see anything except fog. And I'd seen the scene before. He'd opened a door to the heart of the Multiverse itself.

"Still think I can't change your mind, Adamantine?"

I couldn't reply, because there was no oxygen. I had seconds. If he let go… who knew where I would end up? Lost in empty space? Pressure built on my skull. My lungs burned, like I'd stayed underwater too long.

I gasped as air slammed into me, as did all the sensations I had no idea I'd been missing. Even the pain from the bruises I'd picked up was welcome. I shuddered on the ground, his hand locked around my wrist. I twisted over, staggering to my feet, trying to pull away.

He gave me a pitying smile. "You really did think it would be that easy."

The abyss vanished, replaced by Valeria. The view showed a building from above, near the hover train's tracks. There should have been guards there, but the streets appeared deserted.

There was no one here to defend the city, because, if what Kay said was true, they were in the Passages.

"You see, I did think this through, Adamantine," said the StoneKing. "The mageblood leaders are difficult to find, but with the doorway open, even they will be unable to ignore the signs of Royal magic. Once you draw their attention, Adamantine, they will come."

Holy shit. He was planning to bring the war to Valeria.

We were on a level with the rooftops, but as he twisted the world-key in his hand, the view shifted to show the ground.

The street on the other side was deserted. Cordoned off. Blood smeared the metal-coated material that made up the roads and pavements, and the buzz of magic in the air hit me even from here.

"Here we are," he said. "This is the last place magic was used, aside from Cethrax... I believe Valeria's police unsuccessfully tried to subdue some of my Stoneskin people here."

They must have tried to do magic.

The StoneKing grabbed my arm and tugged me over the threshold, and a buzzing crashed over me like a wave, stopping when it hit the place the StoneKing held onto me. *What the hell is that?*

Another Stoneskin followed us, then another. One had held onto the bag of world-key pieces, and the other... I hadn't noticed he held a bag, too, and the buzzing came from inside.

No. If I could feel it even as the StoneKing held onto me, it had to be packing a hell of a lot of power.

"This is our purpose," said the StoneKing, smiling at me. "Now we have the means of drawing Enzar to us."

The other Stoneskin held up a piece of gleaming blue-black rock. Not adamantine.

Another source, charged with power so intense, it lifted the hair on my head and burned my eyes behind the lenses.

"The source contains the energy of Veyak, and all the other places we have gathered it from," said the StoneKing, using his free hand to direct the other Stoneskins to form a circle around us. An unbroken circle, with no gaps. "You will unleash that energy, and the world-key will direct the mage-bloods straight to us. If you don't cooperate, I need only to order one of my Stoneskins to break the circle, and the city will be obliterated. I wonder if any of your friends are still here?"

I glared at him. If looks could kill, he'd be writhing on the ground.

And in that moment, I had my plan.

The open doorway changed from Cethrax to the deep abyss between the worlds again. The StoneKing grinned at me, took the source from the other Stoneskin, pressed it into my hand—and let go.

20

KAY

aster. Even at the highest speed, the hover car didn't seem fast enough. The velocity pinned me to the seat, and behind me, Nell hung onto the back for dear life.

"Do you even know where you're going?" she yelled in my ear. The car skimmed the ground and I pulled a lever to move it higher off the ground, rather than answering. When they activated the world-key, we'd know about it.

"What if they open the door to Enzar?" I asked. "If they try to use her magic, and we can't stop them, what would you do?"

Maybe I was asking myself more than her. But she met my eyes. "We're going to save my daughter."

"I know," I said. "But if you'd been in that position, then what?"

A pause. "Would I have sacrificed her for the sake of the Multiverse? Perhaps."

Some questions could only be answered in practise. It was through acting, not thinking of acting, that you knew what you were really capable of. Consequences came later. If you lived through it.

A flash of blue lit up the sky.

"Shit," I said. The door was already open, the magic rippling outward, and I wondered why I'd ever thought Cethrax was low-magic. The predators had evolved to repel the destructive magic in the atmosphere, destructive enough to rip the world itself apart.

Come on! I pushed the hover car to its limits, pressed flat against the back of the seat.

Two giants loomed ahead, so suddenly I almost crashed into one of them. "Shit," I said again.

I'd forgotten the giant Stoneskins. And damn, they were pissed. Gigantic fists swung clumsily, snarling faces leered at us. I pulled more levers, making the car fly higher and sideways, and narrowly avoided being snatched out of the air. The speed kicked up to a roaring trail that left them in the dust—well, swamp.

Another blue flash lit up the sky. And then we saw it.

The doorway stretched across the horizon, growing bigger even from a distance. Stoneskins disappeared through it in groups, but I couldn't push the car any harder—we were going to lose them.

I cursed to the sky as the doorway closed. We'd missed Ada. Again.

"That wasn't Enzar," I said, turning the car around. "It was Valeria. They were too late..."

And now, so were we. The two giant Stoneskins barred the way back into the Passages, their huge forms easily masking the car-sized doorway.

I hit the stop button, and nothing happened. "Seriously?" I muttered, and hit it again. I twisted the lever to steer sideways, and the car kept moving forwards.

We were going to crash.

"Idiot," Nell snarled in my ear. "You're an amplifier. Use it!"

The sciras. Could I make the effects transfer over to the car?

Not like I had a choice. I tapped into it, expecting the invisibility to fade, but the car itself did its job. The giants stared, stupefied, as the car barrelled towards them. One moved aside at the last minute. The other didn't.

Crash.

The giant staggered back, the car tipped sideways and then upside-down, and I hung onto the side handle, cursing the Valerians for not thinking seatbelts were a necessity in vehicles which had a questionable relationship with gravity. The car ricocheted off the Passage wall, skidding on the metal and landing mercifully the right way up, outside Cethrax's doorway. Even with the sciras protection, I felt like I'd been thrown into a freaking dryer.

Nell groaned, climbing back into her seat. "I am never letting you into a car with my daughter."

"Ha," I said, shaking my head.

Get to Ada. God only knew which world she was in now.

A thud rang through the car and sent us spinning down the Passage again. The stone giant had followed us, and was seriously pissed off. *Crap.* I retook control of the now-battered and half visible wheel and steered the car around the corner, through the staring crowd. "Valeria!" I shouted, without time for a warning before the giants reached the guards.

To their credit, the guards changed direction fast, even to orders given by a hover car-driving lunatic who'd probably smashed every one of the Alliance's laws into pieces in the past five seconds alone.

As the giants lumbered towards the crowd, the Vox's face re-materialised in the air, furious. "You will not trespass on my world again," he snarled, and that was the last I saw of him before I'd driven the car over the heads of the crowd and through the doorway to Valeria.

ADA

Energy surged through my body, sparking off the source's surface. Light overwhelmed my eyes, and the StoneKing stood back, but still within reach. Beyond, I was dimly aware of Valeria's surrounding buildings, but wherever we stood felt apart from all that. Cut off.

The source remained fixed to my hand. I wasn't sure if I could let go even if I tried. No pain, just static, burning under the surface. Waiting to be unleashed.

No. I couldn't draw the magebloods here. Not to Valeria.

Every second stretched out into oblivion. I twitched my free hand. *Move. I can control this.*

Sparks rose, higher, white creeping into the corners of my vision. I turned to the StoneKing, whose grinning face swam into focus.

At last.

Big mistake.

I moved my free hand, sending a rain of sparks through the air, and jabbed two fingers into his eye socket. The jolt shook my hands, and the StoneKing screamed, falling to his knees. I fell, too, but kept my fingers in place—the other Stoneskins moved in, breaking the circle.

I released the charge. My body shook, the metal in my hand vibrated. I knew without a doubt that the Stoneskins were the opposite of the Royals, because while they might be adamantine on the surface, on the inside, they could break.

The StoneKing broke away from me, sparks flying from his ruined eyes, pieces of adamantine crumbling. His hands reached out blindly and grabbed at me, but too late. I put every ounce of strength left into the charge pouring from my fingers, grabbed the world-key from his limp hand, and shoved him into the abyss.

And the screaming started. The others Stoneskins split the circle. Some fell to their knees, openly wailing. The sound of smashing glass resounded as others wreaked havoc on the buildings. I swore and turned around in time to intercept a blow from the other Stoneskin. His free hand lashed out, snatching the magic source. *Oh, hell.* If that thing blew up, the city would, too. I kicked the Stoneskin in the leg, thanking the Multiverse the sciras's effect had held. He stumbled into another Stoneskin who turned on his companion with a roar of anger.

My fist clenched around the world-key. The doorway's scene shifted, from one world to the next, until it stopped on the desert of my homeworld.

The magic signal from Enzar lured me like a siren's chorus. Before I could pull the world-key free, the two Stoneskins nearest to me had crossed over the threshold, hands held high as though hoping the StoneKing himself would fall out of the sky. *He's dead.* But another Stoneskin held the magic source—and he ran over the threshold into Enzar, too.

"Get back here!" I was faster than him, and his surprise let me tackle him to the ground. I couldn't let him unleash that source. Especially not here. We tumbled downhill and came to a rolling stop on the scorching red sand. "Hell," I gasped. Even with the sciras, I felt bruised all over, but the fierce sparks igniting in my veins from Enzar's atmosphere reacted to the source like a magnet, daring me to take it in my hands. My nails bit into my palms instead. *I can't touch it.*

Forks of lightning stabbed through the sky. Enough power brewed here already.

Too much for me to control.

"This is yours, Adamantine," said the Stoneskin, grabbing my hand with a smile as insane as the StoneKing's. "Take it."

"You don't get it, do you?" I said. "I'm not your weapon. I decide how and when I use magic, not you, nor anyone else."

My hand, however, drew closer to the source with every breath, until—

Mine.

The sensation rolled through me like the rumble of a giant's voice, my veins fizzing with magical energy. Like a blindfold had been removed from my eyes, I saw the magic that made this world unique, bright, shaped differently to anywhere else in the Multiverse. A buzzing rose in my ears, and I was barely aware that I'd stood, holding the source high, until the ground trembled and lightning flashed over my head.

Hell. If I drew all the power over here, I'd draw the army, too. The doorway was still open.

I'd bring the war to Valeria myself.

I shook my head, forcing my hand to lower to my side. *Dammit. You know better than this.* I *could* control my magic. Even here. Even as a Royal.

I turned around, forcing myself to step forward. The Stoneskin who'd handed me the source had already moved away, back towards the doorway.

"Get back here."

I threw myself at him. Magic exploded from my finger-tips as I jabbed them into his eyes, still holding onto the source. He was dead, crumbling to pieces, almost before I touched him. *Power.* I could see how the Royals had decimated the magebloods. They only had to touch someone to reduce them to dust. Even an army.

A walking bomb...

I shook my head, again, kicking the Stoneskin's remains aside. Others fought Alliance guards on the other side of the doorway, where the towering skyscrapers of Valeria were still visible above. I had to close the door before Enzar's overflowing magic spilled over into Neo Greyle. But how the hell to do that with a source in my hands?

"Shit," I said, teeth rattling with the magic once again burning within my bones.

I had to end this. But unleashing the power might destroy the world.

"Ada!"

My eyes bugged out. Kay jumped out of thin air, followed by Nell, like they'd teleported into existence. Kay saw me behind the doorway flickering out, and he ran towards it.

The source burned the palm of my hand, and my vision flickered again. *No.*

Nell and Kay both ran through the doorway, and I screamed at them to stop—if they got too close, they'd get caught in the blast.

I couldn't control it.

My other palm burned, reminding me I held onto the world-key. There was something I could do—but if I failed, we all died.

I threw the world-key, and Kay caught it. I didn't dare speak aloud in case the Stoneskins heard, but I willed him to understand—*amplify it. I can't stop this. But I can stop anyone else getting caught in the hit...*

"Ada."

"No," I moaned, falling to my knees. "Stay back—you have to open the abyss." Send me somewhere I couldn't do any more damage. A distant world.

I'd die. But if I held on another moment, until the doorway fully opened, he'd live. The others would survive.

I tried to smile. *It's okay.*

The abyss grew wider, splitting the worlds in two.

Kay was amplifying it. My head filled with buzzing, but I had the vague sense he shouted at the guards to move out of the way—the ones still fighting—and the Stoneskins were falling into the gap, dragged into the abyss.

A slap in the face sent me reeling. Another Stoneskin yelled in my ear, telling me to release the magic. Telling me to blow the world sky-high. I clenched my free hand and hit him hard enough to send him stumbling backwards. Towards the edge.

I followed.

"Ada!"

The magic reached its peak. The world went blinding white, and the Stoneskin tripped backwards, over the edge, and was gone.

Magic sparked from my hands, and I threw myself after him.

Sorry, Kay. I'm sorry.

KAY

The guards on Valeria's side of the doorway had withdrawn from the edge, but those able to stand up to the Stoneskins had caught on pretty quickly. Either push the Stoneskins over the edge of the crater, into the fog, or if not, run like hell.

I should be doing the same—I punched an intercepting

Stoneskin, snapping his jaw back. *Get away, you bastard.* Another hit me back, and the unsteady ground sent me reeling, stumbling over something on the floor. Pieces of—adamantine? I snatched one of them up, and it crumbled, coating my hand in black.

A scream made me look up. Ada. She stood unmoving on the other side of the abyss, magic sparking around her from whatever she held in her hand. Hell—it was a battery, and with the high level of magic on Enzar, it was going berserk.

Shit.

She stumbled forward. I knew what she was going to do. There was so much magic burning inside her it'd blow the world to the sky, so she was going to throw herself over the edge of the abyss.

I kicked the Stoneskin out the way and ran towards her. Another Stoneskin slapped her in the face and rage pulsed through me. I ran, shouting her name, but she'd already hit him back.

Magic sparked higher, making my skin buzz all over. The ground trembled, and I caught myself before I fell over the edge, too. I had to move fast. But Ada was metres away.

The Stoneskin screamed, tripping into the abyss. Ada hadn't touched him, but as she turned to me, her eyes had gone pure white, gleaming. The magic level had melted the lenses in her eyes and the Stoneskin had been blinded.

She jumped as the magic was unleashed in an arc of lightning, piercing the abyss. As it hit the fog, it dissipated into empty space, but it kept coming. She was suspended in the air, eyes wide and unseeing, magic pulsing out of her in waves.

The world-key lay on the ground. If I didn't close the door to Enzar, the magic would spark over the edge.

And Ada would fall into the abyss.

I grabbed the world-key and switched off the amplifier.

The doorway to the abyss shrank rapidly, around Ada. I had seconds before it closed, taking her with it.

I reached out, my hand locking around her ankle, and sent us both tumbling out of the air. We landed on hard desert sand under blinding sun. I gasped as my own magic reacted, sparking to life under my skin like a lit fuse.

Ada lay still in my arms. *God. No.*

"Ada…"

Those bright white eyes opened. "Kay," she said, uncertainly. "Am I dead?"

"No," I said, and would have collapsed with relief if not for the world-key in my hand. We needed to get off this world. Back to Valeria.

"What happened to the source? I must have dropped it." She coughed, blinking.

"Hang on." The world-key was tuned into Valeria, and when I reactivated it, a new door opened right to the same spot the abyss had been. Guards immediately turned towards us, in various states of shock and confusion, staring at the desert.

As I helped Ada cross the threshold, a dozen weapons pointed at us. "What the devil!"

"Hold it," I said. Ada wriggled free of my arms to land on her feet. I put one hand on her back to steady her and closed the doorway with the other.

Enzar shrank to a pinprick, reflected in her eyes as it disappeared.

"What happened to her?"

"What did she do?"

Oh. None of them would have seen Ada's real eyes before.

I had a hell of a lot of explaining to do. Again.

21

ADA

S everal hours of total confusion followed. Half the guards were on Valeria and the other half were in the Passages, and Kay was forced to explain, several times over, my eyes didn't mean I was on the enemy's side. The two of us stood apart from the group, in the wreckage of the plaza the Stoneskins had ruined. A wall of guards cut us off from everyone else. Even Nell.

If anyone hadn't known I was from Enzar before, they sure as hell knew it now. I was too tired, too drained to think what that would mean for the Alliance.

The Stoneskins were gone. Those who hadn't been pushed into the abyss stood blankly staring into space, surrounded by Valeria's law enforcement guards. Most of them seemed lost without their leader. Apparently, the research lab had a bunch of adamantine-reinforced cages waiting for occupants.

While they were taking care of that, and attention was momentarily deflected from me, I asked Kay, "What about the others? The Stoneskins' prisoners? Gervene... there was a woman. I think the Stoneskins… they killed her. They threw her into the swamp. But not all of them died."

"The Alliance sent people to search for survivors," said Kay. "Once they'd dealt with those giants."

"I'm guessing Cethrax isn't too happy."

"Are they ever?"

"Let me at my daughter!" Nell had been pushed back by the guards, but her arguing wore them down and they finally parted to let her through to me.

"You're not hurt?" She wrapped an arm around me, relief etched on her face.

I shook my head. I could hardly believe it. I was… I was alive. Kay had pulled me back from the abyss. I hadn't destroyed Enzar. I hadn't killed anyone.

But I'd put our family in the headlights. I'd put my *homeworld* at the centre of the Alliance's attention. There'd be repercussions. For a heart-stopping minute, I'd thought they'd arrest me for almost destroying the Multiverse. Valeria's media had started swarming around once it was clear the city was no longer in danger from invincible monsters or out of control magic. I didn't have the source, either—I'd dropped it into the abyss, but it had been too late to stop the magic then, anyway.

The magicproof coating on my uniform had stopped Kay from getting hit by the magic, too, when he'd pulled me back from the edge. Had he known how close we'd both come to death?

I turned to him. He watched the police marching the last of the Stoneskins out of sight.

"That was close," I whispered, lamely. "Too close."

"I know."

Nell, thankfully, nodded to me and fell behind to let me talk to him.

"You could have died when you grabbed me before the abyss closed," I said.

"Yeah." He shook his head. "Guess Ms Weston was right. She'll have a hell of a lecture saved for both of us," he said, with a half-smile. "You threw yourself off a cliff. That's worrying."

"Er, you know I was trying to save the Multiverse, don't you?"

"Of course," he said. "And I did have protection, as it happens." He held up the palm of his hand, the one he'd grabbed me with. It was coated in black dust.

"What…?"

"It was on the ground. I picked it up."

"The StoneKing. I killed him and he kind of fell to pieces. I think."

"So much for him being unbreakable," said Kay, wiping his hand on his jacket.

Unbreakable. Adamantine. I turned to Nell as we walked along the pavement. "Why did you not just name me Ada?"

"I did," she said, not blinking. "It's on your official documents."

Well, that was news to me.

"You didn't think I'd put *Adamantine* down, did you?"

"Seeing as it's my name?"

Nell tutted. "It was a terrible idea."

"I've been telling you that for years," I said, smiling despite myself. "Are Jeth and Alber okay?"

"I messaged them, let them know you're alive," she said. "Jeth's in the Passages but they won't let him through—they'll probably send him back to Central. And Alber's managed not to destroy the house even though Jeth left him in control of his computers."

"Ha," I said. "Don't suppose they're going to let us go home anytime soon?"

Another voice shouted, "I do work at Central, you bleeding idiot."

Holy hell. I'd forgotten Aric, who was surrounded by several enforcement officers, walking in the middle of the road. They'd cleared the area of hover-traffic and taped off the parts of the road covered in broken glass.

"Jesus," said Kay. "He wasn't a hallucination. The idiot's really alive."

"Yeah," I said. "I know, right? Must have had the sense to run after all."

"I sent the Alliance a message for you, you ungrateful little shit," he shouted at me.

"Oops," I said, as the officers dragged him away—well, he *did* have several arrest warrants on his head. "Yeah. Forgot about that. I threw him my communicator when I was trapped," I added in explanation, as both Kay and Nell looked at me like I'd announced I was moving to the swamp. "He was a dick, but he was the only person from Earth there, and he wanted to get away. I mean, he was stupid enough to almost get us killed a few times... I'll have to tell Central he helped. It's only fair."

Kay shook his head. "Now I've seen everything. You actually worked with him?"

"I nearly killed him once," I said. "But he did kind of help... that might be the weirdest part of all the insanity."

"Tell me about it," said Kay. "And I spoke to a Vox and crashed an invisible car."

"Invisible car?"

"Valeria's prototype. Not sure the guy who invented it will be happy with me."

We formed an odd group, and everyone stared so much I was tempted to ask Kay for a loan of his Chameleon. Even the world looked strange without my eyes covered up by lenses. Kay, though, didn't stare—not explicitly at my eyes, anyway.

I was too tired and out of it to really take anything in, until we were all gathered in the lab, inside the building the Stoneskins had demolished. There, an unfamiliar machine made of gleaming blue metal not unlike the Passages had opened, and the magic humming from it was enough to make me stare around, wondering why no one was panicking.

"What in the world is that thing?" I asked.

"It's okay," said Kay. "It's a link between the Alliance branches. Guess this qualifies as an emergency."

Walking into the machine took us across the city, directly into a meeting room at Valeria's Alliance. I collapsed into a chair, inwardly groaning when the council started asking for my story. Not just Valeria's council. The doorway port—as Kay said it was called—apparently led to other worlds, too, and I watched in total astonishment as representatives from Alliance branches across the Multiverse came through the doorway, including Ms Weston of all people, along with Earth's council.

Once I'd told the story of my time with the Stoneskins in full, they lapsed into a debate about both Cethrax and Enzar. Kay was dragged into the discussion, given that he'd been the one to talk to the Vox.

War turned from a whisper into a shout as debates raged. Nobody could ignore Enzar any longer, not now a doorway had opened directly there. There'd be consequences.

But I only had eyes for the man who'd risked everything to save me—and the Multiverse. I was too tired to discuss offworld relations, and despite being at the centre of everything, the council didn't seem to want my opinion on Alliance matters. Although Kay didn't let anything show on his face, our eyes met at least half a dozen times. That look was for me alone, and it reflected my own relief, my own gratitude that he'd made it through alive.

Oddly, it was Ms Weston who put her foot down. "Enough," she said, to the arguing council members. "If you aren't going to question my staff, I think Ada should be allowed to return to her family, don't you?"

"Yes," said Valeria's council head, a woman called Alexis Greene. "Of course."

And, mercifully, they let us go. Kay, too, seeing as everyone had listened to his account already. I had no doubt Ms Weston would bombard us with paperwork as soon as we got back to the office, but that was a matter for another day.

Another day. If we hadn't stopped the StoneKing, there might not have been any days left. The shock was palpable, and it was only just sinking in for some people that the Alliance had come a hair's breadth from destruction, and the Multiverse along with it. But we'd escaped. We were both alive. Sweet relief made my knees go weak as I walked alongside Kay, and I wanted nothing more than to fall into his arms right now and let the world slip away.

If it wasn't for Nell on my other side. And I was glad to see her, too. She hugged me again, and I spoke to Alber through her phone as we walked past the guards on the road to the Passage entrance.

"Whereabouts is Jeth?" I asked. "I'll bet they didn't let him in through the doorway."

"Last I saw, he was explaining the sciras booster," said Kay. "I reckon he's either in the main Passage or at Central, but the guards had everyone under questioning."

Nell made an impatient noise. "They're not detaining him. I'm going to find him. Ada, you get yourself home before anyone else can interfere."

"Sure thing," I said.

"And *you*," Nell added to Kay, with startling venom.

Kay's only response was to wrap an arm around me. "I'll take care of her," he said.

"You'd better do that," she said. "Or I won't let you off easy next time."

"Huh?" I said, looking up at Kay. "What's she mean by that?"

He shook his head. "Come on. We'd better get through here before we get ambushed. Pity I don't have another car to distract them with."

As it turned out, one invisible car had caused enough of a distraction in the main corridor. The Alliance had cleared the Passage, and I remembered belatedly that most of Valeria's guards would have been called through to clean up the mess in the city. As for the others, the doorways were closed. Probably a security measure, considering the ruckus. Lucky the Stoneskins' doorway had only crashed into one world.

Lucky. Once again, we'd been at the centre of a cross-world event. When we stepped out into London, I ducked my head, knowing my eyes would attract even more stares here. I might as well have "outsider" tattooed on my forehead.

"Watch it," said Carl, stepping in front of us. "Oh, it's you two." He looked a little battered, but alive.

"Damn," said Kay. "I thought—things looked pretty bad where you were."

"Even a bomb couldn't take care of me," he said, with a hint of a smile. "Guess you were right all along, Kay."

"Didn't the council give you permission to leave?" asked Kay.

"Apparently, nearly getting blown up isn't big enough a deal for him to take the night off," said Raj, who also stood near the gate. "We've got everyone looking out for trouble here, but seeing as you two just came through, I'm guessing it's passed. Unless you have invisible goblins on your tail."

"Nah," said Kay. "Show's over."

Raj shook his head. "Crazy, the lot of you."

"We're going home," I said. "Before Ms Weston makes me write a ten-thousand-word essay on what it's like to be kidnapped."

We walked fast, back to my house. I kept my gaze on my feet. A stupid idea in London's crowded streets, but then again, my real eyes might have caused a traffic accident.

Finally, we reached my street, and the relief sank into my heart again. I leaned my head against Kay's chest as we stopped in front of the door. *Home.*

"I realise this is the lamest line ever," I said, "but I missed you. Even though, you know, I was running for my life and everything. When I thought they'd killed you, I—I had to tell myself you were alive. It was all I could do." I swallowed, turned to face him.

"Ada." He spoke so quietly, and there was so much feeling packed into that one word, it almost reduced me to tears. "I had to come after you. Any way I could."

I smiled a watery smile. "You robbed Central, trespassed in the dangerous parts of the Passages alone, repeatedly defied the council, went offworld when on probation…"

"Sounds crazy to me," he said. "Saki already marked me as 'unhinged'."

"Oops," I said. "Well, the whole Multiverse knows I have freakish glowing eyes."

"Don't be ridiculous," he said. "They suit you."

"Ha. Now you're being ridiculous. Come on. I look like a walking lamp."

"That is *not* a description I'd use," he said, smirking at me now. I lightly hit him in the arm.

"Ow," he said.

"Crap. Did I leave the sciras on?"

"I'm joking."

I rolled my eyes. "Of course you are."

I dug in my jacket pocket. Wonder of wonders, my key had survived the craziness—I always kept it zipped in the small pocket inside my jacket.

"My kingdom for a shower and a change of clothes," I said. "Please. I've got to give props to whoever designed my uniform, seeing as it's survived so much of a beating, but I've Cethraxian swamp water in places you really don't want to know about."

"Hmm," said Kay. "Not sure there's any part of you I don't want to know…"

"Ha ha," I said. Which meant, *God, I've missed you.* "I'm serious, though. I want out of this uniform."

His hand trailed down the side of my face, fingertips lightly brushing my cheekbones. "I wouldn't object to that."

I flushed. "Speak for yourself. Also, I want to kiss you, but I haven't seen a toothbrush in two days. I'll be quick." I drew away from him, though it was an effort, and unlocked the door.

Once I felt vaguely like a civilised human being again, I came out of the bathroom, dripping-wet hair spilling from a towel. I was tired and starving and felt like I'd been run over by a lawnmower, but I was lucky the Stoneskins hadn't done more damage when they'd hit me. I checked my room, but I didn't expect Kay to have gone up there without asking me. I headed downstairs, bracing myself for a lifetime of questions from Nell.

"I'm sure it's not irreparable," Kay was saying, on his communicator in the hallway. "Mostly. Come on, Valeria has bigger things to worry about. At least all the prototypes weren't destroyed."

Ah. The invisible car. Some lucky person had to deal with that. But not us.

"Yes, I know." He saw me and smiled. "Listen, I have to go. I'll explain later."

He hung up. "Simon," he said, in explanation. "Your family are in the kitchen."

"It won't kill them to wait another minute." I pushed open the door to the living room, and was kissing him before we were even through it. *I thought I lost you. I thought I killed you.* He backed up until we were on the sofa, holding onto me like I was the last thing left on Earth.

I pulled back to breathe. "So," I said. Situations like this didn't come equipped with ideal words. "I suppose I could say 'thank you' for crossing a dozen worlds to find me. And don't say *it was nothing.*" I threw my arms around him again, squeezing tight.

"Jesus Christ, Ada." His voice was uneven, almost pained.

I drew back and squinted at him. "You're hurt."

No shit, Ada. I gently touched one of the bruises on his cheek. He didn't say anything—just watched me. Like he couldn't quite believe I was real.

"Was that from the Stoneskins? The first time? I thought they'd killed you."

He rested his head against the back of the sofa, eyes closed. "Yeah… I got lucky. Xanet was still there. You know that girl who healed you?"

"Really? She… she saved you."

"Yeah." He rubbed the back of his neck. "I thought I died. To be honest, I'm still not completely sure of it."

My hands wrapped around his head. "You're definitely alive. You should probably clean that swamp water out of your hair."

"You're probably right." He shifted on the sofa. "I've had bloody enough of Cethrax."

"Was it one of their monsters who did that?" I traced the scrape along his unshaven jawline.

"A chalder vox threw me around a bit."

"Ouch," I said. "Honestly, Kay, I leave you alone for a couple of days and you get beaten up... how many times? What are you like?" I ran my finger over his knuckles. He'd cleaned up the blood, but painful-looking cuts marked both hands. "How bad is it?"

He shifted into an upright position, and I caught the slight hesitation in his movement.

"Come on, let me look."

I pushed up his shirt. Dark bruises patched the taut, scarred skin over his ribs. *Ouch.* I ran my hands over them.

"Nothing's broken," I said.

"If it was, I'd know about it," he said. "How would you like it if I did this?" Next thing I knew, he'd stuck his hands up my top and *tickled* me. I half collapsed on the sofa, laughing and trying to push him away. "Stop it!"

The door opened. "What in the world is going—gah, my eyes!" Alber backed out into the hallway.

"Ah!" I said, jumping off the sofa and tugging my top down.

Alber shook his head. "I can't even tell who was assaulting who, and I don't really want to know. Anyway. Nell wants to talk to you."

"Of course she does." I grinned at Kay. "Come scrape me off the floor when she's done with me. I reckon I'm in for a hell of a safety lecture."

"If it's any consolation, I've been 'invited' to a meeting with the Valerian police tomorrow." He looked more amused than annoyed. "Probably about dangerous cross-world travel."

"Ouch," I said. "Oh well. It was for a good cause. Me."

"Can't argue with that," he said. "I'll wait out here."

EMMA L. ADAMS

I tilted my head on one side. "You're trying to avoid her, aren't you?"

"It was you she wanted to talk to, not me. Suppose I get my lecture later on."

"You better."

Not if I had anything to do with it. Like hell was I letting him out of my sight in the foreseeable future.

I went into the hall. Nell was in the kitchen, elbows resting on the table. Jeth and Alber slipped past, leaving me alone with her, and closing the door.

I drew in a breath. She was as tense as ever, even with me back. I could hardly blame her. A lump grew in my throat. She'd nearly lost me to the very people she'd tried to protect me from all my life.

"You wanted to talk to me?"

"Yes," she said. "I thought it would be a good idea to get it over with. If you don't want to talk about what happened to you, I understand. But I imagine you have some questions."

Well, yeah. "For one thing, the StoneKing said the mage-bloods were *winning* the war, not losing. Is that true?"

She nodded. "These things change, and there are often long gaps between news—and to talk of winning and losing in a war on that scale is not as easy as you might believe. There are more factions in the war than just magebloods and nonmages."

"Yeah," I said, "but is it true about the other Royals? They're all dead?"

A fraction of a second's hesitation. "At last I heard... yes. But that doesn't mean it's true. There are places they can hide, and the methods the magebloods used made it difficult to know for certain. Few eyewitnesses escaped when they bombed the palace, for example."

The palace. The place I'd have grown up, if things had been different.

"My... parents?" I had to force the words out. If the StoneKing hadn't forced me to face the world I'd never be part of again, I would have left the issue in the past, like Nell had always told me to. But given what had happened, I needed closure.

I knew the answer before she spoke: "Presumed dead. They were in the palace when the bombs went off, and I'd know if they used the escape tunnels, because I'm in contact with the people who were watching them at the time. I'm sorry."

I shrugged, torn between disconnection and the nagging sense I should feel something—but at the same time, I'd never known those people. They'd let me be injected with adamantine, and they'd wanted me to be their assassin.

I refused to start thinking about the life I'd have led if things had been one degree different. Because every decision made a difference, however small. If there was one thing I knew for certain after my time with the Stoneskins, after walking within an inch of my own death, it was that. Any moment I could have died, and everyone left behind would have had to deal with the fallout. Maybe I could have prevented the others' deaths. But if I hadn't been there, the StoneKing would have killed them sooner or later. I wouldn't forget them, but I couldn't undo the past.

I hesitated. "The StoneKing... he said something about me being a *nexus*. He told me every world has some kind of main source—the ones with magic, that is. But—he was lying, wasn't he?"

Nell was silent. My heart beat fast, my hands went cold.

"No," I said. "It can't be true. It makes no sense. The—the source of all magic has to *stay* in that world, doesn't it?"

A pause, the longest five seconds ever. Then she breathed out. "It's not true," she said. "The source you were implanted with was a small part of the main deposit on

Enzar. If it *was* true, there would be no more magic on that world."

I breathed out, too. Of course—I'd seen the level of magic on Enzar myself. Seen the destruction.

"But the other part—he said the magebloods would believe it if he told them. They wouldn't, would they? They'd know it was absurd."

This new silence had a different feel. A shiver ran up my back. "It's true? They'd believe it?"

"Ada," said Nell, slowly, "there are a great many people who would believe anything in order to bring an end to the conflict. You're the last surviving Royal—as I heard, anyway —with the magic implant. Of course there will be rumours. It doesn't mean they're true, but belief doesn't require the truth, does it?"

"No," I said. "Guess I get why you wanted me to stay away from there. They'd make me into a weapon or a martyr." I shuddered.

"Yes," said Nell, "but it's no different to what I told you already."

I swallowed. "Guess not. You always said we could never go back. But I can't pretend it isn't a bit creepy. A whole nation would believe that about me."

"To the magebloods, the Royals' powers have always been a mystery. They never knew why they suddenly came to be dominated by the ones they'd once ruled. As recent as thirty years ago, they used to stage public executions via third level magic, and when they caught one of the Royals trespassing in mageblood territory, they wanted to make an example. They were far from prepared for their attack to simply bounce off, killing several of their own. That event triggered the Royals' dominance—until nine years later, when the magebloods retaliated with a weapon of their own."

I didn't even know what to say. "It sounds like the magebloods and Royals were as bad as each other," I said. "I suppose I understand why the Alliance wanted to leave them to kill each other."

"Don't say that," said Nell, her eyes flashing. "Perhaps Enzar is beyond saving, but there are decent people left there. You know that."

"I know." I heaved a sigh. "It's just... it feels like I should do *something*. And I can't. Even with my... power. It's not enough. Hell, it's what caused the war."

"Not just that," said Nell. "The hostilities go back to the dawn of the Royals' arrival on Enzar, after they left their old world. It's the way things are. They were originally the outsiders, but they made themselves gods, in their own eyes."

"Yeah, they sound as deluded as the StoneKing," I said. But it wasn't that simple. Once you crossed one bridge, it was a slippery slope with no clear division between good and evil. In this picture, everyone was a villain, except those too innocent to know any better. And if I'd stayed, they'd have corrupted me, too.

The thought made me sick.

"Enough," I said, aloud. "I don't want to talk about Enzar anymore."

Nell nodded. "I thought not. I wanted to make sure..."

"I know," I said. "But we can deal with that later. I'm just... really glad to be home."

A rap on the door. "Can we come and see our favourite sister?" Alber asked.

"Of course," said Nell.

I yelped as my brothers piled on me in a bear hug. "Guys! Having trouble breathing here."

Alber let go of me, while Jeth loosened his hold.

"Can we skip over the safety lecture?" I asked, before anyone could speak. "Lesson learned, et cetera. I just wanna lie on the sofa and eat takeout and watch Al's crappy ninja films all evening, okay?"

"Deal," said Alber.

My communicator buzzed in my pocket. I'd forgotten I carried it, and my heart dipped a little as I flicked the touch screen. Central were contacting me. *Why? What happened?* My head spun with images of emergencies, or more attacks, or the Stoneskins rising from the abyss. Maybe we hadn't sent them away after all.

I breathed out. It was from Ms Weston, helpfully titled, "This is not an emergency." Couldn't be bad news, right?

KAY

I stared at the message, frozen in shock. Horror and disbelief locked me to the spot, and a roaring sounded in my ears, drowning everything else.

Get out. I stumbled forwards. *Calm down, Kay.*

But the words of the message were imprinted in my head.

"The Alliance have finished negotiations with the Republic of Thairon, and all representatives have since returned to Earth to report to the council. We expect a positive outcome to a conflict that has lasted almost twenty years."

Thairon had opened its doors, which meant only one thing.

My father was coming back to Earth.

ABOUT THE AUTHOR

Emma is the New York Times and USA Today Bestselling author of the Changeling Chronicles urban fantasy series.

Emma spent her childhood creating imaginary worlds to compensate for a disappointingly average reality, so it was probably inevitable that she ended up writing fantasy novels. When she's not immersed in her own fictional universes, Emma can be found with her head in a book or wandering around the world in search of adventure.

Find out more about Emma's books at
www.emmaladams.com.